Tricky
Conscience

A novel

Cenarth Fox

Tricky Conscience

First published in 2017 by Fox Plays
www.foxplays.com
www.cenfoxbooks.com

ISBN 978-0-949175-12-0

Cover design by Ana Grigoriu

Dedicated to the memory of
Marie Ryan
Book lover extraordinaire

1

I have an inner voice that guides me.
Socrates

THE GUN APPEARED. The woman flicked through a *Vogue* lift-out, annoyed at the many wrinkle-free females. At 68, and with a lifetime of smoking behind her, Sheila's skin belonged in the before section of the before-and-after ads for women of a certain age. *Botox be my friend.*

She drained her coffee, put down the mug, and nearly died. The moving gun caught her eye. It waved. Was it loaded? Of course. Then her panic took off as her grinning grandson stepped into the kitchen doorway, and pointed the weapon at his babysitter.

'Bang, Grandma, you're dead.'

Shit.

When holding a loaded gun, the only person more dangerous than a maniac or drunk is a four-year-old playing a game.

Sheila couldn't move, let alone speak. The grinning child didn't know he could kill his Gran. How he found the gun was irrelevant. All that mattered were his aim, and the strength of his trigger finger.

Grandma thought about throwing herself on the floor and screaming, hoping to make Angelo drop the weapon, and come to her aid.

But what if he thinks it's all part of the game?

"I can see you, Grandma," he might say, run towards her and pull the trigger. "Gotcha, Grandma, you're dead." And she would be — literally.

Sheila's life flashed before her.

I've survived a brute of a husband, chemo, two miscarriages, and a criminal son, only to be shot by a toddler. And what if he fires and doesn't kill me outright? What if I die here, blood oozing over the Italian marble floor? My only grandchild will be mentally scarred for life.

Expecting the unexpected doesn't prepare you for this.

Jesus, what now?

Angelo upped the ante as he moved closer to Grandma. His tiny hands grasped the weapon, now with two tiny fingers against the trigger. Sheila's survival instinct kicked in as she reached for her coffee mug.

Must I kill my grandson to survive?

'Listen to me, Angelo,' she said, gripping her mug. 'You must not point a gun at anyone.' The child grinned.

That's a fib, Gran, and you know it.

Angelo scored a water pistol last Christmas, and endlessly fired the toy gun. What's the difference? Same basic shape of weapon, same method of operation — just aim and fire. Mind you, being squirted with a Super Soaker doesn't pack quite the same punch as a .357 Sig bullet from a Glock 31. One of those slugs can tickle your internal organs.

Sheila trembled. She drew the mug closer. It had to be behind her for the throw to work. A flick wouldn't do; only a fair dinkum fling.

Angelo threatened Grandma.

'Put your hands up,' he demanded.

Sheila's thoughts fizzed.

Should I pick up the coffee mug at the same time?

'Gran, put your hands up,' repeated the child, aiming at Sheila's chest.

What a waste. I've beaten breast cancer only to have a bullet do what the cancer couldn't.

She raised her hands, clutching the mug with the "weapon" above her head. Threats were useless, counterproductive.

Keep It Simple, Stupid.

Throw mug.

Hit floor.

Surely he won't get angry and come after me. If I scream like mad, he'll panic and drop the gun. Oh no! What if he turns it on himself?

Angelo loved his new game. Grandma always teased him. Now he could tease her back. He inched closer, the gun stock still. Wee Ange had *potential assassin* written all over him. Sheila forced a smile — just.

'Look, darling, Grandma's got her hands up. You win. Now let's play another game.'

'Not before I shoot you.'

Sheila decided it was kill or be killed. It was throw-the-mug, dive-on-the-floor, and scream-like-crazy time. Angelo prepared to shoot.

Just as he started to squeeze the trigger, the cat jumped from the kitchen bench, and the dog sat up in its basket and barked. Angelo was distracted, and Sheila threw the mug — hard. It struck her grandson in the face. Good shot Gran. Angelo fell back squeezing the trigger.

The cable holding the fake French provincial chandelier in the dining room took a direct hit. The light fitting swayed, and then crashed on the custom-built dining table. The cat and dog fled. Sheila dived.

In the crash tackle, Angelo dropped the gun, and imitated a banshee. Grandma grabbed the weapon, and hurled it down the passage.

'It's all right, little man,' she said, clutching the child, kissing him, stroking him, and weeping more than the boy.

Terror consumed Angelo. The gun's recoil stunned him. The noise of the weapon, the sudden speed of the animals, the surprise and pain of the flying mug, the crashing chandelier, plus the rugby tackle from his desperate grandmother, all delivered Angelo to the gates of Hell. This was the worst game he'd ever played, and all the soothing words, kisses, hugs and pats proved ineffectual — totally.

Shock gripped adult and child. Sheila couldn't stand. Her adrenalin surged. She struggled to breathe.

What have I done to my grandson? What do I do now?

She clung to the child. Their tears joined forces. Time meant nothing, and only became relevant when Sheila's son and his wife came home.

'Hey, Ange, where's my little man?' called his father.

Luciano "Luca" Parisi made money from crime. He owned a restaurant, and claimed to be a professional punter with property investments, but Class A drugs made him rich. His wife, Kellie, enjoyed the trappings of new money, asked no questions, and did as she was told.

Violence was second nature to Luca but even he was rocked at the sight of his mother and son on the kitchen floor.

'Mum,' screamed Luca.

'Angelo,' screamed Kellie.

The child invented a new form of hysterics, as his mother tried to comfort him.

'Who did this?' demanded Luca, helping his mother to sit. Not, "How are you?" or "Are you hurt?" just, 'What happened? Tell me!'

She shook her head. Speechless, her shock became the shakes.

Luca looked at his wife who got the message.

'Come on, baby,' she cooed at Angelo, removing the terrified toddler.

Luca investigated. The cat had knocked over a vase of flowers, the dog had re-arranged his food and water bowls, the coffee mug had bounced off the gun-toting grandson and shattered, chairs lay higgledy-piggledy, and the chandelier, in bits, decorated the dining table and surrounds.

'Tell me, Mum, was it the bikies? Tell me, who did this?

3

Luca had still not managed to ask about his mother's health; revenge his only thought. What's compassion?

Sheila clenched her fists. Anger replaced shock. She glared at her belligerent son, and her belligerence out-muscled his.

She whispered. 'You did.' She roared. 'You did this, you fucken idiot!'

Luca couldn't speak. His brain needed help.

What is the woman talking about?

Sheila staggered to her feet. 'Your son had a gun.'

Luca recoiled in disbelief. 'He what?'

'Your gun; he had your gun with real bullets.'

'He couldn't.'

'Angelo had your gun, and fired at me, and only by some miracle he missed. Your son came this close to killing me because of your fucken stupidity.' She screeched. 'You did this!'

Now anyone who called Luca Parisi "stupid" clearly had a death wish. Obviously, that didn't apply to Sheila. Luca respected his ma although that respect was about to be tested.

She attacked her "boy", raining slaps and blows. Luca was obviously younger, and certainly stronger and fitter. But he couldn't fight back. How can you fight your mother?

True, his hands-on violent days were over, but the man who'd assaulted more victims and rivals than he could remember, couldn't lay a finger on his current assailant. She was his mother — his mia madre.

'Mum!' he cried as she went for him.

He tried to grab her flailing arms. Her language matched her ferocity, and she hurt him. I mean, you cop a decent slap across the head, and see how it feels. Luca grabbed her wrists, so Sheila switched to kicking, and Luca's shins screamed. She jerked a knee, pinpointing the family jewels.

Too much, Ma.

Of course, he'd never strike his mother, but this was an emergency.

With one right cross, he slapped Sheila into next Tuesday. She collapsed. Stunned and exhausted, she resumed her prostrate position on the Italian marble. Her sobbing matched his throbbing — plums.

'Sorry, Mum. You were going mental. I dunno what came over me.'

Yes he did. It was her knee to his nuts. He sat, nursing his knackers.

Silence. Upstairs in his bedroom, little Ange sobbed, being comforted by Mummy. Downstairs, the dog and cat had emigrated. Sheila's laboured breathing dominated. Finally Luca spoke.

'Where's the gun?' She pointed. He limped to the weapon and cursed.

How could I have been so fucken stupid?

4

Luca, or Mr Very Careful, remained free to walk Lygon Street despite his many criminal activities, because he didn't make mistakes. He gave the cops *niente*. He said nothing online or by phone, which could ever help the police. He left no incriminating paper trails for tax officials to follow. He never got his hands dirty. His expertise lay in planning crimes, getting others to do his bidding, and in keeping on the right side of organized criminals back in his Calabrian homeland. Luca desperately wanted to be known as Mr Mafia Down Under.

This business with the gun was a catastrophe. Had the cops arrived with a search warrant, finding the gun would have put him inside with bail refused. His youthful record would see him sent down for years.

I am a moron!

Last night, Luca discussed the weapon with lackey, Alan "The Animal" Darcy, planning a hit on a drug rival. Animal departed, and Luca still had the gun when he went to pee. His wife called, and he entered their bedroom. Being on a conjugal rights' promise, Luca cracked the double.

He was pleased to see his wife, *and* he had a gun in his pocket. Kellie, wearing an off-the-shoulder come-hither look, distracted Luca, who stuffed the gun in the wardrobe beneath his cashmere sweaters, planning to secure the weapon once his baby-making duties were o'er. He so enjoyed the horizontal dancing, he forgot the gun, and the next day, little Angelo, looking for places to hide from Grandma, discovered the lethal object, and the rest you know.

Sheila dragged herself up and sat, slumped across the table. Luca walked past his mother as she decorated the *Vogue* lift-out with vomit.

'I'll be back, Ma,' said Luca, omitting "How are you" or "I'll get help". In the garage, Luca placed his gun in the secret hiding place, made when the house was being built.

At night, alone, the builder did as instructed, and knew that to say anything about this extra job was sealing his death, and that of his family. Luca terrified you, and with his Calabrian connections, Mr Parisi was someone you did not cross — ever.

Luca returned. 'I'm sorry, Ma, that should never have happened.'

Sorry was a big word for Luca. Still no, "Can I get you something?"

'That won't happen again. I'll just go check on Ange.'

And with that, the criminal left his ma pondering her near-death experience, and the almighty whack courtesy of her loving son.

Luca owned the Lygon Street pizzeria his father created. Today it was Luca's domain. He sat at the permanently reserved corner table, and tucked into his gnocchi. At 1950 hours, Animal arrived.

He was the archetypal underling. Luca bossed, bullied and berated his employee who kept on coming back for more.

'Sorry, I'm late, boss.'

Luca ignored him.

'I done that job.'

'And?'

Animal passed an envelope under the table for Luca.

The Italian-Australian didn't make drug baron overnight. He started small, cleaning locomotives before driving them. As a teenager, he ran drugs for anyone who employed him. He saw the wealth in drugs.

His father made money through pizzas, building up the family restaurant, but gambled, and drank away the profits.

He belted his boy, and Luca despised the old man. If Luciano Senior hadn't died of nicotine addiction, Luca might have arranged a hit. His father provided Luca with a perfect upbringing for drug dealing — violence, no mercy, and profit always profit.

The police didn't impede Luca. For him, enemy numero uno were the rival drug barons. No honour among thieves. Kill or be killed.

'I seen them new pushers, boss. They're workin' for that Irish prick.'

'Where's he live?'

'I think in Brunswick.'

'You think?'

'I'll have the address soon.'

'Get it, and then you can borrow my untraceable gun.'

2

A quiet conscience makes one strong.
Anne Frank

BERNIE SLIM WAS NOT WELL-NAMED. His fondness for cinnamon doughnuts and black coffee meant his abdomen and belt often came to blows. At 33, Bernie's stubble was less designer and more homemade. It failed to improve his image, and his marital status of *single* seemed set in stone. By day, he wore a white coat and protective eyewear in his role as a scientist working for the Australian arm of *Labcope,* the international pharmaceutical company.

In a swish laboratory in St Kilda Road, once Melbourne's premiere boulevard, Bernie tested chemicals in the *Research and Development* section, known by some as *R & D,* and by others as *Retire and Die.*

Creating a new drug is expensive. It can take ages, and may produce little of value. Medical research is high risk costing big bucks. It can also trigger gigantic rewards.

Bernie's current project began years ago with scientists, all of whom were now retired or dead. He and a colleague soldiered on, trying to create new drugs for patients with specific mental conditions. At times, he thought he was creating an upmarket pill for migraines. It meant painstaking, repetitious work with seemingly no end in sight.

Late in the working day, Bernie's boss bowled into the lab. He often pulled this trick, hoping to ruin any plans his fellow scientists had for an on-time departure. Mutual hatred thrived between workers and boss.

Not content with a double-barrel surname, Ralph Hetherington-Smythe insisted on a posh pronunciation of his first given name. 'Call me Raife,' he demanded, with a low-budget smile imported from China.

Bernie referred to Hetherington-Smythe as Hyphen — *the* Hyphen. But never to his face. Good God, no.

'Ah, Slim, I need someone to attend the TGA conference on Friday.'

Bernie groaned internally. He hated conferences almost as much as he hated Dr Hetherington-Smythe, but Bernie needed his job, and so produced an insincere forelock-tugging routine.

'*Pharmaceuticals of Tomorrow*,' said the Hyphen. 'Might help you justify your existence in this over-funded backwater. Enjoy.'

The brochure landed beside Bernie, and Ralph departed.

'Wow, aren't you a lucky boy,' said a grinning Lois, Bernie's older colleague. He enjoyed her cheeky barb as she put away her equipment and notes.

'I'm off,' said Lois.

'So what's on, tonight, dear lady? Going clubbing again?'

Lois clubbing? Hardly. She had no social life as caring for her octogenarian mother meant the scientist was fully occupied at home. Lois wanted to retire years ago but needed the money to pay for her mother's carers during the day. Lois felt obliged to keep her mother at home for as long as possible. Meet Lois, her mother's keeper.

Bernie knew about caring. His father suffered life-changing injuries in a car crash, and now lived in a wheelchair. Bernie's saintly mother cared for her husband night and day. When Bernie thought about marriage, which wasn't often, he pondered the lyrics of an old song.

I want a girl just like the girl that married dear old Dad.

'I'll see you in the morning,' said Lois.

'Goodnight,' called Bernie, and tidied his bench. He perused the conference brochure. The topics and speakers held little interest, but two words tickled his fancy — *refreshments* and *luncheon*.

At least these gigs serve quality grub.

Walking home to Cremorne through the Royal Botanic Gardens and Gosch's Paddock, he pondered his evening meal. He needed to "eat healthy". His family stirred him about his "middle-aged spread".

'I'm not middle-aged,' argued Bernie.

'No, but your spread is,' said older sister, Madeline.

It was Monday night after the Garbos. Bernie put away his bins then did the same for an elderly neighbour, who opened her front door.

'Ciao Mr Bernie; how is my kind and lovely friend?'

'Buona sera, Signora,' said Bernie. 'I'm ready for Gary's walk.'

'Oh, did you hear that Gari? Mr Bernie will be taking you to the walk.'

Gari to the Signora, and *Gary* to Bernie, was really Garibaldi, a small dog of unknown parentage, who kept the Italian widow company. She was too frail to walk the hound, and Bernie offered to help. His kindness had a touch of selfishness, as both man and beast needed the exercise.

Not that Bernie ever worked up a sweat. Gary's creaking joints meant the short walk took forever. En route, Bernie collected Gary's droppings, properly disposed of same, then knocked on Signora Conti's door.

'Come in, Mr Bernie, please to come in.'

Bernie did as he did every time he returned with Garibaldi. This small act of kindness meant the world to the widow. She lived alone, and refused to move. Her children and grandchildren had given up trying to persuade their beloved mother and grandmother to live with one or more of them. Bernie's visits became the highlight of her day.

'How was your walk, Gari?' she said to the dog. 'Did you walk nicely for your friend?'

Gari had taken a vow of silence whenever food was within a mile of his senses. He settled for chewing.

'Now I have made some lasagna for you, Mr Bernie,' she said handing her neighbour a container wrapped in a tea-towel.

'Oh Signora, you shouldn't have.'

'You no like my lasagna?'

'Truthfully Signora, I don't like it.' Her eyes widened. 'I love it.' She beamed. 'I just don't want you to go to any trouble.'

'I tell you something, Mr Bernie. The day you have the wife, I stop the cooking for you. Okay?'

Bernie nodded. 'You could be cooking for another fifty years, Signora.'

It took a moment for the meaning to sink in, but then she laughed, and Bernie joined the fun. Garibaldi kept chewing.

'Oh and here is some chicken for your gatto, Alberto.'

Bernie called his cat Albert because of that famous scientist, Herr Einstein. His Italian neighbour had chosen the Italian version of Albert.

The dog-walker now had two items of food to carry home. Both residents in Bernie's Chestnut Street abode would dine well tonight.

The pharmaceutical conference was as expected. Bernie found the first speaker more interesting than his topic. A ludicrous bow tie, speech impediment, and a failure to master elementary button pushing made the lecture almost tolerable. But then came the highlight.

At morning tea, Bernie, with quality black coffee in hand, surveyed the range of edible goodies. No cinnamon doughnuts, but the upmarket biscuits looked intriguing, and those Danish pastries called to him like the Seirēnes of ancient Greece. "Go on, have two Danish," they sang. He was about to yield when a voice interrupted his snack selection.

'Good to see *Labcope* putting in an appearance.'

The woman beside him looked like a model. To have a stunner "chat up" Bernie was so unusual it put him right off his food.

Her hair glistened, and her understated jewellery screamed class.

'We don't usually see you lot at these high-brow events.' Even her sarcasm was subtle, and she nibbled and sipped with style.

Bernie recovered from shock, and attempted to join the conversation. 'You come here often then?' was his pathetic attempt at being funny.

Help me, someone.

'So Bernie, what's your real interest? I would have thought this gig far too sophisticated for a homeopathic juggernaut like *Labcope*.'

Bernie twigged that the gorgeous woman deduced his name and employer from his plastic nametag. She remained anonymous.

'You wouldn't be a journalist by any chance?' he asked.

She smiled, and Bernie's interest in Danish pastries evaporated.

'Do I look like a journalist?'

No, you look like a living doll who is so far out of my league I could be arrested for even standing next to you.

'Well I notice you're not wearing a nametag.'

'Oh that,' she said producing said item from her Gucci bag. All Bernie saw was the name Claudia. 'Mustn't damage the jacket.'

The price difference between Bernie and Claudia's jackets was the equivalent a Third World country's GDP.

'How did you find Professor Bow Tie's address?' he said.

Claudia laughed, and Bernie's mouth went dry. 'Let's just say the thought of a quality coffee kept me going.'

Bliss. This has to be love; a stunning woman who adores good coffee. Say, Claudia, do you fancy a cinnamon doughnut?

He tried a new tack. 'I must admit I'd much rather be back in the lab.'

'Turning out placebo goodies with the TGA's blessing.'

'Actually I'm in *Research and Development*.'

Claudia's face turned serious. 'You have *R & D* for vitamins?'

'I'm working on new meds for mental health issues.'

Claudia's surprise continued. '*Labcope* researches the brain?'

'Afraid so. Beneath all those over-the-counter pharmacy specials, there's a serious scientist desperate to discover some new magic bullet for depression, autism and schizophrenia.'

Bernie's confidence grew. Wrong. He failed to see the danger ahead.

Claudia showed genuine interest.

'I'm impressed. So what's your take on Norman Doidge's work?'

Bernie hesitated. Claudia pounced.

'You're working on brain disorders, and haven't read *The Brain That Changes Itself* and *The Brain's Way of Healing*?'

Bernie tried a pathetic joke. 'They're next on my list.' That died. He dug an even deeper hole. 'Would you believe I'm waiting for the movie?'

Claudia's head shook. 'And I suppose you've not heard of YouTube?'

Bernie groaned. *Shit.* His flippant remarks backfired. Claudia turned her back, and Bernie's mood turned black. Not only had his "date" dumped him, he'd admitted being pig ignorant about the work of a leading psychiatrist doing wonderful things in Bernie's so-called area of expertise. From there, Bernie's conference went rapidly downhill.

At lunch, he spotted Claudia, surrounded by admiring delegates who ignored their vittles, and feasted on her body.

If Lois retires and Claudia takes her place ... ah, dream on.

That night, while Albert slept, Bernie googled Norman Doidge, bought digital versions of his books, and explored neuroplasticity.

Bernie's thoughts kept returning to the lovely Claudia.

Maybe I can still impress Ms Gorgeous. But where does she work?

Online he watched films about examples of the brain healing itself. It was impressive, and Bernie felt ashamed of his ignorance. It wasn't exactly his work area but certainly related.

In one film, stroke patients learnt how to re-do things they once took for granted. Impressive stuff. And this got Bernie thinking. Did it relate to his research? Could chemicals help in this repair work? Could he create some formula to produce a brain changing action?

After a few solid hours, he made more coffee, and flopped on the sofa. Albert refused to budge; perfectly reasonable as it was his sofa.

Bernie flicked on the box, and surfed. Normally an SBS and ABC man, he found their offerings didn't appeal. He landed on some commercial network showing a documentary about true-life villains.

Organized crime figures had no compunction about maiming and murdering, not just their rivals, but judges, lawyers, journalists; anyone who opposed their "business". Innocent bystanders were killed in the crossfire. Their fault. "Serves 'em right for being there".

God, this is so gruesome. Why does anyone watch this?

Bernie did then retired, still tasting lasagna, while pondering the evil humankind heaps upon itself. Deep in Bernie's subconscious, an amoeba of a thought plopped from the mudflat to dry land.

Nice idea, Bernie.

Next morning, he sat in the *Labcope* staff canteen, consuming a cinnamon doughnut and black coffee. Life was grand until Josh arrived.

Every company has a Josh; someone who grates on colleagues, could bore for their country, and yet who thinks they're interesting.

Piss off, Joshua.

'Maaaate,' he oozed, sliding in next to Bernie. 'How they hangin'?'

'Morning,' replied Bernie wanting to stand and depart.

Josh loved himself and, as a *boastard*, (a bastard who boasts about his sexual exploits), could kill a conversation in a nanosecond.

Why do some men boast about their "success" in the bedroom? Mind you, for Bernie to reciprocate, fictional tales would be essential.

'You know that receptionist on the ground floor,' leered Josh, 'the one with the amazing legs?' Bernie knew what was coming.

Just say, "I'm not interested", or "Piss off, dickhead".

And for Bernie, what made these appalling reports worse was that Josh had a wife and children at home.

'I gave Ms Amazing Legs a lift home last night,' gloated the slime ball. He edged closer and whispered. 'She was very grateful.' He winked, and Bernie silently groaned.

To be fair, Josh included his spouse in his Casanova conquests. Whenever the randy boastard persuaded his wife to grant him his conjugal rights, the next morning, in the canteen, Josh would approach Bernie, and tap the scientist on the shoulder. That was the signal.

Last night, I did it with the missus.

It was too much information. Bernie hated himself for being so weak.

I don't like this man. I don't want to hear about his intimate boasts. Or wait. Oh no. Maybe I secretly do. Maybe I stay and listen because I get some perverted thrill at being part of his sordid existence.

Bernie returned to his lab, and Lois looked up. 'Gossiping in the canteen again? What do you men talk about?'

Sex thought Bernie, and resumed his work.

3

My conscience shall dispose of my hand.
Charlotte Brontë

WHEN BERNIE SLIM and Luca Parisi were turning 20, a young Melbourne lawyer started making waves. She had ambition to burn, and balls to boot.

Suburban solicitors were a dime a dozen but Jessica Reid was not suburban. Adversarial by nature, she took to criminal law like a commercial television network to dross. She kept winning. Crims loved Jess because so often the redhead helped them skewer the pigs.

Jessica chose not to be a barrister due to her desire, need even, to do other things. She wanted to play at politics.

The woman was born with a how-to-vote-card in her hand. Her parents belonged to the Sandringham branch of the Liberal Party, and Jessica joined the Young Libs in her first year at Monash University.

She loved the conflicts in politics, the deals, the dirty tricks, and the backstabbing — and that was just within her own party. She fantasized about the power a government minister enjoyed, and craved the top job in her home state of Victoria.

She never missed party meetings, volunteered for everything, and earned a PhD in sucking-up. Jessica paid her dues, and if the Libs had a Rising Young Star Award, she would have been nominated — often.

At 28, as a lawyer and bright young thing, her day job saw her dealing with barristers defending criminals in Melbourne's County Court. She believed her job helped prepare her for a life in politics, and she saw crooks and politicians as being pretty much the same. Oh, except she knew crooks stabbed you in the chest.

A young tearaway and his father entered Jessica's office. The court case beckoned. The villain had been charged with threats to inflict serious injury, and riot, and been granted bail provided he lived with his family. The court case beckoned.

'You sure you're up for this, Miss?' asked the father. 'I mean is there someone more senior?'

Jessica looked at the father. Her expression zapped Mr Sexist, who instantly became Lot's wife. When Jessica's advice and choice of barrister saw the young thug found not guilty, her reputation within the criminal fraternity continued its upward trajectory.

She loved the law but politics more.

Her growing reputation defending riff raff hardly seemed the path to winning Liberal Party preselection, but Jessica disagreed. She liked being different. Besides, rubbing shoulders with criminals taught her survival. She discovered ruthlessness, and shady characters taught her how to bluff, threaten, and lie — excellent attributes for any aspiring politician. If Jessica ever wore a tee shirt, the text would be *Don't Mess with Jess*.

Her parents wished their girl had chosen Wills and Conveyancing, even Family Law. Her mother pleaded.

'But darling, if you must work in criminal law, why not prosecute?'

'Your mother's right,' added Jessica's father. 'You won't win preselection working for criminals. Delegates choose feminine not feisty.'

Jessica didn't argue. The more people pressured her to follow the "rules", the more she rebelled — and triumphed.

With a state election due, she won endorsement for a super-safe Labor seat, lost, but did frighteningly well. Movers and shakers took note. Labor were back in power, and Jessica, although not yet a member of parliament, shone as a future Liberal Party star.

In the meantime, she dealt with drug dealers at the criminal law grindstone. It would be years before another preselection battle.

As the next State election drew nigh, Alan "The Animal" Darcy came to see Jessica the solicitor. A mid-level career crim, never destined for greatness, Alan lived in hope.

'Take a seat, Mr Darcy,' said Jessica. 'Can I get you a coffee?'

'Beer'd be nice.'

'Time is money, Mr Darcy.'

'Call me Animal, everyone does.'

'So, what's the charge?'

She knew but made her clients explain their predicament. This often revealed possible flaws in the police case, and allowed her to perfect her skill of spotting fibs.

What a gift, and what a godsend for any politician. Naturally, her clients lied for a living, and Jessica's antennae picked their porkies. Every politician would surrender his or her chauffeured limo to be able to tell when someone was lying.

'The cops set me up.'

'That's a new one,' she said, watching her sarcasm sail through to the keeper. 'Tell me about it.'

Animal knew this solicitor took no prisoners, and got blokes off.

She's not bad looking. Not the sort I'd take home to meet me Mum, but I'd certainly let her "get me off".

Jessica ignored the looks and comments from crooks. She knew criminal law, and almost always got the best possible deal for her clients. When they offered favours or gifts, she spurned them with ease, and never let villains within a mile of her private life.

Colleagues and friends joked about her sordid cases, and a few heavy-hitters in the Liberal Party began to worry that, by mixing with felons, their rising star would be tainted. 'At least let her prosecute,' they said.

'So, Mr Darcy,' began Jessica.

'Go on, call me Animal.'

'How exactly did the police set you up?'

Animal yielded to the iron maiden. 'The usual way; two cops pulled me over, and planted drugs in the boot of me car.'

'You saw them plant the drugs?'

'Course I didn't. That's how they work. One cop distracts you while the other pretends to search, and then allegedly finds the gear.'

Jessica wondered if Animal could spell *allegedly*.

'And did you handle the drugs in any way?'

'What drugs? I just told you the cops planted 'em.'

Jessica decided that Animal had slightly more intelligence than the average crim. She made notes for the barrister she knew could make the arresting officers squirm. They did — squirm that is.

In court, Animal did exactly as instructed. Jessica's notes and suggested plan of attack were delivered superbly by the barrister, and after the trial, Animal sported a grin not often seen in the County Court.

'I gotta buy you a drink, Miss,' he beamed. 'I reckon you'd be a champagne drinker.'

Jessica checked her phone and read an imaginary text.

'Sorry Mr Darcy. You'll have to settle for Miss Bennet.' She left.

Animal last opened a chapter book in Year 7 — he closed it almost immediately — and today restricted his "reading" to the study of glossy publications featuring female pulchritude. Jessica's comment became a cultured pearl cast before a bore of a boar.

Heading back to the office, her mobile rang. Her excited mater spoke.

'Darling, I've just heard. You've been preselected for Brighton.'

Jessica shrieked, and passersby stopped, thinking someone was in trouble — hardly trouble, more a triumph for the redoubtable Ms Reid. Brighton was a super safe seat, and Jessica had just scored a gold pass entry to the Victorian Parliament. Her political dream became a reality.

The state election drew closer, yet Jessica chose to continue working with criminals. This brought more concern from her folks, and frowns at Liberal HQ. But like Mrs Thatcher, this lady was not for turning.

I've got this far by sticking to my guns. And stick to them she did.

Now there are friends, best friends, and first-best friends. Jessica met Genevieve at uni, and the two clicked. Yin and yang, The Odd Couple or The Bobbsey Twins, the women became the perfect double act.

Genevieve got Jessica elected as President of the Young Libs through a mixture of bribery, blackmail and bastardry. Vote early and vote often. What fool said Labor invented branch stacking? Genevieve was living proof that behind every great woman is a great woman.

After uni, Genevieve became a high-flying banker, and Jessica a high-flying lawyer. The two women kept in touch, and when Jessica was first endorsed as a Liberal candidate, her part-time adviser cum campaign manager just had to be you know who. The main reason Jessica did so well in losing that safe Labor seat was down to Genevieve. So it was no surprise when, three years later, and Jessica won her latest preselection, her first call was to her right-hand woman.

They met after work in Jessica's office.

'Now listen, darl,' said Jessica, 'this is serious.'

'The Honourable member for Brighton,' mocked Genevieve. She pronounced *Honourable* and *Brighton* with exaggerated sarcasm.

More laughter.

'Decision time, babe. Tis time to ditch that shaky career in banking.'

'Shaky!' scoffed Genevieve. 'Let's compare take-home pay, and the size of my bonuses — plural.'

Their joking couldn't hide the pending lifestyle changes both now faced. Jessica would soon become a member of parliament, but would Genevieve become the power behind the throne?

Jessica desperately wanted Genevieve on board. But the banker had built a brilliant career, and didn't want to back a loser. If Jessica remained a backbencher, especially in opposition, or at best reached junior minister level, where was the fun in that? Big drop in salary, no such thing as a bonus, and no joy in being close to the woman 26th in line to the throne. Both women loathed failure.

'You know I want you as my campaign manager and Chief of Staff.'

Genevieve roared. 'Campaign manager in an unlosable seat, and Chief of Staff to an opposition backbencher in a broom cupboard.'

'Every Premier's gotta start somewhere.'

More scoffing from Genevieve, but the laughter covered the crunch question. Will the banker switch to politics? The laughter subsided. They sipped their chardonnay and fell quiet.

'I'm serious,' said Jessica.

'Duh,' replied Genevieve.

'Think about it. Have a chat to what's-his-name ... Jason.'

They both roared as one. 'Justin!'

This was a running gag. Jessica pretended to forget the name of Genevieve's husband. For once, the gag wore thin. More silence.

Then the banker announced her switch to politics — subtly.

'I've been thinking about your next move,' said Genevieve.

Jessica sparkled. *Welcome aboard Genevieve.* This is what the would-be pollie wanted, needed; her bestie onside, doling out pearls of wisdom.

'I'm all ears,' said Jessica. Genevieve hesitated. 'Well, come on.'

'Get married.'

Jessica was struck dumb. This she didn't anticipate. New wardrobe, new hairstyle, join the board of certain charities, even sponsor an African orphan, were all possibilities. But wedlock?

'Married?'

'It's part of the big picture; Joe Stalin's Five Year Plan. Know what you want tomorrow, create the tactics today, and then do the business.'

Getting hitched wasn't on Jessica's radar. She oozed sarcasm.

'So is this a big church wedding or a quickie in someone's backyard?'

Genevieve remained deadly serious. 'Your marital status is irrelevant to your parliamentary colleagues. If you're running for a leadership role, they'll vote according to what's in it for them.'

'Running for leader? Even the state election's not till next year.'

'But Joe Public and the missus will warm to you more if you've got the little man by your side. Their thinking is that she's not a man-hater, and she sure as hell ain't a lesbian.'

'God, you're serious.'

'Life is full of choices, sweetie, and winners take action.'

'Okay, I'll make a diary entry. Attend Court, speak at the Young Libs conference, and then find a husband.'

'You asked for my advice.'

Genevieve knew Jessica better than the lawyer well. Jessica had pushed her motherly instinct aside, unlike Genevieve who had a husband and two kids. Jessica's two kids were her careers — the law and politics.

She remained stunned. 'Any other gems like that?'

'Only the name of your future husband.'

Jessica's sails went limp. 'Bloody hell, Gen, you've got to warn me about this stuff.'

'You know me, darl. Tell it like it is and the sooner the better.'

Jessica paused. 'Well go on. Who's the lucky fella?

When Genevieve replied, Jessica's jaw dropped.

'Myles Lane! Are you kidding? Isn't he gay?'

'It's the perfect match. He's a rising star in the corporate world held back by archaic traditions. You're a rising star in the political world needing to tick all the right boxes.'

'You're talking about an arranged marriage.'

'So?'

'*So?* This is the twenty-first century, woman, and not some medieval union of two royal houses.'

'But that's exactly what it is. Two tremendous talents working alone may struggle. Together, those two talents can become a powerful, hugely successful partnership. This is quintessential synergy, darl. Carpe diem.'

Jessica shook her head. It's not often she was lost for words. 'Whatever happened to love?'

'A good title for your memoir. Now this will only work if both parties abide by the rules.'

'Oh, and what pray tell are they?'

'Come on, Jess, you're a big girl. No scandal, no playing away from home, and no letting the domestics discover the couple's pre-arranged sleeping arrangements.'

'Unbelievable.' Jessica puffed her cheeks and exhaled. But because her trust in Genevieve was so deep, so locked in, she couldn't reject the idea out of hand.

'So he *is* gay,' stated Jessica.

Genevieve held up her hands. 'There are fifty shades of sexuality, and anyway, who cares?'

'Me. I care. And I'm the one in white, remember?'

Genevieve grinned. 'Bags be matron of honour.'

Jessica clenched her hands and grimaced. Her friend had been right so many times before; never wrong in fact. Why would she propose this move if it wasn't in Jessica's best interest? There was a long pause broken finally by the lawyer.

'I think I've met him once.'

'Yes, at my dinner party.'

'You conniving bitch.'

'I was simply testing the waters.'

'You even had us sit together.'

'And?'

'And?' Jessica pondered. 'All right, he was pleasant and charming.'

'Congratulations. He said the same about you.'

Jessica pointed at her friend. 'Now you're taking the piss.'

'Come on, babe, it's cards on the table time. You want the top job. As a single woman, you'll lose points to the prejudiced men and women who judge a politician by their lifestyle. With a talented but out-of-the-picture gentleman sharing your life, you're "normal" and definitely more electable. Tick all the boxes.'

Jessica suddenly felt sick.

'Please don't tell me you've already told him about this crazy scheme?'

'Oh come on, give me *some* credit.'

The women fell silent. Genevieve worried their relationship might be irreparably damaged. Jessica worried she had to take one for the team — her team.

Again silence dominated. Finally Jessica spoke.

'So how do I get him to ask me?'

Myles Lane had a lot going for him. He was clever, poised for a stellar career in international law, wealthy in his own right, and the sole heir to his father's squillion dollar estate. Add to that his wit, his passion for music theatre and felines, plus his innate charm and urbane nature, and Mr Lane became a magnet for any society dame's unmarried daughter. True, he was no oil painting, and he did bat for the other side — albeit always as 12th man — but hey, nobody is perfect.

Jessica took advice from Genevieve, and met Myles a second time at yet another dinner party arranged by Jessica's bestie. If Myles thought he was being set up, he said nothing, and went along for the ride.

Soon after, Jessica found herself asking Myles for a huge favour. Would he, could he, please compere a fundraiser she arranged for one of the largest animal shelters in Melbourne?

Are you kidding? He's Mr Ailurophile. Of course he could and would.

From there, the relationship between Myles and Jessica took root. No suggestion of *a* root because this was a marriage in name only, a marriage of convenience. They dined together in public. Gossip in various wealthy postcodes set off spot fires and, when the couple announced their engagement, fire engines began racing around Toorak, South Yarra and Brighton. Genevieve high-fived herself.

Jessica agreed to marry Myles, a wealthy, well-closeted gay man, and both knew the deal. They gave one another a cover story, and agreed that their lack of any issue was down to God giving Jessica (or was it Myles?) imperfect reproductive capabilities. Blame God — he never blabs.

Each saw their union as a new and rewarding adventure. Pecks on the cheek became frequent, morphing to soft kisses on the lips. Their friendship grew, and both found fondness to be fulfilling. Could respect and affection ever become love?

It was an expensive wedding with every guest sucking on his or her BYO silver spoon. The honeymoon in the Bahamas was relaxing and brief as Jessica had business back home.

In November, the good burghers of Brighton gave Jessica a resounding tick of approval, and she won her seat in a canter.

Jessica Reid MLA — she retained her maiden name — increased the Liberal vote, and became an elected politician. But not all was bliss. The other mob won — again.

Jessica became a humble backbencher with Genevieve her trusted PA. Genevieve thought long and hard about throwing away the wealth and prestige of a senior post in a major bank. But hey, if her instincts were correct, her friend was destined for much bigger things.

As Jessica began her parliamentary career, a youthful Luca Parisi started a one-man drug empire in Melbourne's inner north; a youthful Ulsterman, Brendan Murphy, prepared to swap West Belfast for Melbourne; and an equally youthful Bernie Slim was a final year science student at Melbourne Uni.

Once parliament began, Jessica was delighted to score a minor shadow portfolio. It had less to do with her potential, and more to do with the Liberals having lost so many seats. Almost everyone got a gig.

'Are they trying to be funny?' asked Jessica. 'The Shadow Minister for Families and Children has nil issue and never will.'

Genevieve frowned. 'Not so loud,' she mouthed.

'I was hoping for something with a bit more bite. Surely it makes sense to allocate Police or Corrections to an experienced criminal lawyer.'

'You have got Family Violence.'

'God, I'd love to be Attorney-General. I could give the old crime-and-punishment platform a right good seeing to.'

'I think it's called crawling before you walk into the top job.'

Jessica went back to reading the day's political commentaries, while Genevieve had other fish to fry. Her ideas bubbled; ideas to position her "boss" for promotion, publicity and power.

'We need to discuss a few tactics, madam,' said Genevieve, opening a notebook and sitting in front of Jessica's desk.

Jessica's heartbeat accelerated. Nothing gave her a greater thrill than learning about her friend's schemes.

And so it began. Two intelligent women, planning their way to the leadership of the state Liberal Party, and then, to the all-powerful position of Premier.

Within the Liberal party, many people noticed Jessica Reid. Within the general public, she was Ms Anonymous. That situation continued until the day of her first big break.

It took three years for Jessica to hit the headlines, and hit them she did. *Youngest Shadow Attorney-General in State's History* ran one leader.

Years ago, nobody imagined that mixing with crims, and defending their wicked ways, would earn Jessica such a prestigious reward.

Her new office was bigger, her staff numbers doubled, and the Attorney-General suddenly found himself confronting a feisty and intelligent shadow who knew about lying and bully-girl tactics. Go Jess.

There was a reason Jessica won such a prize with so little political experience. It was step #2 in Genevieve's manifesto — *Dig up dirt.*

The then Shadow Attorney-General had shares in a relative's building company which collapsed leaving hardworking Victorians with half-finished homes.

Genevieve's banking contact tipped her the wink, and the former Shadow AG suddenly developed a stress-related condition. He stepped aside but with a plan to return once his condition improved — of course.

Jessica became the new Shadow Attorney-General. After not even three years in Spring Street, she had slid up the greasy pole, and if anyone could slide upwards, 'twas Ms Reid.

The next election came and went, bringing mixed results. Jessica increased her majority, the Liberals increased their number of seats, but alas, not in sufficient numbers to seize government.

'Shit, bugger, bum,' vented Jessica. 'More opposition and more wandering in the bloody wilderness.'

She and Genevieve drank to drown their election-loss sorrows. It was late, and Genevieve's mind was never idle.

'I've been thinking about our next four-year plan,' she said.

'More of the same, Gen. If we lose the next one, there'll be a leadership spill, and then I might, *might* be a chance for deputy.'

'Forget the wing-and-a-prayer approach.'

Jessica became tetchy. 'There won't be a spill before the election.'

'But if there is, are you ready?'

'Oh come on, Gen. I might be on some accelerated promotion gig, but it's way too early to run for any leadership role.'

'I've got an idea to enhance your appeal.' Jessica finished her drink.

'Another husband perhaps? Or what about a gender switch; Jessica Reid becomes Jesse Reid?'

'Listen ma'am,' — Genevieve had taken to addressing Jessica in regal terms when she thought her friend got ahead of herself — 'you don't have to take my advice but lay off the petulant sarcasm.'

Oops. A chill settled in the office. Jessica felt bad.

'Sorry. You were saying?'

Genevieve paused then lobbed her latest grenade. 'Adopt a child.'

Jessica held back. She was used to her friend's out-of-the-blue suggestions but this one knocked her for six.

'What, so now I'm a cross between Madonna and Angelina Jolie? I nip off to Africa and pinch a tribe of orphans?'

Genevieve persevered. 'If you adopt a young child, a toddler, and bring him or her up as your own, you will earn kudos with a lot of voters. You'll have no labour pain but cause Labor pain. Motherhood's a winner. Make some statement about you as a couple being unable to conceive — leave it blank, don't identify the misfiring party — and explain how you both desperately want a family.'

'More lies.'

'Think of your Christmas cards — family photo with the politician, the banker and their darling offspring and pets.'

Jessica shook her head. She never wanted kids. She worried sometimes that a lack of a motherly instinct meant she was somehow not a proper woman. Her drive for power swamped her drive for procreation. Her lust for promotion was barely concealed. Genevieve continued.

'Before you reject the idea, talk it over with hubby. If he's keen, you'll be mad to say no.' Jessica said nothing. 'You know, you might actually enjoy being a mother.'

Genevieve was right — again.

When Jessica broached the subject with Myles, he came alive. He longed to have a family but dared not raise the topic believing his ambitious wife would ridicule the suggestion. So enthusiastic was her husband's response, Jessica agreed.

That Christmas, their greeting card included a family of five. Rufus the labradoodle and Vera the moggie were there together with toddler, Simone. She swapped the orphanage for the palace, and her plastic spoon for one of the silver variety.

4

BERNIE KNEW WHEN to tease Lois, and when to say nowt. This morning his colleague looked terrible, and any joke about her clubbing last night would be dead out of order. He plumped for safer ground.

'How's your Mum?' Wrong question.

Lois turned away and didn't answer. Bernie winced.

Surely not death. Lois wouldn't be here if Mother had carked it.

A muttered reply saw both scientists resume work. Seconds later, Lois, with her back to Bernie, spoke in a shaky voice.

'My mother punched me last night.'

Bernie gasped. How does one respond to such a statement? He touched Lois on her arm. Her mental torment led to tears.

'I'm sure she didn't mean any harm,' whispered Bernie.

'Oh yes she did, and she hurt me,' whimpered Lois.

Bernie rubbed her arm. Giving her a hug seemed a step too far.

'It might be an age thing,' he said. 'Maybe her health problems cause frustration, and she just reacts in that way.'

Lois let rip. 'I've sacrificed my life for her. She never thanks me. She constantly complains. Nothing I do is ever right, nothing.' She took deep breaths. 'I don't think I can take much more.'

Bernie crunched eggshells beneath his size nine brogues.

'Perhaps it's time you considered putting her in care.'

Lois laughed sarcastically. 'Oh that would give her the greatest pleasure. She'd tell the staff I only wanted her money, and couldn't wait until she died. Then, when I'd visit, she'd perform.' Lois mimicked her mother. 'Oh, so you've finally bothered to show up. How lucky am I? Look everyone, it's my loving daughter.'

Lois wept.

Bernie felt helpless. Comforting his six-year-old niece, whose doll was broken, proved tricky. Comforting a 63-year-old spinster, whose mother doubled as a tyrant, proved impossible. He was about to suggest they go for a walk when Lois revealed her most hurtful experience.

'She's now accusing me of being selfish. Me, selfish.' Again she repeated her mother's words. 'You're punishing me by going to work and leaving me with all these faceless people.' Lois mimicked her mother by shouting. 'They're not my family!'

Suddenly embarrassed, Lois shut down. At least her outburst had some cathartic benefit. In a small way, she felt better, although inside her turmoil thrived. Outside, she looked a mess.

'I'm so sorry,' muttered Bernie.

'I think of your mother, bending over backwards to care for your father in his wheelchair, and never once complaining. Your mother's a saint. Mine's not even remotely human.'

Bernie sat on his stool. This was not the time to return to work.

'Have you considered some form of psychiatric assessment?'

'For her or for me?'

Things got worse as the silence lingered. Bernie was fresh out of ideas. He settled for a safe option.

'How about I get some coffee and cinnamon doughnuts?'

Lois looked at him with glistening eyes. 'You mean, how about you do what you always do only an hour earlier?'

They both smiled. Bernie felt a little better, and started for the door. Disaster. Wonder boss Ralph, "Call me Raife", the Hyphen, swept into the lab. Lois turned her back.

Ralph looked peeved. 'What's this? An even earlier lunch?'

Bernie wanted to humiliate his superior by explaining his colleague's predicament, but knew Lois would hate her private life becoming public knowledge. Besides, being keen to emasculate the R & D section, the Hyphen would relish any excuse to sack Lois.

'What can we do for you, Doctor?' asked Bernie in his best monotone.

'I haven't seen your report from the conference, Slim. I assume you bothered to attend.'

Bernie removed a folder from his satchel, and handed it to his boss.

'Conference attended and detailed report completed — sir. I was about to come to your office. Thank you, for saving me the trip.'

Bernie lied well. The Hyphen bristled. He expected Bernie would fail to complete a report, and wanted to belittle him — again. Bernie and Lois took delight in seeing their supervisor falter.

'Oh, right,' he mumbled. 'Okay.' He left. The words *thank you* remained unspoken.

Bernie was thrilled to have shafted the Hyphen but far happier to see Lois distracted. She even winked as Bernie departed for the canteen.

Lois was no doughnut lover but indulged Bernie on this occasion even if for only half the confection. He was anxious to talk shop.

'Lois, what do you know about Norman Doidge and neuroplasticity?'

'Norman Doidge,' she gushed. 'Oh he is exceptional, fantastic; my idea of the perfect psychiatrist. He breaks new ground, explains things in clear and concise terms, and he's just so personable.'

'Right,' said Bernie, not expecting such an answer.

Suddenly Lois became anxious. 'Don't tell me he was at the conference? Oh Bernie, why didn't you say?'

'No, no, he wasn't there. His name came up in a discussion.' Bernie felt a warm inner glow as his mind replayed an image of Claudia.

Lois changed from morose to motivated. 'Now if *he* gave a paper, I'd be there in a flash.' They sipped their coffee. 'I didn't know you were interested in neuroplasticity.'

'I wasn't, until I met a woman at the conference.'

'Ah, I see. And did Norman Doidge become interesting because the woman in question just happened to be a bit of a looker.'

Bernie laughed. 'A smidgeon above gorgeous,' he said, and the coffee consumption continued. She caught him eyeing her half-eaten doughnut.

'Go on, I know you want to.'

His cinnamon addiction took control. Between chews, he asked what had been bugging him for hours.

'Lois, can I ask you a question?'

'Of course.'

'Are we wasting our time?'

'Eating doughnuts or working in *R & D*?'

'I'm ashamed to admit I've never really studied neuroplasticity — no, let's be honest, I knew bugger all about the subject — but last night I did some research, and then had this crazy idea.'

'Well, you know what Samuel Langhorne Clemens said. *A person with a new idea is a crank until the idea succeeds.*'

Bernie added the name of Mr Clemens to that of Professor Doidge on the list of people he needed to investigate. He continued.

'Our drugs help people with depression, anxiety, schizophrenia and the like. But can we create a drug to change people's behaviour?'

'Sorry?'

Bernie didn't understand her question. He thought about re-wording it when she interrupted.

'Bernie, that's the purpose of our drugs. Surely you know that.'

26

'Yes but you're talking about people with mental health issues. I'm talking about healthy people who behave badly.'

Lois raised an eyebrow. That stopped her. 'Okay, give me an example.'

Bernie took a punt. Would it backfire? He jumped in.

'As an example, let's take your Mum.'

Lois sucked air through clenched teeth, and Bernie felt sick.

Why did I say that? Lois has stopped talking about her nasty mater, and now I've dragged my colleague back to her trough of despair.

'I wish you would,' replied a subdued Lois. 'I'll even pay the postage.'

'As far as we know, she's not mentally ill, but treats you terribly even though you're bending over backwards to give her the best quality of life.'

Lois rediscovered sadness. Bernie felt lousy but prattled on, hoping Lois would stay calm and breakdown-free.

'Does your Mum know her behaviour is wrong?'

Lois blew air. 'I know she's in pain with arthritis and osteoporosis, and her glaucoma's getting worse. She hates being old, and lashes out from fear or frustration or ... whatever.'

'But is she ashamed of her behaviour?'

Bernie made Lois think. The issue of her mother being ashamed had never entered Lois's thoughts. She thought she knew why her mother did what she did, but not if the behaviour troubled her mother's conscience.

'I've no idea. Is she ashamed?' She shrugged. 'Who knows?'

'Have you ever asked her?'

Lois shook her head. This was new territory. Bernie continued.

'Have you ever challenged your mother; told her you think she's being unfair, unkind or boorish and rude?'

'You really don't understand, Bernie. If I stood up to my mother, she'd call me a bully, or worse, or have a heart attack, real or fake. And if I say nothing, I'm weak. Whatever I do, I lose.'

Bernie moved on tippy-toe. This subject was super sensitive for Lois, and Bernie's idea was vague and untested. It had no substance. It was a momentary thought, a wild idea, a crazy notion.

But can Lois test my theory? Possibly, but what is my theory?

Bernie took the plunge.

'Do you think your mother would act differently if her moral compass controlled her behaviour?'

'Her moral compass?'

'What if we developed a drug which impacted a person's conscience; a drug which helped a person know right from wrong?'

'Define right and wrong.'

Bernie nodded. 'Okay, I agree some issues involve value judgments, but many are clear cut. I mean, is child abuse right or wrong?'

'Silly question.'

'Is bullying or making racist remarks, or cheating, right or wrong? Is your mother physically and mentally abusing you, right or wrong?'

Lois jumped in. 'Okay, I'll play. They're all wrong.'

'Of course there are grey areas but many actions are clearly good or bad. I mean if I murdered the Hyphen, would that be good or bad?'

'That's definitely a grey area.'

They failed to laugh because something interesting began to happen. Bernie struggled to control his enthusiasm.

'If we could develop, let's call it "a conscience drug", people would see the difference between right and wrong, between good and evil.'

'That's one big if. And anyway, knowing something is evil doesn't stop evil being done. Criminals know murder is wrong but their conscience is non-existent, or buried within their hatred and greed.'

'Let me finish. There could be two parts to this new drug.'

'Two parts to a non-existent drug that could take decades to create.'

He paused. 'Do you want me to stop?'

She paused. 'Do you want *me* to stop?'

Bernie shook his head. 'No, please, shoot me down.'

'Okay, fire away.'

Despite her cynicism, Lois was giving Bernie's idea serious thought. His excitement grew as he continued to explain.

'First, the patient is clearly able to define right and wrong. Second, they come under terrible pressure if they don't follow their conscience.'

'Whoa, whoa, whoa. Terrible pressure? Your drug *causes* pain? What physical or mental? And please don't say both.'

'Yes but it's good pain.'

'*Good* pain? Bernie, that's lunacy. You want to create a legal drug which actually injures the patient?'

'Pressures rather than punishes, helps rather than harms.'

'This is thinking way, way, way outside the box.'

'But you have to consider the benefits. And remember, the patient only suffers if they continue doing the wrong thing, acting against their conscience. If they respond to their conscience, the pain disappears.'

'But what if their conscience is wrong or their brain is scrambled?'

'Look, I didn't say it was perfect. I don't even know if it's possible.'

'At least you're honest.'

'And hopefully realistic.'

Lois persisted. 'Okay, so what's the major benefit?'

'You know; it's obvious.'

'Really?' She stared at him forcing him to explain.

'Ah, this so-called wonder drug aims to cause people to mend their wicked ways. Your mother wouldn't need a lecture from her GP. The new drug would cause her to treat you with respect. How's that for a benefit?'

They paused, thinking, and then both started on the jokes.

'I'll take a dozen,' said Lois.

'A dozen conscience tablets? Certainly madam,' grinned Bernie.

'Not a dozen tablets; a dozen cartons.'

More enthusiastic laughter; Bernie had no idea if his idea could or would work. Lois believed it had great potential as a thriller starring Matt Damon. She chose not to tell Bernie about her proposed movie.

Bernie remembered his TV viewing from the previous night.

'Just imagine if hardened crims took a drug which made them see their behaviour as evil, and, and this is the crucial part, imagine if they suffered mental torment if they continued to go against their conscience, and kept breaking the law, and this torment only went away if they stopped doing evil. I mean, if that happened, society would change for the better all over the world.'

Shock from Lois. 'Change society for the better? Are you mad? Bernie, Big Pharma, our magnificent employer, doesn't exist to improve society.'

Bernie wasn't sure if this was sarcasm. He soon knew.

'We exist to make profits.'

Bernie twigged. 'I like your cynicism, madam, but what of the idea?'

'You sure you're not talking science fiction?'

'Do you think it's science fiction?'

Lois made a face and shrugged. Bernie tackled the second doughnut still thinking out loud, and spoke with food in his mouth.

'If a drug stimulated an understanding of right and wrong, and your Mum took this drug and it worked, she would see her behaviour towards you as cruel, wrong and counterproductive.'

Lois paused. 'Now *you're* being cruel. You're offering me false hope.'

'And if that same drug caused anyone who went against their conscience to suffer mental anguish, people would stop being baddies.'

'You hope.'

'They may not become goodies but hopefully they'll stop sinning.'

Lois instantly became a telly-evangelist. 'Hallelujah brother.'

'So what are our chances? Can we create a Moral Compass Pill?'

'What's this "we" business? It's your idea, Mr Slim.'

'You can slip a pill to your Mum, and I'll slip one to the Hyphen.'

Lois smiled. She knew Bernie meant well even if his idea was to the right of loopy. She humoured him. 'Now you're talking.'

'Give me a time. How long will it take to find the right formula?'

'Is your name Methuselah?'

Bernie laughed. 'I still think it's an interesting idea,' he said.

'Create that drug, sir, and I'll buy you a life's subscription to Cinnamon Doughnuts Inc.'

Bernie purred. The more he spoke about his idea, the more he liked it. It might be pure fantasy and, for a scientist, his behaviour was unscientific, but as Lois seemed to take him seriously, his enthusiasm grew. It got busy when she remembered something.

'There was a scientist here when I first arrived, oh, thirty odd years ago. She worked on some birdbrain idea like yours.'

'So now it's a birdbrain idea.'

Lois turned serious. 'Sorry. I'm not quite myself this morning.'

'Lois, I didn't bring this up to take your mind off your Mum.'

'I know that.'

'I spent half the night studying Norman Doidge and neuroplasticity, and thinking about criminals reforming their wicked ways.'

'Can I swap your night life for mine?'

They looked at one another. Both were glad they'd spoken out. Lois needed to unload her misery and rage, and Bernie needed to share his ridiculous idea with a scientist he trusted. Lois turned serious.

'You know that some of the greatest scientific discoveries started life as an idea which at first was ridiculed within an inch of its life.'

Bernie grinned. 'So Samuel Langhorne Clemens got it right?'

'You mean Mark Twain.'

Lois grinned and Bernie laughed. He enjoyed having his leg pulled. She liked him, and the feeling was mutual.

He became inquisitive. 'So tell me about that former scientist.'

'God, what was her name? She was short, Hungarian, and weird, and worked on coercing the brain to respond to one's behaviour.'

'What happened?'

'No idea. But her research should still be in the archives.'

Bernie mimicked his future speech to the firm's librarian. 'Excuse me, Madam Librarian. I'm looking for research notes created 30 years ago by a weird Hungarian midget.'

Lois threw an empty plastic cup at Bernie. Bullseye.

In the company library, Bernie found the research material created by the Hungarian scientist, Dr Annuska Eszes, PhD. Talk about fascinating.

Then he located said person, very much alive but retired, and residing in suburban Melbourne. Bernie telephoned, and made an appointment.

Next Saturday he stood outside a solid Victorian house in Balaclava. The gardener's name was Run Riot, and Bernie pushed aside vegetation en route to the front door. He rang the doorbell, and heard footsteps.

The door opened revealing an extra from *The Hobbit*.

'You must be Bernard,' she said, her teeth downstage centre. 'As my Scottish grandfather used to say, "Come away in".'

The former scientist had more Hungarian blood than British, and vast reserves of energy. She was quicker to jump over than run round, and had masses of grey hair often mistaken for terrified steel wool. Despite its octogenarian status, her brain remained super active.

Bernie met Annuska's friend of 53 years. 'This is my lover, Bernard,' chirped the scientist. 'She's Dorothy, a friend of Dorothy on the distaff side.' Dorothy sighed having heard the so-called joke a million times, and Bernie had never felt more at home.

He and Annuska chatted about *Labcope* while Dorothy fetched tea and expensive biscuits. Black coffee, and you know what, would have made this the perfect visit.

'I am intrigued, young man,' said Annuska. 'Why would anyone be interested in my research? The company wasn't. And why now?'

Bernie gave a vague description of his conscience drug idea. She seemed trustworthy but secrecy in science is more vital than vital. He gently probed Annuska who had no such fear of secrecy.

'Years ago I had this idea about drugs being able to control the brain and our thinking. The management laughed at me. "It can't be done. You could take 50 years to discover it won't work. There's no money in it. *"Migraines before miracles"*, they used to say.'

'I must admit I found your research notes extremely interesting.'

'Now Bernard, please. Phoney flattery or more likely flattery with an interior motive demeans you.'

Interior motive?

She continued. 'The truth is you have a crazy idea and want to pick my brain to see if your boat will float.' Bernie froze. 'Or you're a *Labcope* spy sent to see if I've continued my research since I left the company.'

Wow.

'I'm afraid, Dr Eszes, you give me far too much credit.'

'Do I? You could be a spy. They don't all look like Alec Guinness.'

Bernie's heartbeat quickened. This woman promised a goldmine of information with a touch of lunacy thrown in gratis.

'So which is it?' she asked.

Dorothy entered. 'Don't bully the boy,' she said carrying a tray.

'I assure you, ladies, I would make the world's worst spy.'

Annuska replied. 'So your flattery does mask an interior motive.'

'Ulterior motive,' said Dorothy. 'Milk, Mr Slim?' He nodded.

'You could be the best scientist in the world, Bernard,' continued Annuska, 'but *Labcope* is only interested in profit. You want my advice?'

'She'll give it, young man, whether you want it or not,' added Dorothy.

'Work alone, away from the company, and trust nobody.'

Bernie blanched. 'Work alone?'

'Any one of your colleagues could be a spy for the company.'

'I really don't think so,' replied Bernie, thinking of Lois.

'You think I am crazy?'

'You *are* crazy,' added Dorothy, passing the tea.

'I could tell you stories to make your hair stand very tall. If you make a discovery, the company will know everything. They will use your discovery, not to help mankind, but to make money. People above you will claim it is *their* discovery and you will be drafted.'

'Shafted,' added her partner.

'So,' said Annuska, 'did I tell you what you wanted to hear?'

Bernie hesitated. 'I believe I should respectfully decline to answer on the grounds I might incriminate myself.'

The women warmed to their young visitor. Annuska continued.

'Perhaps when you have developed your idea, and think I can be trusted, you will call again. Slowly is how to make your theory proved.'

'Prove your theory,' corrected Dorothy. 'Have a biscuit, young man.'

Going home, Bernie's mind fizzed.

Are there spies at Labcope? Surely not.

There were. As Bernie headed back to Cremorne, the Hyphen sat in his South Yarra home, reading an email from the *Labcope* librarian. Her report detailed Bernie's recent inspection of Dr Eszes' research notes.

So Slim of R & D is looking at research produced by that whacky Hungarian dyke. Why? What is that smug prick up to?

The Hyphen reached for his phone, dialled a number then spoke.

'It's your *Labcope* contact. I have another job for you.'

5

LUCA PARISI knew the drug trade well; he knew how to obtain drugs, sell them, "clean" the takings, and, most importantly, how to avoid the law. But Luca had a new rival, Brendan Murphy. Born and bred in Belfast, Murphy excelled at hatred and violence.

The Irishman attempted a takeover of Luca's patch. His associates approached the druggies, the worker ants, who sold Luca's goods.

'Want some gear?'

'How much?'

'Try before you buy.'

Genius marketing. The addict snaffled the free sample.

'Nice,' said the addict. 'Emma chisit?'*

(*Australian for 'How much is it?')

'Usual price but we give credit.'

More genius marketing. Talk about an offer too good to refuse.

And so Murphy moved in, and Luca's drug income collapsed.

It was payback time.

At Luca's next meeting, his "staff" looked nervous. An angry Luca made everyone nervous. The word from the street was all about Murphy, the Irish prick who muscled in on "our" territory. Luca seethed.

'Irish prick. Who the fuck does he think he is?'

'He's givin' away free samples and free credit,' said Animal.

'You want we match the offer, boss?' asked ex-builder's labourer Jim, so-called because his mates couldn't pronounce Giambattista.

'No way,' snorted Luca. 'We fight fire with a fucken cruise missile. Where there is fear, there is respect. Scare 'em, Animal, give his pushers a slap, something special.'

Animal grinned. Other people's pain was his drug of choice, and that night Luca's army waited by an inner-city lane. Animal paced in the shadows, pretending to be a druggie on heat. A Murphy car pulled up, and one of his pushers approached Animal, Luca's phony addict.

The pusher had barely started his spiel when the sounds of breaking glass and terrifying screams exploded. The pusher spun around.

Using a tomahawk and sledgehammer, two of Luca's crew smashed the windows of Murphy's company car. The driver lost control of his bodily functions, and the top of a couple of digits for good measure.

Alas, the driver was not alone in Trouble City. As the pusher turned to the commotion, Animal thrust a knife towards Murphy's minion.

Now there are conditions and diseases of the buttocks, which can be bloody unpleasant, but few provide as much exquisite pain as a blade plunged into one's gluteus maximus. The screaming of Murphy's men reverberated in stereo.

By the time the cops arrived, the weeping wounded, along with Luca's entourage, had fled, although only one team repaired to St Vincent's Emergency. The hospital staff called the police. Unsurprisingly, the victims couldn't remember anything about their attackers.

When told the news, Luca and Murphy had vastly different reactions.

Therefore, war was unofficially declared between two crime lords, the Italian and the Ulsterman. They were raised good Catholics although both now only attended church for a funeral, of which there were plenty.

The gendarmes were chuffed the crims were at war with each other. So long as collateral damage didn't raise its bloody head, crims killing crims meant bodies were interred, not incarcerated — savings all round.

Luca seldom swore in public. Unlike most criminals, he worked hard at looking like a good citizen. His theory being that if he dressed and behaved as a law-abiding and polite member of society, his neighbours would trust and accept him, and the cops would be less inclined to consider him a person of interest.

Hardly. To the cops, Luca was a ravenous wolf in sheep's clothing, and various law-enforcement agencies had well and truly marked his card. But being on their radar was not the same as Luca being inside.

Like many a top crook, Luca remained at large. He maintained clean hands, using lackeys at the coalface to perform his criminal activities. If they got caught, these low-ranking lawbreakers knew that to grass meant death to them and their family.

Luca had two goals — to make as much money as possible, and to impress his Mafia connections back in Calabria. Luca wanted to deal with his Italian fellow criminals, the 'Ndrangheta, not just because they could supply quality gear or knew where he could find same, but because he wanted respect. Luca just had to become the Down Under Don.

Dealing drugs wasn't easy. He faced competition — the Belfast boy a prime example — and Luca found demand for drugs constantly changed.

From heroin in laneways to cocaine in penthouses; from good old pot to ecstasy and ice, and from Bute to Carfentanil — which drugs would be fashionable next year, next week? Should Luca import the finished product, or make his own? God it was tough being a crime lord.

But the boy done well. Washing the money through his Lygon Street restaurant and gambling forays became the final link in the chain.

Until Murphy made waves, Luca's money rolled in, the cops couldn't nail him, and if they tried, Luca believed in the 'Ndrangheta proverb: "The only thing that can't be bribed is the weather".

Brendan Murphy became Luca's sworn enemy. Murphy and Luca had identical investments and, in the words of many a cowboy in many a B grade Western, "This town ain't big enough for the two of us".

Murphy played dirty. He had anger, vengeance and fear tattooed all over him — literally. He saw Luca as a dago, an Iti, a feckin' spaghetti-sucking wog. For Murphy, ruling Melbourne's underworld was less important than smashing Luca's empire. Hate is a powerful stimulant. Murphy, the ex-IRA street fighter, went in hard with his simple plan.

Because Luca offered no credit when selling drugs, he avoided outstanding bills but left himself open to a takeover. Murphy took over.

Murphy's free samples and credit whacked Luca's hip pocket hard, and the Italian wasn't having it. The bashing and brutal maiming of Murphy's men was a statement of intent, a textbook example of payback.

Murphy knew all about tit for tat. He grew up in Belfast. And so it started. You pinch my patch, I smack your boys. You smack my boys, I smack your family. A code between warlords didn't exist, but if it did, the only rule would be, "there ain't no rules".

Of course Luca knew Murphy would hit back hard, but even Luca didn't expect the double whammy the Irishman had in mind.

It was the perfect *tit* for Luca's *tat*. It scared the shit out of the Italian, but worse, it brought the cops to Luca's front door. Bugger.

News of Luca's savage attack on Murphy's men caused the Belfast boy angst. He fumed. His blood pressure surged. His motto in life could be found in the "biblical" verse hanging on his parlour wall.

An eye for a feckin' eye.

We all have different types of sleep. When we experience deep sleep, we are harder to wake and, if woken, we might become disorientated. Some reckon 3am is the time of deepest sleep with our body clocks in lock-down. It's the perfect time for unrighteous villains to ply their trade.

If you're planning a hit, the fear a 3am attack creates is greater than if the victim is awake or nearly so. Deep sleep, plus sudden and life-threatening activity, equals serious fear.

Murphy's hitman had clear instructions. The target was tattooed on his brain. The driver repeated Luca's address, and explained his exit route with the skill of a London cabbie reciting The Knowledge.

Luca and his family slept soundly; deep, deep sleep. Suddenly their world exploded as bullets smashed through windows and doors. The noise woke the suburb. Dogs barked, babies cried, and parents panicked. Luca leapt out of bed, screaming at his wife.

'Put Ange under his bed and stay down.'

Luca raced downstairs. He needed a weapon. How could he protect himself and his family without a firearm? He stopped.

Shit. People have already rung the cops. They'll be here in my house. An innocent victim would call the cops.

He left his gun in its hiding place, grabbed his mobile, and called triple zero. He gave his details to the dreaded pigs.

The filth arrived pronto. They walked, sauntered even, around his home; uniforms first, then detectives, and finally forensics.

The fucken police are standing in my lounge room.

'And have you any idea who may have done this, sir?'

'Not a clue, officer,' replied Luca. 'Perhaps hoons on a joyride, or criminals with a crap GPS.'

Luca loathed this interview and crime-scene situation. His plan to be a "normal" citizen blew up in his face.

How the hell can I remain low-key with a pile of cops in my home?

Murphy played a blinder. He frightened the life out of Luca's family, but far worse, he exposed his rival to the cops. Murphy handed the police an open invitation to walk into Luca's home, and look at everything. No need for a warrant. This was a crime scene to be investigated. Murphy had logic in his lunacy. Luca couldn't decide which scenario he hated more — Murphy's attack or the cops invading his home.

This drive-by shooting was tit for tat 101. Luca bashed Murphy's boys. Murphy shot up Luca's home. So now it was game on. The ball was back in Luca's court. But how would he return serve?

The police departed and Luca relaxed a touch. Big mistake. If he thought getting rid of the cops meant the end of his misery, he was deadset wrong.

His troubles multiplied. First his wife, and then his mother fired both barrels.

'Our son could have been killed,' screamed Kellie.

'I was in the kitchen just before the shooting.' Sheila berated her son. 'Five minutes later and I'd be dead.'

Luca had no time for bawling women. 'Go back to bed, I'll fix it.'

'Fix it! You couldn't fix a lid on a fucken jar,' yelled Sheila.

Luca began to crack.

I've hit you before, Ma. Don't tempt me.

The adults eventually retired. Luca would have been warm to cuddle due to his boiling blood. Sheila wanted out, but where? Kellie turned a blind eye to hubby's business activities, but not when her home became a war zone. She too wanted out, but where? Luca faced a mutiny.

And then there was Murphy and his treachery. Good luck, Luca.

Murphy loved a fight. As a hardened criminal, he took great satisfaction from revenge. And in his mind, he proved his manhood by accepting reprisals, and wore any wounds as a badge of honour.

But hang on. What about a double whammy?

A lightbulb pinged in Murphy's bald head. He buzzed, remembering the Belfast priest who coached Murphy's football team. Before the game, the priest tried to stir his players.

'Now den lads, let's be gettin' y'retaliation in first.'

Of course. Hit Luca again before he responds to my shooting. But this time make the response a deadset killer.

Murphy's plan was simple. He would frame Luca for murder. It sounded perfect, and often the simple plans are best. All Murphy needed was a body, shot dead of course.

Now Luca wouldn't kill one of his own, unless they grassed. But Luca would willingly murder one of Murphy's men. Luca would love that.

So to frame the Iti, Murphy needed one of his drug runners to top himself with Luca's gun in Luca's home, and have the cops rock up.

Feckin' unbelievable thought Murphy. *That'd be twice the cops had strolled into Luca's joint, and this time they'd find a murder victim. Oh, Luca, me lovely boy, get y'self out of that shite, y'wog bastard.*

Murphy needed to keep his plan secret. If someone discovered the plan, his business, his life, was over. He couldn't trust anyone to carry out the plan. He had to do the job himself.

He asked his cronies about Luca's home.

'No chance, boss,' said Noddy, so-called because he had big ears. 'He's got cameras, alarms, and probably fecking landmines. Italians are big on family, and there's no way the prick would ever put his kid in danger.'

'What about his restaurant,' asked Murphy?

'He's there most nights,' added Shorty, who was six six in socks.

'What you planning boss?' asked Noddy.

Murphy paused. His crew hung on his every word.

'I'm gonna top that feckin' Iti m'self.'

There was a murmur of surprise and delight followed by something amazing — a round of applause. Hardened crims actually put their hands together. They were rapt. It was a trifecta. Luca would be dead, Murphy's empire would rule Melbourne, and the boss himself was to do the deed. If only they knew Murphy's real intention.

The Belfast boy chose his youngest and least experienced gang member.

'Don't take him, boss,' pleaded Noddy. 'The kid's a deadset liability.'

'He's small enough to get over da fence and in dat back window,' replied Murphy. 'Just make sure you're ready once Luca's been hit.'

Noddy's big ears twitched with concern.

The three men waited till near midnight. It was a Monday, and the restaurant would be empty or nearly so. The plan was to break into the back of the restaurant, bail up the kitchen staff, have one of them call for Luca, and then, when the drug lord arrived, hit the prick with a few rounds where no surgeon need ever go.

That was Murphy's public plan. His other plan remained secret.

The teenager, Hoops, smaller than a jockey, accompanied his boss. The duo crept down the Carlton lane. Both were carrying. Murphy had the weapons, Hoops the steps. They stopped at the back fence of Luca's restaurant. Murphy gave Hoops a bunk up. He scaled the fence, couldn't handle the locks, so Murphy used the steps. Once inside, Murphy handed Hoops a gun.

Lights from the kitchen lit the yard, and the intruders crept towards the back door. Inside, pots and pans rattled and banged. An Italian song played on a flour-dusted radio. Garlic smells lingered. Suddenly the back door opened, and Murphy pulled Hoops back against the wall. A kitchen hand dumped food waste in a bin.

A click disturbed the employee, who looked and, in the dim light, saw Murphy's gun pointed straight at him. His scream died.

'Call out and you're dead,' hissed Murphy.

'Don't shoot, please,' he begged.

'Is Luca inside?' The kitchen hand nodded. 'In da restaurant?' More nodding. 'You got a weapon in da kitchen?'Even more nodding.

'Where?' demanded Murphy. This time nodding wasn't an option.

'There's a pistol behind the knives, and a shotgun in the freezer.'

'How many people are in da kitchen now? Show me fingers.'

The terrified worker gave a V for Victory sign. Murphy moved towards the man who dropped to his knees and wept. Murphy whipped his pistol across the victim's temple, and the man fell, knocking rubbish bins.

Someone called from the kitchen. 'What's going on?' The chef appeared, saw his fallen co-worker, and knelt. Terror sprang from the darkness as Murphy's pistol pressed against the back of the chef's skull.

'Shut da feck up.' The chef's hands shot up. He was familiar with Mafia rules. 'Stand slowly, *slowly*,' ordered Murphy.

The chef entered the kitchen where a man, washing dishes, saw the trio. Even the suds fell silent as the third employee copped instant fear.

Murphy spoke to Hoops. 'If dey move, shoot 'em.'

Murphy crept towards the knives on the work surface, and collected the hidden gun. He gave orders to the chef.

'Get Luca to come to da kitchen. Tell him dere's a problem wid da oven. And make it feckin' believable. Warn him and you die.'

The chef and dish washer endured chest pain. Murphy nodded.

The chef moved to the swing door leading to the restaurant, opened it a little, and called.

'Hey boss. We got a problem with the oven. She no good.'

'How bad?' called Luca.

Murphy pointed his gun straight at the chef.

'We is gunna need the main man. She broke bad.'

'Okay,' yelled Luca. 'I'm coming.'

The temperature in the kitchen raced into the red zone. Luca's footsteps got louder. Hoops had never killed anyone or anything before, and his trigger finger had the shakes. The chef decided to call out just as Luca pushed open the door.

Hoops fired first but missed. Murphy fired twice. It was your typical chaos when criminals discharge firearms without fear or favour.

Luca dived back inside his restaurant, scrambling for cover, when suddenly a gun slid towards him. He grabbed it, and prepared to return fire. The shooting stopped.

Silence. The seconds ticked by. Luca yelled.

'Tony? You okay?'

The chef was not okay. He was without war wounds, but desperately wanted to puke. He croaked his words.

'It's okay, boss. They gone.'

Luca crept towards the kitchen, and took a quick peak through the round glass window in the door. No bandits. He pushed open the door, and ducked inside, pointing his gun in different directions.

The chef was only partly correct. Murphy had gone but not so Hoops, and he was not going anywhere.

The Italians surveyed the scene. They checked the corpse. Then the wail of a police siren made Luca sick to his guts.

This time the police came with guns drawn. Luca wanted to throw up. It was stunning stuff as Murphy whacked Luca twice; stunning because of the surprise element, and stunning because the cops arrived en masse.

Crims expect revenge but not a double serve. After the drive-by shooting on his home, Luca planned his payback. While he planned, Murphy struck again; he got his retaliation in first.

The Irishman was doubly smart. Luca now had cops crashing through his privacy, and arresting him for murder. Murphy framed his rival, and did it well. The boy from Belfast now ruled the Melbourne drug scene.

Hoops lay dead on Luca's kitchen floor. The pint-sized teen took two bullets from Luca's gun, which had Luca's prints all over it. Wearing flesh-coloured gloves, Murphy had "accidentally" killed his own man, and boy was he cut up about that — not.

Murphy raced back to his car. En route, he called triple zero on a pay-as-you-go mobile, and sent the cops to Carlton —'dere's been a murder,' he screamed, gave the address, cut the call, and later dumped the phone and steps. He leapt into the car blabbing about Hoops being shot.

'Hoops is dead?' whined Noddy.

'I'll kill dat feckin' Iti wid me bare hands,' growled Murphy, while secretly grinning inside, knowing Luca was up to his eyes in shit.

'Just drive, *drive*,' screamed Murphy. He was home free as the cops burst into Luca's HQ.

The police saw what they saw.

Yes, it was a robbery or an attempted hit, or both, and yes, Luca had every right to defend himself and his staff. But this didn't look good.

Luca knew the police would seize any chance to nail him. He knew his so-called squeaky-clean image didn't wash with the pigs. The whiff of a set-up counted for nothing.

I spy the smoking gun and you, chummy, are going down.

In the interview-room, a detective spoke. 'Look at the facts, Mr Parisi. We have a dead man in your restaurant, shot with your gun which has one set of fingerprints — yours. What can you tell us about that?'

Luca remained mute. His solicitor spoke.

'My client has nothing further to add to the statement he's already provided. Please officer, either charge or release Mr Parisi.'

The police turned off the recording equipment, and left the room.

'It's bullshit,' snapped Luca, pacing the room. 'No way can they charge me with murder. Three witnesses saw Murphy shoot his own man.'

'Two witnesses; one was out cold.'

'He will say he was pretending and playing dead. He will swear he saw Murphy shoot his own man — three eye witnesses.'

'Of course we fight any murder charge. But having unregistered and unsecured firearms on the property is trouble, Luca. You'll be charged.'

Luca kicked a chair. 'Fines, a slap on the wrist.' He pointed at his solicitor. 'Just make sure there's no fucken murder charge.'

There was. The police woke a sleepy Office of Public Prosecutions lawyer then returned. Luca's ears expelled steam.

The detective spoke. 'Mr Parisi, you will be charged with murder. You can apply for bail before the magistrate in the morning — but I wouldn't hold your breath.'

Luca thought about screaming abuse, about lunging at the police, about threatening to kill Murphy, but remained outwardly calm — just.

He ordered his solicitor to be at Luca's home first thing in the morning to explain matters to Sheila and Kellie. They would not be happy. Then Luca called Animal.

6

BERNIE EXPERIMENTED in his father's shed. For 31 years, Gus taught science in secondary colleges until his devastating car accident. He gave son Bernie a love for all things scientific and, as a wee lad, Bernie explored chemistry with his father in this backyard bungalow.

Tonight Bernie beavered away mixing chemicals, heating them, testing reactions, and making notes.

It was a fortnight since he first met Annuska. He went a second time, and they hit it off. She gave him copies of her private notes on drugs influencing the brain. By night he digested them, re-read Norman Doidge's texts, read more generally about drugs affecting the brain, and even threw in ideas from his own training.

He rang one of his father's friends, a neurologist. He picked people's brains about brains, and all this enabled Bernie to create a formula with equal amounts of guesswork, hope and science. He clung to his wild idea of a conscience drug.

He worked alone. Annuska's message about spies rang alarm bells. Everything he did was offline, at home with Albert, or here in the old man's shed. Bernie and Luca Parisi had something in common — no paper trails and nothing online.

Bernie heard a strange sound, and stopped work. It got louder. Bernie waited. Had the company spies tracked him here?

'It's only the poor, old cripple,' called Gus.

Bernie relaxed, opened the shed door, and helped push his father inside. The wheelchair only just made it.

'Dad, this is crazy. There's mud all over your tyres. Mum'll have a fit.'

'Long time since we were in here together.'

Bernie nodded. His father's shed held heaps of happy memories.

'You sure you don't mind me being in here,' asked Bernie?

'Mind? I'm delighted, but curious to know what you're doing.'

Bernie grew nervous. What possible reason could his father have to slip and slide through the backyard? Any chat could far more easily occur indoors. He originally told his father he wanted to "fix" the shed so he could teach his parents' grandchildren about science. Then Annuska's warning jarred his brain.

Is my father a spy? Hardly.

'Ah, I'm just testing a theory on a new drug for the brain.'

'In here? You have a million dollar research lab, and you choose this ramshackle garden shed?'

'It's the nostalgia, Dad. It's my lucky charm locale.'

'Well I hope you're a better scientist than you are a liar.'

Bernie grimaced. He'd been sprung.

'I could never fool you, Dad. If I broke a window, and tried to blame Maddy, or told you I was out with the boys when I was with a girl, you always knew.'

'It wasn't me being clever; it was more you failing the baloney test.'

They laughed. Gus examined his son's apparatus and concoctions, becoming nosy in a polite and genuinely interested way.

'So what's the real reason you're working out here?'

'You won't believe this,' said Bernie. 'I really am testing a theory on a new drug for the brain, but I'm working here because my crazy idea is not part of my job, and I think there are spies at work.'

Gus looked at his son. This time the boy spoke the truth.

'Spies — as in Russian diplomats and spooks?'

Bernie shrugged. 'More your lackeys-for-the-management spies, but yes, people who check your work and tell others.'

'Have you told your boss?'

'Ah, therein lies the problem.'

The old man's eyes widened. 'Your boss is a spy?'

'Well, perhaps the collator of data delivered by his spies.'

'So what's this theory of yours? No, don't speak. You could say, but you'll have to kill me.'

They laughed again but without enthusiasm.

It was time for a role reversal with Bernie asking the questions.

'You haven't come out here to inspect my chemistry.' Bernie looked at his father. 'What's up, Dad? Are you okay?'

'I'm fine.'

Silence filled the shed. Bernie sensed bad news but hesitated to ask. Ignorance is bliss. Finally, Gus spoke about his wife, Daphne.

'It's your mother. She's not well.' Bernie's heart sank.

'She can't be sick; she looks terrific. I've never seen her looking better.'

43

Gus hesitated. 'Physically she's tickety-boo.' More silence. 'But I'm afraid she has early signs of dementia.'

Wow.

Tears appeared in the old man's eyes. He became numb, and grasped the arms of his wheelchair, turning his knuckles white.

Bernie slumped. Words failed. Finally, he spoke in a whisper.

'Are you sure?'

Gus nodded. 'The GP told me the other day. Maddy knows.'

'But Mum's your carer. How can she cope with all your needs?'

'Oh that's not a problem. We'll swap and I'll become *her* carer.'

Bernie looked at his pathetic father. His black comedy sense of humour thrived. But this once active, proud and loving man now lived in a wheelchair, needing help to perform even the most basic of tasks. Bottom wiping was barely within his remit.

'Why haven't you told me this before?' pleaded Bernie.

His father shrugged. 'At first it was just the odd thing. She'd forget someone's name or ask me a question, and then five minutes later, ask me again. I forget things. I thought it was just old age.'

'You and Mum aren't old.'

'I talked to the GP who arranged tests. The results came back and ...'

Gus couldn't finish the sentence. He didn't care that Daphne would no longer be able to care for his crippled body. He cared because the woman he loved was no longer the woman he loved.

Bernie squeezed his father's shoulder. Gus squeezed his son's arm. They weren't big on hugs, and the wheelchair didn't help, yet both found the activity natural and comforting.

Emotional?

You bet.

They went inside and Bernie knew his instructions. Say nothing. Treat your mother as if everything is normal, and everyone is fine and dandy.

They found Daphne with Madeline and her two kids.

'What were you doing outside, Uncle Bernie?' one asked.

'I was being a scientist in Pa's shed. I can teach you two all sorts of things about science. Would that be cool?'

His nephew and niece bubbled with enthusiasm.

'But not now,' said their mother. 'Show Gran and Pa your projects.'

The children proudly displayed their school material. Gus was delighted and made all sorts of positive comments. The room buzzed with excitement until an innocent six year-old asked a question.

'Do you like my project, Gran?'

Daphne looked at the artwork, then at the child, and then dropped a bombshell when she spoke.

'What's your name?'

The silence was deafening. Gus looked at his adult children with tears in his eyes. Madeline took control. She told her kids to kiss their grandparents, then bundled her offspring out the door. Bernie kissed his mother, and shook his father's hand with both hands.

'Bye Mum. I'll call you tomorrow, Dad.' He looked straight at his father, nodded, and then followed his sister.

In the street, the grandkids sat strapped in the car, while the adult siblings stood in the street not able to look at one another.

Madeline cried. Bernie embraced her, struggling to offer comfort.

'It's Dad I feel sorry for,' she wept. 'Mum has no idea.'

'Probably,' said Bernie.

'Probably?'

'We can't be sure how much knowledge dementia patients have about their condition.'

Conversation proved tricky. Madeline had problems of her own, and her mother's condition exacerbated her woe. She unloaded her grief.

'Poor Dad. He sits there, helpless, and watches the woman he loves fall apart in front of him. It's not fair.'

'I know,' whispered Bernie.

'I'd like a word with God. Surely one disabled parent's enough. Why two? And what are we going to do?'

'Dad told me they'll switch roles; he'll become Mum's carer.'

Madeline looked at her brother in disbelief, and cried the more. The black comedy quip fell flat. Bernie was nervous but felt he had to ask.

'How's Bruce?'

The loaded question intensified Madeline's suffering. Her unhappy marriage now had a rival; her mother's dementia. Bernie promised to call his sister the next day when they would have a full-on discussion about this latest crisis. Suddenly Bernie's wonder drug idea lost its relevance.

Bernie rang Annuska and asked if he might visit. She agreed. When he arrived, Annuska opened the door almost as wide as her smile.

'Bernard, it is so lovely to see you again.' He handed her a bunch of flowers. 'And flowers too.' She stiffened and spoke in a mock threatening way. 'Are they for me or that floozy, Dorothy?'

'I heard that,' said Dorothy entering the hall.

'For both of you, of course,' replied Bernie.

The trio entered the lounge room where Annuska indicated a chair for Bernie. He remained standing, waiting for Dorothy to sit.

'I'm not staying,' she said. 'I'll pop these in water, and then fetch your black coffee and cinnamon doughnut.'

The stunned look on Bernie's face caused the women to laugh with gay abandon. Annuska was well ahead in the volume stakes, and the mirth took some time to subside. Dorothy departed.

'How on earth did you know?' asked Bernie.

Annuska tapped her nose. '*Labcope* are not the only ones who have the spies. Do you know Bruno in the basement?'

'I do, and he's a lovely man.'

'We Hungarians stick together, no? He did some exploring for me and we found your only weakness.'

Bernie sat and purred. 'I'm afraid I have many weaknesses.'

'Good, these we can explore later,' added Annuska with a wink.

'Dr Eszes, thank you for all your help. Your notes have been fantastic.'

'Dr Eszes? Please, I tell you to call me Annuska.' She slipped into a Marlene Dietrich voice for the last two words. 'Or else, *my darling*.'

'Annuska,' grinned Bernie.

'But that previous conversation on the telephone, my friend, must be our last.' Bernie frowned. 'You forget my warning about spies?'

The penny dropped. 'The lines are tapped?' he gasped. 'Are you sure?'

'I tell you everything what happened when I worked at *Labcope*. You can then decide for yourself.'

Dorothy entered with that favourite snack.

Bernie munched as Annuska told stories. They blew his mind. If only half were true, *Labcope* was a hotbed of intrigue. If the Hyphen was a sneaky bastard, some of Annuska's bosses were positively Machiavellian.

'If we talk on the phone in the future, Bernard, we discuss the weather and our love lifes.'

'Love *lives*,' corrected Dorothy.

'Oh take no notice of her, Bernard. She is not like you and me. We are still full of romance with a passion for love, yes?'

She winked and, for a moment, Bernie thought he was in some drug-induced fantasy.

'And we know what they say about those who talk about it,' added Dorothy.

Finally, barbs and boasts aside, they turned to Bernie's proposed formula. He opened his backpack, and handed Annuska his notes. She started to read, fascinated with the contents. Occasionally, without looking up, she threw in a comment.

'That won't work ... it's the *right* side of the brain ... you are wrong here ... that is something I never would have thought about ... I'm not sure that's correct ... Ez a csodálatos.'*

(*Hungarian for 'That is amazing'.)

After what seemed like ages, she stopped reading, removed her glasses, and handed Bernie his notes. She didn't speak.

'Well, put the young man out of his misery,' ordered Dorothy.

'You have taken my work and added something new,' said Annuska. 'I think you may have found a stunning new way to treat the brain.'

Bernie found it hard to breathe. The lump in his throat got lumpier.

'I'm not saying it will work, mind, but maybe,' said Annuska.

'That's very encouraging, thank you, Annuska.'

'However, you have one major problem.' Bernie's happiness stalled. 'You know that animals help us to understand many results and side effects when we trial a new drug. And you know that testing a drug on animals can be unreliable, sometimes impossible. But your situation is far worse. With your proposed drug, we are talking morality, and physical pain caused by mental torment. To put it sharply ...'

'Bluntly,' said Dorothy.

'To put it bluntly, Bernard, your guinea pigs will have to be human.'

Smack! Bernie felt as if Annuska had slapped his face. He argued.

'But I must work with animals first. To start with human testing is against everything a scientist does, not to mention illegal.'

'Do you like the irony?'

Bernard paused, not sure of the question.

'It's all right, Bernard,' said Dorothy. 'This time the good doctor's grasp of irony is, ironically, perfectly correct.'

'Thank you, Dotty,' added an appreciative Annuska.

Bernard realised. He planned to make a drug for the conscience, yet had to test it in an unconscionable way.

Ralph Hetherington-Smythe drove his BMW, entering the darkened car park of the Black Rock Yacht Club. Soon after, another car arrived, and parked thirty metres away. Ralph stared towards the Bay. He heard footsteps, and checked out the person standing next to his vehicle. He released the internal lock.

The other driver opened the passenger door, and climbed in beside the *Labcope* CEO. The visitor had a firm handshake.

47

'Nice to see you again, Doctor.'

'Good evening.'

Small talk did not appeal to the Hyphen.

'You have another job for me?' asked the passenger.

'Where the usual conditions apply,' said Ralph. 'You report only to me. You'll be paid by me, the same fee as last time. This is our last face-to-face meeting. *Never* come to *Labcope*. Use the same dead-letter drop, the same web site to inform me of a drop, and the same pen name. No text messages, phone calls, emails or snail mail. Understood?'

'Yes.'

Ralph handed the spy a page of handwritten notes.

'Read this and start immediately. Once read, destroy. Questions?'

'No.'

'Target A is a current member of staff. Target B is a former member of staff. I assume they meet at her home. I want to know why and what they discuss. Questions?'

'No.'

'A recording device at one target's address might mean a bonus. A recording device at both addresses guarantees that bonus.'

'Thank you.'

'And, as always, if you're caught or implicated in any way, you've never heard of *Labcope* or me.'

'I'm sorry?'

'What?'

'Who are you?'

Ralph twigged. He liked the spy's professionalism, which meant only relevant data was collected with never any trouble for the employer.

'I'll start work tonight.'

'I want this information yesterday.'

The spy smiled and looked at the CEO. He didn't smile.

Ralph started his engine giving the spy three seconds to exit, and close the door of the BMW.

The Hyphen left. His spy perused the screed, made notes in a phone, destroyed the screed, then drove to Cremorne, parked illegally in Chestnut Street, and wandered past Bernie's house.

'Piece of piss,' murmured the spy.

Inside, Albert slumbered. Outside, the spy cased the joint. Annuska was right. Spies and *Labcope* were secretly best friends.

That night Bernie dined on Signora Conti's superb chicken cacciatore casserole. His taste buds celebrated but his mind was science bound.

He collected even more notes from his own experiments, factored in Annuska's comments, and re-read serious amounts of relevant literature on drugs which affect the brain and human behaviour.

He fine-tuned his formula. He placed the ingredients on his kitchen table, and looked at his mortar and pestle. He placed a laboratory beaker and holder beside the gas stove, took a deep breath, and made drugs.

On paper, his formula seemed logical. But how would he ever know? Who would ever volunteer to try the drug? The only people who should be given this drug would run a mile from any opportunity to take it.

Then an idea struck.

Test the drug on myself.

He wouldn't be the first person to trial an invention with the creator as guinea pig. Dr Jekyll turned into Mr Hyde when the good doctor ingested one of his own drugs. And another famous doctor, Arthur Conan Doyle, the publicity agent for Dr Watson's tales about Sherlock Holmes, tested a drug on himself — and lived to tell the tale.

But did Bernie have a problem with his conscience? Was there something about which he felt bad? Because without something nasty, illegal or evil in his past, taking the drug would be useless. Only with a guilty secret could Bernie seriously trial his invention.

Then he remembered. How could he forget? He cheated during his final year Chemistry exams.

It was a terrible time. He broke up with his then girlfriend. He borrowed money from his parents to invest in an app designed to teach toddlers to read, and lost every cent. Then his father was in that horrendous car accident, and spent months in hospital. Bernie's life had spiralled out of control, and he fell behind in his academic studies. Failure in his final year would have been catastrophic.

In the university library, he spied a swot from his class. The guy was a good student, and got high marks in every essay and thesis.

The student went to find a book, and Bernie acted on impulse. He moved to the table and, making sure nobody was looking, quickly used his phone to photograph the student's notes.

Bernie went home, and used those notes for his essay. He passed.

To this day, at different times, his conscience still troubled him; not in a massive way but enough to make him think badly of himself. His conscience flared whenever he ran into the student at reunions.

That incident could test his conscience drug.

If it works, I'll feel terrible unless I confess about my cheating.

He looked at the first batch of his formula. It was in loose powder form. He'd pinched some empty drug capsules from work but couldn't be bothered with presentation right now.

He placed a small amount of his unproven drug in a glass of water and stirred. He picked up the glass. He stared at it, believing he could hear his heart beating. He raised the glass and drank.

Next morning Bernie woke, and immediately felt his head. There was no pain, just the appearance and disappearance of follicles. He had more on his face and fewer on his scalp. Hello baldness, my old friend.

But where was the stress, the mental anguish, the pain caused by his conscience being pricked? It didn't exist.

He fell out of bed, disturbed Albert, and felt terrible.

My brilliant idea is useless. Mark Twain was right. Lois is right. Annuska is right. It's pure science fiction, my son.

He prepared for work in a fog and a funk. *What was I expecting?*

Arriving at work, he felt terrible; terrible at his useless and time-wasting wonder drug, and terrible at having to tell Lois the result.

But wait, no Lois. The switchboard rang to advise that "Mother" had fallen, and been taken to hospital. Nobody knew when or even if Lois would arrive at *Labcope*.

Bernie plodded on with his 'real' job. He couldn't stop thinking about Lois and her mum, his mum and dad, and about his failed drug test.

But hang on. If I'm thinking about that essay where I pinched someone's notes, doesn't that prove my drug works?

No, it proved nothing. There was no mental torment, and no prompt to make a full confession. Then a thought hit him.

What if I make a full confession to that outstanding student? If that removes any lingering feelings of guilt, maybe the drug works after all.

He started searching for Grant Littlejohn. He found him easily on LinkedIn, located his current employer, and tracked him down.

'Grant, g'day. It's Bernie Slim from uni.'

'Bernie, nice to hear from you. How y'going?'

'Good mate; yourself?'

'Fine. This is a coincidence.' Bernie froze. 'Are your ears burning?'

Bernie spoke with a feeling of dread. 'Ah, should they be?'

'Would you believe only yesterday I bumped into a couple of guys from our final Chemistry class, and your name came up?'

'Really?'

'Freaky. So what's news? You still at *Labcope*?'

'Yep, still here.' Bernie lied. 'And that's why I called. I've got a tricky research project, and wondered if I might pick your brain.'

'Sure, happy to help if I can.'

'Great.'

They met in the Cherry Tree Hotel, a short walk from Bernie's abode. A beer and a handshake got things rolling, and Bernie cut to the chase.

'Listen, mate, I've actually got you here under false pretences.' Grant looked intrigued. 'Nothing weird, just a small confession.'

'So it *was* you,' smiled Grant. Bernie's heart sank. 'The boys reckoned you were the one who put that sulphur in old Furtwangler's satchel.'

Bernie pretended it was him. 'Guilty as charged, but listen. I need to say something.' He drew a breath. 'I copied your notes for that final essay in Chem 4. I am really sorry. I felt bad about it then and still do now.'

'Join the queue, mate.'

'I hope you aren't too pissed off.' Bernie stopped. 'Join the queue?'

Grant was grinning. 'You weren't the only one.'

Bernie didn't follow. Grant explained. 'I pinched the notes. So did three other guys. You were just one of many, mate. And we all passed.'

Bernie looked puzzled. 'So whose notes were they?'

'Have a guess.' Bernie shook his head. 'Only that gorgeous blonde Fiona what's-her-name.'

'Not Stretch-Jeans Fiona?'

'The very same. Remember how she'd sashay to the front of the lecture room with every guy staring and drooling.'

'I'm still drooling.'

'You and me both.' They laughed.

'Perhaps I should make my confession to the lovely Fiona.'

'Bit tricky, mate. She's inside.'

'Inside?'

'The slammer. What a waste. She had the body of a goddess and the brain of a genius, and ended up with some scumbag who led her astray.'

'Damn. I wish she'd led me astray.'

They laughed again, enjoyed their drink, and left promising to keep in touch. Bernie had a short walk home.

Maybe his drug didn't work because his conscience didn't need a jolt. Maybe his guilt had been spread thinly between all the other cheats.

Nah, that's baloney. The drug doesn't work.

7

THE NEW SHADOW ATTORNEY-GENERAL made waves. She attacked the government, and especially the Attorney-General. She raised issues the public found troubling. She asked tricky questions about riots in youth prisons, home invasions, and the threat of terrorism in the state. She put the government on the back foot. People noticed.

But despite her success in wounding the Government, the polls were not good for the Opposition. Could leader, Trevor Rand, unkindly known as Trevor Bland, turn around the *SS Liberal*? He trailed the Premier, and didn't look like making ground. *A safe pair of hands* and *trustworthy* were the characteristics the party machine applied to dear old Trev. He never rocked the boat; in fact, he never even set foot on the jetty.

Rumblings grew within Liberal ranks.

'We can't lose this year.'

'Not another term of Labor rule.'

The Opposition Treasurer, Michael Riley, made no secret of his leadership ambitions, which were insipid at best. He couldn't backstab a corpse, and with the election in nine months, Riley had to challenge now.

Jessica and Genevieve watched this maneuvering from afar.

Over a lunchtime takeaway, Jessica dropped a bombshell.

'I forgot to tell you. This morning I was asked if I had any interest in running for deputy leader.'

'By whom,' snapped Genevieve?

'Some lackey. He works for Riley who, by the way, thinks he's a shoo-in to replace Trevor.'

'And of course you gave the scripted answer,' threatened Genevieve.

There was a pause. Genevieve's face contorted. She blurted.

'You didn't? Oh Jess, there are double agents everywhere. They work for Bland, sussing out where you stand in any challenge.'

'Keep your wig on,' said Jessica. 'I did exactly as Mother told me.' Jessica had taken to referring to her adviser as Mother. 'I laughed a lot making the whole thing a joke, and that way I kept them guessing.'

Genevieve relaxed. 'Good girl. Listen, I've been thinking.'

'Here's trouble,' replied the wannabe Premier.

'If we do nothing, we lose. If we do something, we lose.'

'Ah, the logic of genius.'

'Many will vote against Trevor if there's a credible alternative.'

Jessica mocked herself. 'Just call me *Credible Alternative*.'

'I reckon the best way to challenge Trevor is to make you the victim.'

Jessica was clueless. 'The victim of what?'

'I have a plan but as I've so often told you, timing is everything.'

'Yes, yes, what's the plan?'

'If we launch now and win, there's too much time for Trevor's mates to leak and damage us leading to the election.'

'Assuming we win.'

'Oh we'll win, kiddo, trust Mother.'

'Fine, just tell me the plan.'

'If we delay much longer, we won't have enough time to show the electorate you're the answer to a maiden's prayer.'

'If you delay much longer in telling me this effing plan, you'll be a maiden in *need* of a prayer.'

Genevieve paused. She couldn't say the words. Jessica sighed, her frustration palpable. When Genevieve spoke, Jessica felt ill.

'Your husband's a paedophile.'

Genevieve made many suggestions, but this latest took the biscuit. Jessica finally managed mouth the words represented by the letters WTF. Genevieve calmed her friend.

'Don't panic. Of course it's not true.'

'Of course it's not true,' hissed Jessica. 'So why would you say it?'

'All's fair in love and war, my dear, and to smash your opponents, we need an axe, not a feather duster.'

'This had better be good.'

It was. When Genevieve explained her statement, and the reasoning and strategy behind it, Jessica became calm; well, relatively.

'You are one devious bastard, Genevieve Kovács.'

Her advisor shrugged, and agreed by not speaking. Before they could continue, a staffer came in to say a member of the public was outside asking for Ms Reid.

'What do they want?' asked Jessica.

'I'm not sure, but he said something about a murder.'

'Call Security,' ordered Genevieve.

'The guard's with him now.'

'This is beautiful,' said Jessica, smiling. The others looked at her. She rubbed her hands together. 'Oh I miss the underworld.'

'I'll deal with this,' said Genevieve, heading out to Reception.

Last month, Brendan Murphy carried out an audacious sting on rival Luca Parisi. The Irish drug baron stitched up the Italian drug baron with Luca arrested for murdering short arse Hoops, one of Murphy's minions.

The cops were rapt to nail the crook they'd been chasing for years. Luca seethed. Animal went to visit his boss in jail, where Luca explained the sting, and Animal choked with rage.

The boss's murder charge was bullshit. Murphy framed Luca, and Animal and his mates could do nothing legal to change the situation. If they hit back, the cops would clobber even more of Luca's gang. But doing nothing wasn't an option, and Animal had a brainwave.

He remembered a chick with red hair, a solicitor, who got him off a drugs charge years ago. She was bloody good. He went to the CBD, and the legal chambers he once visited.

'Good morning, sir,' said the receptionist.

'G'day. Look I come here a few years ago and saw a solicitor, and she give me some help when I had a bit of trouble with the cops.'

'And who was the solicitor?'

'Ah, her name was Jessica something. She had red hair and her office was down there,' said he pointing.

'That's Ms Jessica Reid, sir.'

'That's her, Jessica Reid. Can I see her? It's real important like.'

'I'm afraid Ms Reid doesn't practise here anymore, sir. She's still a partner but today is a member of parliament.'

Animal's dial displayed confusion. 'Parliament? In Canberra?'

'No, state parliament, here in Melbourne. In fact Ms Reid is the Shadow Attorney-General.'

Animal wondered how anybody could be a shadow but didn't wish to advertise his ignorance.

'So I can't see her?'

'I'm afraid not, sir. But I can recommend other solicitors. May I ask the nature of your issue?'

'Murder,' said Animal, looking straight at the receptionist.

'I see,' she replied, shifting in her seat. 'Well if you'd like to take a seat, I'll get someone to see you.'

Animal thought about it. 'Nah, you're all right. Thanks.'

And with that, he turned and headed for that place the bird said. He asked an old geezer in a suit where the state parliament was, and took off for Spring Street. He located the offices of Her Majesty's Opposition. A receptionist loomed large, and a security guard hovered nearby.

The receptionist smiled. 'Good morning, sir. How may I help you?'

'Does Jessica Reid work here?'

'She does. What is the nature of your enquiry?'

'Ah, she helped me once, and I need her help again.'

'Well if it's a constituency matter, sir, you'll need to contact her office in Brighton.' She reached for a card with the Honourable Member for Brighton's details, but stopped when Animal spoke.

'It's about a murder.'

The security guard came alive. The receptionist had never had a member of the public raise such a topic, certainly not before lunch.

'I'll ask for help,' said the receptionist beckoning to the security guard.

'Could I ask you to step over here, sir?' asked the guard in more of an order than request. He gently took Animal's arm to escort him outside.

Animal growled. 'Hey, what's with the hands?'

The guard backed off a tad, noting that Animal had muscle, and an attitude similar to that of an almost-sleeping wild animal. Had Animal been wearing a nametag, it would have read *Do Not Disturb*.

'You'll need to follow me, sir,' said the guard, hoping the visitor would.

'Listen mate, all I wanna do is see Jessica Reid. It's no big deal. Okay?'

Not okay. Animal's request needed to be vetted, and the further away from VIPs and innocent citizens the better. Just when it appeared that force would be required, a voice interrupted proceedings.

'Is there a problem?' Genevieve came out of her office at the pointy end of the dispute. 'Can I help you, sir?'

'Yeah, I want a quick word with Jessica Reid; just five minutes.'

Genevieve took control. Telling the man to get lost or having him forcibly removed might spell trouble. A quick chat to resolve the problem should have the gent depart a happy camper.

'Will you come this way please, Mr ... '

'Animal.'

Genevieve led the visitor to her office, and indicated a seat.

'Now Mr Animal, what can I do for you?'

Genevieve was good. She didn't have Jessica's naked ambition, but her people skills were top drawer.

'Me name's Alan Darcy but everyone calls me Animal.' Genevieve smiled. Animal got the message. 'Ah, well a few years back, Jessica got me off a police charge, and I want her to do the same for me mate.'

Genevieve felt relief. *He needs legal aid. I can handle this.*

'Okay, I think I understand but I'm afraid I have some bad news.'

'Look, this is really serious. The cops have fallen for a con job. Me mate's been framed for murder, and there's no way he done it.'

'If I might finish, Mr Darcy. The bad news is that Ms Reid no longer practises criminal law. I'm afraid she can't help you.'

'What about if I ask her meself?'

Genevieve sighed. *The silly bugger's persistent.* 'Just not possible.'

'So is she something in the government then?'

'She is. Jessica's the leading law officer in the State Opposition.'

'Would she be interested in police corruption?'

Good question. Bloody good question.

If this person has something important which Jessica could use to her advantage, then we're in a completely new ball game.

'She may well be interested, Mr Darcy, but first I need some details. What exactly is this police corruption?'

'Listen, no offence, lady, but I want the boss, not the cleaner.'

The gatekeeper discovered demotion. Genevieve liked the putdown.

'I tell you what, Mr Darcy. I'll have a word with the Shadow Attorney-General, and get back to you with her reply. How's that sound?'

'When?' asked Animal.

'Well she's a busy woman.'

'Is she here now?'

Genevieve didn't have to answer as the door to her office opened, and there stood the Shadow Attorney-General. Animal's face shone.

'G'day Miss,' grinned Animal, and Jessica saw a flashback.

'Are you insane?' asked Genevieve after Animal left. 'You cannot touch this case with a barge pole. You haven't the time, and what is ridiculously worse is the fact that the accused and his buddy have criminal records as long as your Cartier necklace. Parisi's a drug dealer and extortionist. I can't believe you'd even consider this.'

'Have you finished?'

'No, but you will be if you get involved.'

'I like a challenge.'

'Jesus, Jess, grow up. Get a grip, woman.'

56

'I'm disappointed, Gen.' Her friend stood gobsmacked. 'If this Luca Parisi's been framed, I can have that overturned. It'll prove I fight injustice for everyone, including the crims.'

'Oh, that's a clever career move; how to impress the world by defending a man who makes his living out of other people's misery.'

'So the Law only applies to the good and noble?'

'The next Victorian Attorney-General does not defend drug barons. Listen to me. If you take on this case, the cops will hate you.'

'They do already.'

'If you get the bastard off, the cops will become your sworn enemy.'

'Do the cops vote for the next leader of the Liberal Party? Well?'

Genevieve stared at her friend. Jessica got serious.

'If I expose a police cockup, the public will thank me big time, and my colleagues will see a strong leader. This case just gave my leadership aspirations a serious leg up.'

Genevieve struggled for an answer. 'Okay, get involved, but stay out of sight. Work behind the scenes, give advice to another solicitor.'

'And where's the fun in that? You know I love a party.'

Genevieve looked like she might explode. Office staff could hear the argument and pretended to be busy. When Genevieve stormed into the outer office, every head was down.

Jessica did get involved. She relished being back in the world of criminal law. She met Animal back in her old chambers. He told Jessica about the feud between Murphy and Luca, and all the gory details of how Murphy murdered his own man to set up Luca.

Jessica felt fantastic knowing she still had the skills she once used daily as a solicitor. She took statements from Luca's kitchen staff. She found witnesses who identified men in the lane behind Luca's restaurant. She had a former cop visit Noddy, and put the frighteners on him for protecting his boss who murdered one of his own.

'Did you drive the getaway car, Noddy? You're an accessory to murder mate. The murder of your little pal, Hoops.' Noddy felt sick. Pressure.

All this information was building a strong case for doubt in the jury's mind should the case proceed. Jessica took her favourite barrister, a man the cops hated more than Jessica, to the Office of Public Prosecutions.

The OPP knew Jessica well from earlier times, but this was a first. The Shadow Attorney-General acting for the accused in a murder case.

She had her brutal legal chum heap pressure on the OPP with alternative possibilities backed by logic and bravado. It worked.

The OPP dropped all charges, Luca was released, and the cops invented new curses. 'The murder investigation is continuing,' announced the police through gritted teeth and vowed revenge on Ms Reid.

Genevieve was right. The police hated Luca and Murphy, and all they stood for and did. But the cops had a bigger target. They hated the politician who overturned the murder charge against Parisi the crim.

If Ms Reid ever attains office, she'll be the Attorney-General most loathed and opposed by the constabulary.

Genevieve couldn't believe the OPP would drop the case. She was certain Jessica would ruin her career. Now, with all the publicity about Jessica's win, here was a golden opportunity to maximize the would-be Premier's position. Strike while the publicity iron's hot.

Genevieve's plan involved leaking the appalling lie that Myles Lane, devoted husband to Jessica, and loving father to their adopted daughter Simone, had a secret life; a perverted interest in child pornography.

Hail the dirty tricks. But they must leak to the right person. Genevieve knew a journo sans conscience. Ah, the depths to which politics can sink.

She sat in the wine bar frequented by journos, politicians and their staffers, sipped her white wine and waited.

Bliss thought Genevieve when her favourite victim spotted her.

'Hello me darling,' said Gordon; 'all on your lonesome? Where's that flaming redhead bosom buddy of yours?'

'Piss off, Gordon.'

'Now don't be like that.' He sat and sipped his beer. 'We don't usually see you in here. Lovers' tiff was it?'

'If you don't go away, I'll kick you in the balls — if you've got any.'

'Oooo, who's rattled your cage? Come on, you can tell Uncle Gordy.'

Genevieve had performed in university revues and the odd play; very odd. She invoked her thespian skills, hesitated, than dropped her voice.

'You know, you bastard.' Gordon grinned. He had no idea what Genevieve was talking about but he sure as hell wanted to know. 'I might have known you'd know. You probably started the rumour.'

'Ah, so it's only a rumour. I could've sworn it was true.'

Gordon luxuriated in gossip, with sleaze an essential ingredient. Genevieve hooked him good and proper, and she milked the moment.

'Defending that drug baron killed her. She upset the cops, and now they're going in boots and all.'

'And so they should.' Gordon paused. *She isn't going to say. I'll ask.* 'Going in over what?'

Genevieve switched tactics. 'Ah, you don't know,' she sneered. 'Well maybe we'll be okay after all.'

Gordon mixed salivating with frustration. *What don't I know?*

He tried again. 'So our wonderful Shadow Attorney's in a spot of strife. It couldn't happen to a nicer bitch.'

Genevieve played her ace. 'Actually you could probably help us, Gordon. Being such a liar, if you spread the rumour, no-one'll believe it.'

Being immune to sarcasm, irony and criticism, Gordon grinned. 'Try me,' he whispered exuding aromas of alcohol, tobacco and halitosis.

Genevieve hesitated, looked around, and then spoke quietly. 'The cops are so pissed off at the Shadow Attorney-General, they've decided to go after her husband.' She sat back.

Gordon felt hopeless. 'Is that it?'

'And you didn't hear it from me.'

'Didn't hear what? You haven't told me anything.'

'It's crap, complete bullshit. Jess's husband has legitimate concerns about child pornography from an international legal point of view.'

Child pornography? Gordon suffered a meltdown.

Genevieve tapped her nose with a finger. 'We don't know if the cops will go public before or after Jessica challenges for Leader.'

Oh my sainted aunt's bicycle clips. Gordon copped both barrels. Jessica making a challenge was enough to incinerate his briefs. To have the cops arrest her hubby for kiddy fiddling set fire to Gordy's gonads.

He skulled his beer, patted Genevieve's hand then fled.

Don't shoot the messenger; salute the messenger.

'The cat's among the pigeons,' said Genevieve to Jessica. 'I told Gordon the Gossip you were to challenge, and Myles is under police investigation.'

Jessica wanted to vomit. The hare was running. She struggled to speak. 'So, how do we play this?'

'I suggest we don't reveal the specifics until the very last.'

'You want me to announce the lie that my husband's a paedophile?'

'Listen to me. The plan can work if we hold our nerve.'

An email pinged in Jessica's inbox. She read it aloud.

'Party room meeting tomorrow at 10am.'

'They're worried.'

'Me too. How can I rally support before then? They know I've not been canvassing, and they reckon they'll catch me ill-prepared.'

'Ah but you're not,' said Genevieve. 'You've been planning this move for years and you hold the unknown ace — the sympathy vote.'

8

BERNIE STARED at his kitchen table. The mixed ingredients of his Moral Compass Pill — he decided to call it the MCP — stared back at him. The first batch was born. But one question kept tapping on his brain.

How the hell can I effectively test it?

He thought about Lois and her Mark Twain quote.

A person with a new idea is a crank until the idea succeeds.

He filled a few capsules, and a small airtight container with his "pixie dust", popped on its lid, stored the creation, and retired.

Next morning Lois was back at work with her mother now recuperating in hospital. Bernie saw a spring in his colleague's step. Not having her abusive parent at home made Lois almost chipper.

They discussed her mother's health, and then got on with their work until Lois could not contain her curiosity any longer.

'So, Professor Slim, what progress on the new wonder drug? When do you administer a double dose to our beloved leader?'

Bernie laughed. He hadn't contemplated the Hyphen as a guinea pig.

Bloody hell, imagine if the MCP worked, and on Ralphie boy.

'Slow progress I'm afraid,' replied Bernie. 'And I regret to say I'll not be able to speak about it again.'

Lois looked puzzled. 'Oh?'

Bernie tapped his nose. 'Spies.'

Lois laughed in a way Bernie had never heard before. 'Spies?'

Bernie dropped his voice. 'Here in *Labcope*. Maybe even in *R & D*.'

Lois liked Bernie teasing her, but a sliver of curiosity stirred in her brain. Did his attempt at humour mask something serious?

'I think you're over-doing the cinnamon doughnuts, young man.'

He enjoyed Lois calling him "young man".

'Speaking of which,' he said, 'addiction and the canteen calls. Sure I can't tempt you?'

Lois gave her usual "thanks but no thanks" answer and Bernie left. In the canteen, his order was stored in the barista's brain.

'Morning Bernie,' chirped Enrico.

'Morning sir,' replied the scientist. Bernie alone called Enrico "sir".

'Your usual,' said Enrico producing the coffee and doughnut.

Bernie paid with the exact money — always. 'Molte grazie,' he said, and headed for his usual table. Talk about Mr Habitual.

He sipped, chewed and thought; *my kingdom for a human guinea pig.* Suddenly his day got worse. Josh the boastard burst into view. He hadn't yet seen Bernie who considered sliding under the table. Too late.

'Maaaate,' greased the phantom shagger, joining Bernie. Josh winked, then leant forward and whispered. 'Have I got two tales for you?' He tapped Bernie's shoulder. 'I'll be back with a ball-by-ball description.'

Josh fronted the barista where he called Enrico, "my man". The serial womaniser was officially a gilt-edged scrote.

Bernie worried about his own character. Surely, a stronger person would tell Josh to get lost. Playing disinterested would never work.

Josh must think I actually enjoy his company. Who will rid me of this troublesome twat?

The boastard returned, and launched into the gory details of his latest sexual conquest, then stopped to sip. 'Shit, no sugar.' Bernie pointed to the next table. 'Nah, I want that dark stuff.'

Josh returned to Enrico. Bernie's brain pinged. He hesitated for a few seconds then decided. He removed the container holding his magic powder, checked to see if anyone was looking, then sprinkled a serve on Josh's coffee. The powder sat on top. Panic. Josh headed back. It was too late to stir the brew. 'Sink, sink, sink,' silently cried Bernie.

Surely, he'll notice.

Josh sat, and Bernie cringed awaiting an accusation of poisoning or attempted murder — or worse. Josh spotted the MCP.

'What,' said the confused sex maniac? 'He *has* put the damn sugar in.'

'Must have been hiding behind the froth,' opined Bernie.

Josh shrugged, added the "extra" sugar, stirred his drink, and sipped. Bernie trembled with a solid serve of horror.

Then the salacious storytelling commenced. Josh described his latest conquest whilst drinking his now drug-laden coffee. The coitus chat meant nothing to Bernie who was spellbound, watching Josh's face.

Will he break down and weep? Will he clasp his head as his conscience shouts "repent"? Will he nothing?

Josh kept prattling, with no sign of any response to the drug.

First guinea pig report — fail.

Pity, because Josh was the ideal candidate. If ever anyone needed their conscience pricked, it was Josh the prick.

Bernie returned to Lois. He he injured, or laid the groundwork for murdering the womaniser. What if he dies, and there is a post mortem?

Shit. What have I done?

'You look worried,' said Lois. He *was* worried but diverted the other scientist by asking more about her mum.

'All being well, she'll be home this weekend.'

Bernie wanted to say, "Enjoy it while you can", but found his brain preoccupied with Josh from *Marketing.*

'I'm dreading my mother coming home,' said Lois in a soft voice.

'Good,' said Bernie, thinking of other things.

Lois too was preoccupied. She wanted to ask Bernie a favour.

After work he shopped for milk and cat food. Signora Conti provided abundant "extras" for Alberto, but not his favourite dry food.

When shopping, Bernie always bought things he didn't need. One day, science will discover the be-kind-to-grocer gene.

With a planet-destroying plastic shopping bag in each hand, he bowled along Swan Street when something hit his leg from behind.

'Oh no,' said a voice, and Bernie found himself being surrounded by oranges and lemons. The bells of St Clement's remained safely in their belfry as a young woman apologised.

'Sorry,' she said, trying to gather her runaway fruit. Bernie joined in. 'Thank you so much,' she added as Bernie placed some of the cheeky chaps in her cloth bag. One of its straps had broken free, and the pieces of fruit took advantage to make their escape. She put her bag on a bench, and looked around for any pipped stragglers.

'I think that's all,' he said. 'But I'm afraid your bag needs a service.'

'I'll be fine, and thanks again.'

'You can have one of mine,' said Bernie, placing the contents of one of his bags in the other, and handing the woman the now empty bag.

'Are you sure?'

'I'm positive,' smiled Bernie.

'Well that's very kind of you.'

There was a pause as the strangers checked out one another, then Bernie launched into an old Graham Kennedy joke his father taught him.

'I think you're supposed to say, "Only fools are positive".'

The woman didn't understand.

She thinks I'm a fruitcake. I am a fruitcake.

Bernie wished he hadn't started but now felt he had no choice.

'You said, "Are you sure", and I said, "I'm positive," and you're supposed to say, "Only fools are positive", then I reply, "Are you sure?", and you say ...'

'I'm positive,' said the woman, and they both laughed.

They looked at one another, and Bernie liked what he saw. He had his next line ready but felt that hitting on a woman in the street was uncool.

'Well, good luck with your fruit carrying. Bye.'

He set off as the woman called, 'Bye. And thanks again.'

Bernie waved his one free hand and felt good.

It was decision night. Bernie and Madeline had agreed a plan to rescue their parents. Their wonderful mother had dementia, and her caring days were over. Their parents' world had been turned upside down. It was time to sell the family home, and move the folks into care, together. Their father understood the situation, but the others could only guess as to their mother's state of mind. The siblings sat in Madeline's home.

Bernie's brother-in-law Bruce, known to Bernie as Brutus, was out drinking, so with Maddy's kids asleep, the siblings got talking.

'I've investigated homes with dementia patients,' said Madeline.

'Costs, vacancies, what's available?'

'Hang on. We agree that Dad has to be in the same place. But that's where the problems start.'

'No wheelchair access?'

'Just shut up and let me finish.'

'Sorry.' Bernie fell silent.

'Dad's classified as "high care". Yes, his brain's as sharp as a tack but they ask questions about his mobility, if he can manage washing, going to the loo, getting in and out of bed, etc. Dad fails just about everything.'

Madeline's emotions became too much. She wept in silence.

'It's just not fair,' she whispered.

Bernie waited for her to settle. 'I know.' He squeezed her arm.

'I mean with Dad's body wrecked, they were fine because Mum looked after him, and loved it. Now God in his wisdom has played funny buggers with her brain, and their lives are a total mess.' She continued to cry.

'Do you want me to check some more places?' asked Bernie.

She recovered. 'I've found two strong possibilities.' She handed her brother a piece of paper with details of nursing homes.

'Bloody hell, that one's in China.' Madeline began to cry again. 'Sorry,' mumbled Bernie, ashamed to be so negative.

Madeline knew her own mind. 'Dad has to make the final decision.'

'Of course,' agreed Bernie.

'He knows they need fulltime care, but where they go has to be his call. If they have to be separated, he needs to make that decision.'

Bernie thought of his Italian neighbour. 'If we were southern Europeans, we'd be fighting to have our parents live with us.' They paused. 'Why do we call Oz the lucky country?'

They fell silent until Bernie had a thought. 'Even if they're in the same place, they may be in different areas.'

Madeline's head slumped. Bernie groaned in silence. *Hardly helpful, Bernie.* With Maddy's spirits so low, Bernie changed the subject.

'So how is big, bad Brutus?'

Wrong. Madeline gave a gasp of pain, and lapsed into more crying.

'He still goes out with his mates, drinking and gambling.' She sobbed.

Bernie felt miserable. What a night.

Let's have a cosy chat about our seriously ill or disabled parents, or alternatively, let's have a laugh about a troubled marriage.

They discussed the nursing home option at length, and then agreed to act on their father's wishes. Neither wanted that conversation.

'I'll ring Dad, and tell him we'll be over tomorrow night. Okay?'

'Fine,' nodded Bernie. He stood then stopped. His brain raced. From his pocket, he withdrew a small container with his infamous pixie dust.

'Listen, Maddy,' he said, 'we've developed a new drug at work which is not yet on the market. It's designed to help people think about their behaviour, and how it affects others.' Madeline stared at him. 'It may not work, but I thought if Brutus lost interest in boozing, maybe that might help things at home.'

He held out the container. She paused then took it.

'And this stuff really works?'

Bernie lied. 'Well, it's early days but you've got nothing to lose.'

'Do you have any arsenic?'

'Just stir a small amount in his tea or coffee. But don't tell him.'

'I'll pour the whole lot down his bloody throat,' she replied. 'Thanks.'

Bernie departed wondering if he'd soon be in serious trouble.

Have I helped my sister kill her husband? Have I given a work colleague a fatal dose of an unproven drug — my drug?

Back at *Labcope* next morning, Bernie couldn't concentrate. He was helping Lois in a joint project but she kept asking for his response.

'What's up Bernie? Why are you taking so long?'

'Sorry, I'm miles away; a bit of trouble at home.'

That was true with his parents facing upheaval, and his sister enduring a shaky marriage. But his main concern was his MCP.

One, possibly two healthy males had ingested his unproven drug. If something bad happened to either man, for Bernie, losing his job and his career would be the least of his worries.

'I'm sorry,' said Lois. 'Anything I can do?'

'No, thanks,' replied Bernie cracking on with his work.

After a long pause, Lois spoke. 'Can I ask you something?'

'Of course.'

Lois looked serious. 'I'd like to use my mother as a guinea pig for your conscience drug.'

Wow. Bernie gulped.

'Right,' was all he said.

'Are you shocked? Have I offended you? Do you think I'm being cruel? Tell me, honestly, please.'

'Ah, shocked, a little; offended, not at all; and cruel, definitely not.'

'I assume all your ingredients are used in different drugs for the brain, albeit for different reasons. So if I trial it on my mother and it doesn't work, then hopefully, there's no harm done.'

Bernie didn't like the word *hopefully*.

Lois continued. 'I think your idea is mind-blowing, Bernie, and if I can help test your theory, I'd like to try.'

'That's fantastic. Thank you, Lois, I'm touched.'

'But it must be a secret, no mention of anything to anyone.'

'Of course,' replied Bernie, 'that goes without saying.'

'You must be frustrated not having found any human guinea pigs.'

Bernie thought about his response.

Should I tell her I have two already?

'Yes, it is a bit frustrating.'

Lois hesitated. 'So, can you give me a sample, please; just a small one? I'll give it to my mother once she's back home.'

'Of course, but I must stress the importance of a low dose.'

'I promise to be extra careful. And I'll keep notes about her response.'

Bernie hid his panic. 'I don't think that's a good idea.'

'No notes?'

Bernie shook his head. Lois nodded. From his bag, Bernie produced a small container with a label, *MCP Batch 001*. He hesitated then held out the container. Lois hesitated then reached out and took it.

'Thank you.' She looked at the handwritten label. 'MCP?'

'Moral Compass Pill.'

'Nice title.' Neither knew what to say next. 'I guess you're a little worried,' said Lois.

'Perhaps a bit,' lied Bernie.

'I mean if you tell the company about your drug, they'll take total control and, if it works, you'll probably get nothing financially.'

Bernie nodded. 'There's no probably about it.'

'Is that why you mentioned spies within the company?'

Oh God, thought Bernie. *Lois is a spy and she's setting me up to hand over the formula.*

'No, that's because I spoke with an experienced scientist who told me about the need for secrecy here at *Labcope*.'

'Is that the Hungarian woman I told you about?'

Bernie felt sick. He was supposed to say nothing, yet already he'd mentioned spies and Annuska, the one person who told him loose lips sink ships. *Annuska will be horrified. Shut up, Bernie.*

'Lois, let's not talk about the conscience drug while at work ... please.'

Lois saw fear in Bernie's eyes. 'Of course, Mum's the word.'

'Mum indeed,' said Bernie, 'guinea pig, Mum.'

There was a pause before they grinned then laughed. The door opened and in came the Hyphen. Lois hid the container marked *MCP Batch 001*.

'Well, I do like to see a happy staff.'

The *Research and Development* team's laughter vanished.

'Good morning,' said both Lois and Bernie.

'How can we help you, Dr Hetherington-Smythe?' asked Bernie.

'You could start by letting me in on your wonderful joke.'

'Not so much a joke, sir,' replied Lois. 'It was more a friendly remark about my dear mother.'

The Hyphen knew he would get no more.

'I'm telling staff that the next budget will likely have cuts. Unless each department can nominate areas where expenditure might be trimmed, I'll make the decision for you. Let me know by the end of the week.'

The Hyphen left. His supercilious smile continued grinning until it realised its owner had departed and then, in a panic, raced after him.

Both *R & D* scientists now knew one of them was facing the sack.

Bernie went for a walk at lunchtime. He needed fresh air. His parents needed serious assistance. His sister needed saving from her boorish husband, and Bernie needed saving from himself.

His whacky idea about a conscience drug had taken flight. He opened a can of worms. The wrigglers sprinted in all directions. *Bloody hell!*

Sitting in the lunchtime sunshine did not help. Bernie headed back, opened the *Labcope* front door and stepped back to allow free passage to a woman making her exit. He smiled, as did she, and then they twigged.

'Oh, hello,' said the clumsy fruit carrier from Swan Street.

'Hello again,' replied Bernie and stayed outside to chat.

'You'll notice I have complete control of my possessions,' she said, indicating a classy art portfolio.

'I'm impressed,' said Bernie. 'Do you work here? I mean I do, and I've never seen you before — apart from the other day I mean.'

'When I failed lemon juggling.'

They laughed. For the moment, Bernie forgot his worries, and savoured the eyes of his fellow conversationalist.

'No,' she continued, 'I'm a freelance designer, and have been trying to impress your *Marketing* department with some of my designs but, as usual, I got the standard "thanks but no thanks" answer.'

'Well if there's anything I can do,' added Bernie, a little too quickly. 'I mean I'm a scientist, but I know one of the guys in *Marketing*.'

Immediately Bernie felt sick.

What the hell am I saying? The one person in the world, in the universe, I would never introduce a woman to is Josh the Boastard.

'Gee that's awesome.' She held out her free hand. 'I'm Kate Naismith.'

'Bernie Slim,' he said sucking in his gut. 'Let me give you my number.'

She produced her phone and added his number. Bernie kept chatting.

'If you'd like to give me a call, say, tomorrow, I'll see if I can get *Marketing* to give you another chance.'

'That's brilliant. And I'll send you my number, if that's okay.'

If that's okay? Whadaya mean, if that's okay?

'No problem,' said Bernie trying to maintain a cool demeanour. 'No promises, mind, but I'll certainly give it a go.'

'Thanks heaps. That's two favours. Do you believe in reciprocity?'

Being a lapsed Presbyterian, Bernie had doubts about any religion.

'Sometimes,' he said, trying to bluff his way out of his ignorance.

'Well I do, and you're due a double serve.' She again held out her hand and they shook. 'I'll call you tomorrow, Bernie Slim. Bye.'

She left with Bernie staring after her and wondering.

A double serve of what?

It was hard for Bernie to concentrate. Things to ponder included his parents, his sister's depression, his colleague wanting to dope her mother, possibly two men walking around with his unapproved drug inside them, and now, Ms Oranges and Lemons promising a serve of reciprocity.

What's work?

Needing to pee, he pushed open the door to the *Gents*, and regretted his move. Josh from *Marketing* fronted the urinal.

'Maaaaate,' he smirked.

Oh no, don't stand next to him. He'll want to compare appendages.

Bernie greeted his colleague, and moved to the end of the urinal.

At least he can't tap me on the shoulder from down here.

'We can't go on meeting like this,' grinned Josh. Bernie forced a grin, hit the flush button, and moved to a hand basin with his back to Bernie.

I'll pretend I haven't finished, thought Bernie. *He'll leave and I won't have to speak to him. There's no way I'll introduce him to Kate. Come on, come on, leave*, thought Bernie.

But Josh remained hunched over his basin. Then a weird sound began. It was like someone in pain or certainly in distress.

My God, it's Josh.

With his face close to the bowl, Josh kept making this unusual howling, moaning, or something.

Bernie moved. 'Josh? You okay?'

'No,' wailed the *Marketing* man who slapped the hand basin in frustration. 'Do I look okay?'

Bernie felt confused. Then a young chemist bowled in.

'Get out!' snapped Bernie.

The young chemist looked surprised. 'But I need a pee.'

'Get out!' roared Bernie, and the bloke went elsewhere.

'Help me,' begged Josh. He grabbed Bernie's white coat. 'Help me.'

'Okay. Do you need a doctor? Are you ill?'

'Something terrible is happening.'

'I can see you're upset. But what's wrong?'

'I don't know. I just feel awful. I hate myself. For years I've been cheating on my wife, and all of a sudden I feel guilty.'

Bernie became excited. 'But why feel guilty now?'

'I don't know. That's what makes it so scary. I felt strange last night and worse this morning. Now it's really bad, and all of a sudden, I can't forgive myself. And my head feels like it's going to explode.'

'Have you told your wife?'

'Are you mad? She'll leave me and take the kids.'

'Are you sure?'

That stopped Josh. He wasn't sure. 'No, I'm not sure, but I've been unfaithful so many times.'

'So?'

'*So?*'

'I mean cheating is cheating. Once or many times, it's all the same.'

Josh struggled. 'Maybe; what are you trying to say?'

'Do you have to name every woman?' Again Josh stopped. 'If you just say you've got to get something off your chest, that you've cheated with a woman, that it was a huge mistake, you're really, really sorry, and beg for her forgiveness, that might be enough.'

Josh changed. He stopped crying. He looked pathetically hopeful. 'Do you really think so?'

'Are you sincerely sorry?'

'I've never been so sincere in my whole life.'

'Then apologise, tell your wife you love her, and promise never to cheat again.'

Josh almost begged for the answer. 'But will the pain go away?'

'I don't know. Is it still bad?'

Josh touched his head. 'No ... no, it's ... better, definitely better.'

Bernie shrugged. 'It's worth a try.' Josh tried to smile. 'But I think you'll have to follow your conscience in the future.'

'Why? Do you know something about this condition?'

Bernie decided to wing it. 'It's just a guess but perhaps your cheating caused your conscience to become active, and that caused your pain.'

Josh looked at Bernie in a new way. The advice seemed sensible, even right. He gripped Bernie's hands and spoke with a passionate sincerity.

'I'll do it. I'll go home early, and confess and apologise tonight. God, I feel so much better. Thanks mate, you've saved my life.'

He moved forward and hugged the hapless Bernie just as the company accountant opened the door. He didn't need to be told to leave, he just did. Two blokes hugging in the *Gents* sent a certain signal. *Pee elsewhere.*

Josh wiped his tears, smiled at Bernie, and spoke with feeling.

'I'm a new man. Thank God for my conscience.'

He left, giving a thumbs up at the door. Bernie looked in the mirror.

What the hell have I done?

The visit to his parents that night became super stressful. Maddy had good news. Their cousin Chloe, a favourite niece of their parents, having sold her apartment, was heading to London in a few weeks. She needed short-term accommodation. When Maddy phoned her about Aunt Daphne, Chloe jumped at the aunt and uncle-sitting gig.

Madeline was there when Bernie arrived. The family sat in the kitchen although Daphne fussed and made tea.

'So why are you here?' she asked Bernie.

'Do I need a reason to visit my favourite mother,' replied Bernie.

Once that remark would have drawn a laugh and a witty retort from his clever mother; not tonight.

'My darling,' began Gus, 'how would you like to go on a holiday?'

'You go,' said Daphne. 'I need to stay here and look after our children.'

"Our children" looked at their father. His eyes brimmed with moisture.

After the cuppa, Gus told his wife her much-loved TV show was on, and she and Madeline went to watch it. Father and son got chatting.

'Dad, we're going to get through this, all of us. Maddy and I will take responsibility for both you and Mum.'

'Thank you,' whispered Gus and gripped his son's arm.

'Everything from finding the right place to live, selling the house; everything. You don't have to do a thing. Okay?'

Gus nodded. He couldn't speak. Silence ruled. Bernie continued.

'We're trying to find a place where you can be together, have the best professional care, and your kids and grandkids will visit non-stop.'

The man in the wheelchair nodded. His throat went dry, which made talking tricky. Bernie spoke.

'It'll mean selling the house, but we'll look after that. We'll use the money to set up you and Mum for life.'

Gus smiled his appreciation. 'Sorry about your inheritance.'

Bernie looked in shock at his father then saw the familiar twinkle in his eye. They laughed as Madeline came into the room.

'Mum's nodded off. Just sitting in her favourite chair, she fell asleep.'

'She's doing that a lot these days,' said Gus.

'So what have you two villains been talking about?'

'All sorted,' said Bernie. 'Dad's happy for us to arrange everything.'

Madeline gave her father a hug and sat beside him, rubbing his arm.

'I've just apologised to your brother for spending your inheritance.'

Madeline playfully smacked her father's arm.

'I'll start looking for estate agents tomorrow, Dad,' said Bernie.

'And I've started looking at top nursing homes,' added Madeline.'

'Thank you,' said Gus. 'Thank you both.'

'Dad,' said Madeline. 'We can't leave you and Mum alone now. It might take weeks or months to get you moved.'

Gus grimaced. He knew this issue had to be sorted immediately.

'We could get some professional care, Dad,' added Bernie.

Maddy smiled. 'No need; cousin Chloe has sold her flat, and going overseas. She needs somewhere to stay. She'll be here in the morning.'

'That's fantastic,' beamed Bernie.

Gus couldn't speak. His gratitude overflowed. The "kids" tidied the kitchen, and helped their folks prepare for bed. Their mother became childlike and retired without a murmur. In the street, the siblings chatted.

'Well done on finding Chloe. What a perfect solution.'

'Just lucky, and we needed a break. But what I still don't understand is how Mum got so bad so quickly.'

'She didn't. Dad just kept the early stages from us.'

'Typical Dad, thinking of others.' Bernie nodded. 'Now we have to move fast on this. They need help right now.' Bernie agreed.

'I'll find the estate agent; you find the nursing home.'

'I prefer retirement village but needs must.'

Both siblings were under stress, especially Madeline. Bernie was afraid to ask. He did. 'So how are things at home?'

She looked at him, and then tears appeared, and rolled down her cheeks. Bernie felt terrible. Brutus the Bastard still lived up to his name. Suddenly Madeline threw her arms around her brother, and hugged him so tight it almost hurt. She sobbed.

'Thank you, thank you, thank you,' she cried.

'Whoa, what's happened? Maddy!'

She relaxed her grip. 'I cannot begin to tell you how grateful I am.'

'Why? What's happened?'

'Last night, Bruce knelt and begged for forgiveness.'

Bernie's heart rate accelerated. 'He what?'

'He apologised profusely for treating the kids and me so badly.'

'He apologised?'

'He told me he loved me, and said he wants to become the best husband and father in the world.'

'Bloody hell.'

'Your new drug, brother dear, has changed my husband overnight. He is back being a kind and loving man. You have saved our marriage.'

She hugged Bernie again as his mind started spinning.

That's two guinea pigs and two magnificent results.

9

THE PARTY ROOM meeting buzzed. A leadership spill didn't happen every week. With the polls showing Labor well ahead, and the next election due in nine months, whispers of a serious challenge sparked tension. It filled the room. Trevor stood.

'Good morning.' The parliamentarians mumbled their response. Then the big shock floored everyone.

Trevor had slipped into a phone box, and changed his costume. It was bye-bye Mr Bland, and hello no more Mr-Nice-Guy. He let rip.

'United we stand, divided we fall. Yes, it's a cliché but yes, it applies to all of us. I've called a spill of leadership positions because of the cowards in our party. Some of you have been undermining me for months, but never to my face. Well this treachery stops right here, right now.'

Wow. What's happened to Trevor? He rarely displays passion. Out of nowhere came Mr Fiery. Now was not a good time to challenge the boss. He moved up a gear.

'I want to clear the air. I intend to nominate for Leader. If I am returned, every member of caucus will give me total loyalty. This is your final chance before the election to accept or reject my leadership. Do I make myself clear?'

Nobody replied. Silence dominated. The shock of Mr Bland becoming Mr Grandstand stunned everyone. Had his handlers advised him to flick the nasty switch?

Go heavy, Trevy. Silence your critics and win over the undecideds. Besides, Riley's a wimp, and the Bitch has serious personal issues. Do it.

Trevor looked around the room. He was riding roughshod over procedure. There needed to be a chairperson, and a call for nominations for the various leadership positions, but Trevor used his status as Leader to dare anyone to challenge. Incumbency rules.

'Well as there is no challenge to my leadership, I suggest we move to the position of deputy leader.'

'Just a minute.'

Three little words, but oh the power therein. It was Jessica Reid, sitting near the back of the room. Heads turned and people stared.

'Ah, Jessica, what a surprise. I thought we might hear from you. An explanation of your current "difficulties" perhaps?'

'I thought the correct procedure involved calling for nominations.'

'Of course, how naughty of me. I simply wanted to clear the air, and get on with the business of winning government. I'm sure you want us to win the next election. Now is that all you have to say?'

'Only that I wish to nominate for the position of Leader.'

Oops.

Jessica's live hand grenade rolled down the aisle, and stopped at the feet of the Leader of the Opposition. Members counted the seconds before the device would explode. Trevor smiled. Any body language expert would define Trevor's facial expression as forced.

'Good for you,' he said crushing the grenade. 'Anyone else fancy their chances?' Not a sound was heard. 'Brother Riley, tossing your titfer in to the ring are we?' Riley shook his head. 'Right then, Ms Reid, it's a two-horse race. Care to make your pitch? Ladies first, and all that jazz.'

Jessica moved to the front of the room. 'Thank you, Trevor. I'm happy to face the new ball.'

Every eye stared at her. Every mind gave her their undivided attention. She nodded at Trevor who secretly gloated.

If you don't reveal your husband's nasty little secret, sweetheart, I'll be delighted to do it for you.

'Good morning,' began Jessica. 'As you know, I've always done things my way. When practicing law, I've often defended alleged criminals. Only recently, I defended a man the police believe is a major supplier of drugs here in Melbourne. The police got their murder charge wrong.'

This was clever. She talked about what others talked about behind her back. She owned her own actions, and took pride in what she did. Impressive.

'I've always ignored advice from Liberal Party elders, my parents, my colleagues, and particularly my opponents. So many people have urged me to take a certain course of action, and invariably I do what I believe is right.' She paused. 'Not sure what that makes me.'

'A lawyer,' called a voice, and everyone laughed.

'Thank you,' said Jessica, 'but let's be specific. I'm a woman, and we all know the difference between a female lawyer and a pitbull is the lipstick.'

An even bigger laugh filled the room, and Trevor shifted in his seat.

The bitch is making them laugh, not at her, but with her. Shit.

73

Jessica was on a roll.

'Let me tell you what you will and won't get from me as your leader. What you will get is access to me and not my advisor, my willingness to listen far more than I speak and, when I do speak, straight-talking sans bullshit.'

Trevor's collar tightened. Jessica was good, getting better.

'What you won't get from me are promises I can't keep, offers you'd be crazy to accept, and a pat on the back when a boot up the backside is what you deserve.'

She paused. It was live theatre, tense, and with the audience hooked.

'Two other things. First, some of you may have heard a vile rumour about my husband. It's patently untrue, it's a typical tactic of desperate politicians trying vainly to maintain their status, and, should I hear of anyone, *anyone* so much as breathe a word of said rumour, they will face the full force of the law led by the Pitbull herself.'

Jessica paused, and a you-could-hear-a-pin-drop hush took root.

'And second. My main goal, my *only* goal should you elect me as your leader, is to hammer the current government in ways they cannot even imagine, to expose their lack of vision and achievement, and to give Victorians the progressive and caring Liberal government they deserve.'

Jessica had her audience enthralled. She relaxed, and dropped the volume of her voice. This became an intimate chat. Everyone, well, apart from Trevor and his tribe, felt they were alone with Jessica.

'If I don't like your work, I'll tell you to your face, and in private. I won't spread rumours about you. I won't send colleagues to suss out your voting intentions pretending to represent one person while secretly working for another.'

Ouch. Everyone knew this was a Trevor tactic. Jessica delivered a classic put-down without naming names. Clever.

Then she began a subtle crescendo. As her volume increased, she stood. She made eye contact with her colleagues. She was a natural leader inspiring her troops.

'I'm a hands-on leader. I'll back you all the way. I'll delegate giving you the power to make decisions without having to run everything by me first. That's what you'll get from me as your leader.'

It was time for the denouement; the final pitch beckoned.

'I'm a winner; losing is not a part of my DNA. I'll fight fair, mostly, but damn hard to knock the bloody socialists off their perch. I'm only in it to win it, and *when* we win this year, I want you to be part of the team.'

The breathless hush seemed reluctant to leave. She turned to Rand and smiled. 'Thank you for the opportunity ... sir.'

She headed back to her seat in silence. Then, as a shaken Trevor stood to make his pitch, spontaneous and strong applause began. It kept on keeping on. Big Trev died inside. Out of left field came an opponent who was smart, witty, and with the oratory skills of a fiery preacher cum life-coach. The current leader had suspected Jess was good. Now he and everyone knew that, and Trev was in serious strife.

Will I play the hubby-is-a-paedophile card? The bitch is a lawyer. So is her pervert of a husband. But do I have my facts confirmed? What if I make the claim and I'm wrong? I'll be sued from here to Texas. Bitch.

Bitch, bitch, bitch!

Trev tried to be everything to everyone. He tried to be funny and clever. Fail. He tried to be statesmanlike. Fail. He simply came across as yesterday's man. He knew it, and his body language betrayed his fear at losing the top job. Even his closest allies voted against him.

Jessica Reid became the new Leader of the Victorian Opposition.

When the news reached government members, the word *bugger* and its numerous synonyms came readily to the lips of all concerned.

Jessica's first press conference turned hectic. The fourth estate turned up in numbers the Premier envied. The new Opposition Leader was female, young, controversial and different. My God she was different. From Trevor Bland to Jessica Fiery could not have been more striking.

But had the rumour about her husband reached the press gallery? Were they there for the kill? Jessica waited for silence.

'Thank you, ladies and gentlemen. I'm delighted to become the new Leader of the Opposition. I wish to publicly thank Trevor Rand for his outstanding service to the Liberal Party, and to the state of Victoria.'

'I say to the people of this wonderful state that the Coalition will offer sensible, affordable and appropriate policies to improve your quality of life. All our policies will be revealed in the coming weeks and months, together with detailed costings. Now, I'm sure you have questions.'

Several journalists spoke at once. Jessica refused to speak. They finally stopped talking. Subtly, she nodded, indicating one of the journalists. Jessica became teacher, mother, nanny and traffic cop rolled into one.

'What did your husband say when you told him your news?'

Leading question. The eagerness of some journalists seemed to surge.

'What he usually says. What time will you be home, and where are the tea towels?'

After a moment of bewilderment, the press re-launched their simultaneous babble. Jessica again refused to speak, waited for silence, then nodded to another journalist.

'If you become Premier, will you continue to defend criminals?'

The tricky question bulged with landmines. Jessica stayed calm.

'I think you mean alleged criminals.' Ouch. 'If they are members of the ALP or the fourth estate, then no. Everyone else is most welcome.'

Pens scribbled, thumbs texted, cameras whirred, flashlights popped, and observers smiled. If nothing else, it seemed that Victorian politics had entered the Comedy Festival. The Premier and his cronies worried.

Late that night, Jessica and Genevieve were alone. Much had been said and done. Celebrations now were muted and the women pensive. They kicked off their shoes, which lay where they landed. The women lounged, their posture dreadful. They didn't care. They'd taken a giant step towards their ultimate goal. Jessica was one election away from becoming Premier.

'When are you moving into Trevor's office?' asked Genevieve.

'Whenever,' shrugged Jessica. 'Losing didn't suit him. Let the poor bastard depart at his own pace.'

'What did Myles say?'

'Who?'

They laughed a little. These women had husbands and a child or children but those family members were part of the chorus, performing upstage. The two political females were the main players, the stars, and the perfect team. One without the other wouldn't work. In fact, each wouldn't exist without the other.

'So have you thought about portfolios,' asked Genevieve?

'You handle it.'

'What?'

'Do you speak English?'

'Me?'

'What part of "You handle it" don't you understand?'

Genevieve loved working with Jessica. Genevieve's gamble to ditch a top job in banking, and throw in with an Opposition backbencher all those years ago now looked like a stroke of genius. Genevieve was literally the power behind the throne. In a few months she might well be the kingmaker; well, the feminine version thereof.

Myles was still up when Jessica came home. She entered the subtly lit kitchen where he twisted a bottle of champagne in a bucket of ice. It wasn't cheap. And the champagne cost a bomb too.

'Congratulations, again,' said the husband.

'How's Simone?'

'Dreaming about her famous mother.'

Myles popped the cork, which frightened Rufus, poured two glasses of *Veuve Cliquot*, and handed one to his wife. He proposed a toast.

'To the outstanding lawyer, the wonderful wife and mother, and the next Premier of Victoria.'

Glasses clinked, and the couple sipped their champers. Then Jessica put her glass on the island bar in their stunning kitchen, took her husband's glass, and put it beside hers. He wondered what was happening. *She* wondered what was happening. It sure was unusual as Jessica did something for the very first time.

She stood close to Myles, put her hands on either side of his head, and gently pulled his face towards hers. She looked into his eyes from this intimate distance then kissed his lips with a tenderness neither knew she possessed. Ever so slightly, Myles recoiled.

They looked at each other in a new way, in a way they never thought would happen. Then, without hesitation, they kissed each other for seconds, and then more seconds. They had to break because Rufus started barking. He'd never played this game before.

Myles was a tad confused, but nice confused. Jessica felt bad or sad or both. Was her kind but unusual behaviour driven by guilt? Did Jessica Reid have a tricky conscience?

10

'HELLO. You are talking to Doctor Eszes.'

'Annuska, hello, it's Bernie. I'm sorry to call you so late.'

'Bernie, how good to hear your voice. Tell me, how is your love life?'

He hesitated.

Is this woman a clairvoyant as well?

He spoke cautiously. 'How did you know about that?'

She hesitated. 'I don't understand. I asked about your love life.'

Bernie twigged. 'Oh, I see. Yes, thank you for asking. My love life has suddenly become very interesting.'

'Really? Can you call to see me and tell me all your news?'

'I can. When would you like me to visit?'

'Why now, of course.'

'Now? It's not too late?'

'Too late? Bernie, for lovers like you and me, the night is young. I will powder my nose and elsewhere in anticipation of your visit. Viszlát.'*

(*Hungarian for 'see you soon'.)

She hung up. Bernie smiled. A woman in her 80s, presumably a lesbian, spoke in a way, which both fascinated and frightened him.

Outside his parents' Hawthorn home, he used his Uber app, and then climbed into a VW Golf in Burwood Road, and twenty minutes later knocked on a certain door in Balaclava.

'Ah, it's my favourite caller,' grinned Annuska. 'Come away in.'

They entered the cosy sitting room where Dorothy worked on *The Age* crossword.

'Good evening, young man,' said Dorothy. 'Had I been given more notice, I would have offered you at least one cinnamon doughnut.'

They sat and Annuska gushed. 'I am hoping my nosy neighbour saw you arrive. I want to make her jealous.' Bernie didn't know what to say, and Dorothy rolled her eyes.

Annuska became impatient. 'News, you said you have news. Your love life is booming?'

'Blooming,' said Dorothy, not lifting her eyes from the puzzle.

'It is,' said Bernie, both the literal, and the other one.' Annuska looked confused. Even Dorothy turned to see Bernie. Annuska spoke.

'What other one? You have *two* new drugs?'

'No, I have one new drug, and one new girlfriend.'

Annuska fell into deep shock. 'Oh Dorothy, did you hear that? Bernard is cheating on me already.' She dropped her voice. 'So tell me everything, especially about the sex.'

Bernie hesitated then celebrated. 'First the drug, Dr Annuska Eszes, it works.' He almost shouted. 'It works!'

Dorothy forgot her crossword. Annuska sat forward and beamed.

'You have found a human guinea pig?'

'Two,' said Bernie.

'*Two* human guinea pigs!' exclaimed Annuska.

'And both have been an outstanding success. More than we could have hoped for.'

Annuska was spellbound. 'You have a trial result already?'

'I have. Both subjects are men who have been treating their families badly. The men were given the drug surreptitiously.'

Annuska's face showed confusion. 'They did not take it orally?'

Dorothy explained. 'Yes orally; surreptitiously means they didn't know they were taking it.'

'Of course,' said the Hungarian. 'I did know that. Please continue.'

'It took up to 24 hours for the drug to work. Both men became seriously stressed and unhappy. I saw one with my own eyes. It worked, right in front of me, just as you predicted.'

'Me?' replied Annuska. 'I predicted nothing. You are the genius who created the drug.'

'But based on your research and notes, and with your advice, and your leads and recommendations.'

'Congratulations, Bernard,' said Dorothy.

'Yes, congratulations,' added Annuska who suddenly became worried. 'But who else have you told about this? And please don't say you have told someone at *Labcope*.'

'I haven't, although ...' Annuska groaned. 'There is a third human guinea pig yet to take the drug, and the person administering it works with me.'

'She's a spy,' said Annuska.

'No, no she's not a spy. I trust her. And we've already spoken about the need for secrecy.'

79

Silence filled the room. Bernie was thrilled to be able to share his news with the woman who gave him invaluable advice. Her previously ignored and long forgotten research notes played a major role in the creation of his drug.

Dorothy stood. 'I'll put the kettle on.'

'Coffee?' boomed Annuska. 'This calls for champagne.'

'No, Nussy. You know what happens when you drink champagne. And we don't want to embarrass our guest.'

Bernie pondered that last remark.

How does an octogenarian embarrass her guest?

They settled for coffee and cake. Annuska wanted all the trial details. Bernie provided same, and Annuska showed great interest in Mother.

'So you say this lady is old?'

'In her eighties,' replied Bernie.

Annuska scoffed. 'That is not old. Young man, I am 85 and ...

'86,' said Dorothy arriving with orange cake.

Bernard couldn't believe Annuska's age. It wasn't so much her appearance but her behaviour. How many women in their mid-eighties display the *joie de vivre* this retired scientist exudes?

Annuska changed tack. 'Now Bernard, I am worried that you did not obey the code when we spoke on the telephone before.'

'Yes, I'm sorry. I was confused because you asked about my love life and, by coincidence, I've only just met a young woman.'

'A young woman,' exploded Annuska. 'You mean I have a rival.'

'Ignore her,' said Dorothy. 'Imagine what she's like with champagne.'

Bernard smiled and saw Annuska's grin grow bigger and brighter.

'That is the most excellent news, young man,' she said. 'Now please, I would like verse and chapter.'

'Chapter and verse,' added Dorothy passing the cake.

'Well her name is Kate, she's a graphic designer, and I hope we'll be having dinner this week.'

'You must bring her to me.'

Bernie choked on his cake. Dorothy became annoyed.

'Forgive my friend, Bernard.'

Annuska acted as if Bernie was absent and addressed her lover. 'Mr Slim is my protégé. I have a responsibility to ensure he is happy, and not mistreated by anyone, especially someone of the female species.'

Bernard looked at Annuska and then at Dorothy, who spoke.

'There you are, Bernard. Apparently you're dating a species.'

The trio paused and then laughed *con brio*.

Bernie couldn't sleep. There were messages on his phone from estate agents about his parents' house. There was a text from Lois about her mother coming home on Sunday. And, best of all, there was a *thank you* text from Kate promising to call him tomorrow. It finished with *xox*. And she included her mobile number, just in case he'd lost it.

Bernie didn't speak advanced *Emoji* but knew the shorthand for a kiss and a hug. Was that part of the promised "double serve" of reciprocity? Roll on tomorrow.

He went to work, chatted with Lois, then went upstairs to *Marketing* worried that Josh may have died, had a relapse, or quit *Labcope* because his wife had thrown him out. Bernie developed a twitch.

Once the effect of the drug wears off, will the patient lose their moral compass? Is backsliding the default position?

All was well; better in fact. Josh came over wearing a smile with bells and whistles. He led the scientist away from the other staff, and grasped Bernie's hand. There was no tap on the shoulder, no weeping or wailing, just a look of deep gratitude.

'Great, great news, mate. My lovely wife still loves me.'

'That's brilliant. So how's your head?'

'Fine, perfect, never felt better. Once I confessed, and she saw I was sincere, once she got over the shock of course, she said she forgave me.'

'That's fantastic news.'

'Mind you I had to promise to never cheat again, and you know what, I wanted to make that promise.'

"I'm really happy for you, mate.'

Josh became nostalgic. 'It was the first time I cried in front of the missus since the Pies won the flag.'

'Go Pies,' said Bernie, who followed Carlton, and always enjoyed a rush of schadenfreude every time Collingwood lost.

Bernie struggled to believe the success of his MCP.

'And look, Bernie, thanks for coming to see me. I really appreciate it.'

'No problem. Actually, I've got a small favour to ask.'

'For you, buddy, anything.'

'I have a friend who's a graphic artist. She pitched her work before, but I wondered if she could bring more of her samples to show you guys.'

'Absolutely, be happy to see her. Get her to give me a call. If she's a friend of Bernie Slim, I'm sure she'll be brilliant.'

'Thanks Josh, I appreciate it. Her name's Kate Naismith.'

Bernie shook hands with his guinea pig colleague and left. In the corridor, he took out his phone and called Kate.

'I was just about to call you,' she said.

'Well I thought I'd let you know that *Marketing* are happy to let you pitch your ideas again whenever it suits.'

'Really? Bernie, that is fantastic. You are such a star.'

'No promises but at least you've got your foot in the door.' He gave her Josh's number. 'And make sure you mention my name.'

'I will. I'll ring him today. And now it's reciprocity time, Mr Bernie Slim.' He liked the sound of that. 'I insist on taking you out for dinner, tonight, if you're free.'

Bernie quietly bubbled.

'Sure, that'd be great.'

They decided to select one of the eateries in Swan Street, and planned to meet by the Dimmeys' mural at seven.

When Bernie entered the lab, Lois looked at him.

'Now I know what the cat that got the cream looks like.'

Bernie found it easy to laugh.

Upstairs in his executive suite, Ralph hit the link to a web site on recipes. He clicked on *Recipe of the Day* and scrolled down to the section marked *Comments*. There he found a response from Peregrine. Ralph read.

I found this recipe delightful, and have shared it with my friends.

This was code for "News is available". Ralph closed his computer, and went for an early lunch. The nearby Royal Botanical Gardens attracted tourists and locals alike, and the CEO joined the masses. He headed for his dead-letter-drop location.

Making sure nobody saw him; Ralph collected the envelope, and moved to a garden bench. He read the contents.

Target A spending time at home of Target B. Listening device
set in Target A home, with device in Target B home due soon.

The Hyphen destroyed the note. Meet Mister Meticulous.

Bernie panicked. He couldn't make his dinner date. *Shit*. He had no choice. Dealing with his parents took priority. Putting off estate agents to go out with a new "girlfriend" just wasn't on. He made appointments to see agents at his parents' home at 6 and 6.30, and sent Kate a text asking if they could meet at eight instead of seven. She readily agreed.

Madeline was spending more time with her parents now, and felt great. Her children were safe in the care of their father, Bernie's second guinea pig triumph, Bruce, the man who recently apologised profusely for his wayward behaviour. So far, Bruce's promise to be a great husband and father held firm.

Cousin Chloe was the perfect aunt-sitter, and having his wife well cared for made Gus a happy camper.

Bernie dealt with both estate agents and, after discussion with his sister and father, chose the second. A contract was signed.

In the street, Bernie spoke frankly to the chosen agent.

'The reason we're selling is pretty obvious. My Dad has health issues but now, sadly, so too does my Mum.'

'I'm sorry,' said the agent.

'Can I ask that you tread carefully when bringing prospective buyers to the house? Our cousin is living here, so please give her, or me or my sister, plenty of warning before you arrive.'

'No problem. We'll be super sensitive. I'm in charge of the sale, and I'll make my colleagues fully aware of your situation.'

'Thanks,' said Bernie and meant it. He switched on his phone. 'Sorry, I've gotta fly. I have a date with a gorgeous girl, and need to call a cab.'

'Where are you heading?'

'Richmond.'

'Perfect. I live in Cremorne, and I'm heading home. Jump in.'

'That's great,' said Bernie checking his watch. He had 20 minutes so sent her a text.

On way. See u soon.

He wanted to put an *x* or an *o* or both but decided against it.

Maybe she's taking me out to dinner to say thanks, and doesn't fancy me at all.

The car pulled up by the Dimmey's mural. Bernie shook hands with the agent, and felt excited. The agent came across as a real pro, and Kate's smile gave Bernie's heartbeat a serious boost.

The couple strolled along Swan Street, and chose Chinese. The food was great and the girl even better. Bernie spoke naturally. He didn't try to impress but he did, and that made him even happier.

They chatted about work. Kate was a Sydneysider who followed her boyfriend to Melbourne. Bernie's stomach lurched at the word *boyfriend*.

'But things didn't work out,' said Kate. 'He's back in Sin City, and I've decided to try my luck in Melbourne.'

'His loss,' said Bernie, and meant it.

There was a pause as they looked into each other's eyes.

'I'm staying in a hotel off Bridge Road before moving in with my cousin, who is about to lose her flat mate.'

Bernie liked the use of the female pronoun.

'And you spoke with Josh in *Marketing*?'

'Yes, and I have an appointment next week. He sounds really nice.'

Bernie had a flash of Josh's rampant womanizing. 'Oh he is.'

'So tell me about *your* work, Bernie. Are you a boffin who lives in a laboratory, and teases mice?'

Bernie laughed. He felt good. He wanted to talk about his work. He wanted Kate to like him, to find him interesting and fun. His mind buzzed but confusion reigned.

My work is boring. The only exciting thing I've done is create a new drug, which might make a person do good rather than bad. In short, I may have made an amazing scientific breakthrough. Or not.

But Bernie couldn't speak about that. He kept hearing Annuska's warning about spies, so he stuck to the standard script. Kate seemed interested, and asked questions.

Ah, but is she just being polite?

They finished their meal, Kate paid, leaving Bernie feeling a tad awkward, and he offered to walk her home.

'But you live that way,' she said, pointing south.

'True but I need the exercise,' said Bernie. They wandered along Swan Street, and headed up Lennox.

They talked about family, and Bernie found himself opening up about his folks. It must have been Kate's friendly nature or her ability to listen, because by the time they reached the hotel, she knew everything about Gus and his wheelchair, and Daphne's dementia.

'Your parents are lucky to have such a caring son as you, Bernie,' she said and leant forward and kissed his cheek.

Wow. Move, my son; keep the action flowing.

Before he could initiate any follow-up activity, Kate got in first.

'Are you interested in art?'

'Ah,' Bernie struggled.

'There's an exhibition I want to see, and I'm going tomorrow. It might not be your cup of tea but ...'

'I'd love to come,' said Bernie, his adrenalin getting busy.

'It's just over the river off Chapel Street. I'll be walking so can pick you up if you like. How does three o'clock sound?'

'Sounds great,' said Bernie. He told her his address. 'And thanks for the meal.'

'It's the least I could do. Till tomorrow. Good night.' She smiled, blew him a kiss, and disappeared into the foyer.

Bernie waved, and walked home. His mind got busy.

How do you read the mind of someone you find attractive? She asked for a second date. But is that because I helped her get work? I'm hardly Bachelor of the Year, more Bachelor of the Wet Weekend.

First thing on Saturday morning, Bernie went to his see his folks. The agent, called Jackson, had a couple who were very interested in the property, and wanted to inspect at 11.

They loved the Slim home, and with Madeline there, plus Chloe keeping her aunt and uncle happy, the inspection was a breeze. Later, the agent got Bernie and his sister alone.

'That couple have been on my books for weeks, and are super keen. I have many other buyers just like them, but I'm wary about an open inspection knowing your folks are not well.'

The siblings liked this attitude. Jackson continued.

'How do you feel about developers?'

The siblings looked at each other. Both had questions.

Madeline let rip. 'You mean, have the family home demolished and replaced with some mock Georgian monolith?' Bernie cringed.

Jackson shrugged. 'I know they're not for everyone, and maybe you don't want your folks to see their treasured home being bulldozed.'

'Is there any interest,' asked Bernie?

'I could sell it tomorrow to any number of developers.'

Madeline spoke her mind. 'The right price is what matters. Who buys it is irrelevant. Mum won't have a clue, and Dad understands what some people call progress.'

'I agree,' said Bernie. 'Find out what they're prepared to pay. We have to sell and the sooner the better.'

Bernie was back home by 2pm and checked his appearance. Knowing zilch about art, his plan was to say as little as possible. For him, the big question involved the activities after the exhibition.

It's my turn to take her out for a meal.

He tidied his lounge room for the third time, changed his jacket twice, and applied a touch more aftershave.

God, how is my breath? And am I wearing clean jocks?

The doorbell rang. He took a deep breath and bounced along the passage. He felt a smile coming on as he opened the door. There stood a woman but not the one he expected.

'Signora Conti.'

'Ciao, Mr Bernie. Come stai?'

'Bene grazie, Signora. Is something wrong? Can I help?'

'Nothing is wrong. I have just made some lasagna for my daughter who is now the grandmother for the first-a time.'

'That's wonderful, Signora. So now you are a great-grandmother.'

'Si, I am a bisnonna.'

'Congratulations.'

She held out a tea-towel-covered pyrox container. 'I have some leftovers and I say to Gari, this is for your friend, Signor Bernie.'

Bernie took the dish. 'You are too kind, Signora. Mille grazie.'

Before either could say another word, Kate appeared by the garden gate. Bernie paused with home delivery in hand.

'I've found you,' said the smiling visitor.

The bisnonna turned and saw the vivacious Signorina Naismith.

'Hi,' managed Bernie. 'Signora, this is my friend, Kate.'

Kate stepped through the gate, and a beaming Signora Conti, now with hands free, stood on tip-toe, and kissed the visitor on both cheeks, then threw in a third smacker for free.

'Ciao, Signorina Kate,' she said. The elderly Italian went into the street, and turned back to Bernie. 'Maybe the fifty years is come very soon, Signor Bernie. Ciao.'

Her eyes sparkled as she waved, and went home to Gari.

'Come in,' said Bernie.

'Something smells delicious.'

'Yes, my neighbour is very kind.' He put the lasagna in the kitchen, and joined Kate in the lounge room. She seemed curious.

'What did she mean about the fifty years?'

'Oh, it's an old joke; nothing important. All set?'

Kate smiled. Bernie grabbed his father's ancient golfing brolly because showers were forecast, and Albert had been cleaning himself.

The art lovers crossed the Yarra, and headed up Chapel Street.

The exhibition featured charcoal drawings of realistic portraits. Bernie hoped for abstract art, feeling better equipped to comment on something difficult to understand — well for him, anyway.

Some of the models pictured were naked, their body shape similar to that of Mr Slim, with a few being positively Rubenesque. Bernie sucked in his cinnamon doughnut gut, and tried to be interested in the exhibition. He found it much easier to study his companion.

They went for coffee then turned for home. They reached the Church Street Bridge when the weather changed. Bernie unfurled his brolly. Kate moved in close and slipped her arm in to his. *Thank you, God*, thought Bernie as nature gave his romantic plans a shove in the right direction.

The rain delivered a friendly overture, which soon became a nasty first act. By the time they reached Bernie's place, the rain was going hammer and tongs. He didn't have to ask Kate to come in, she had to.

They sat on the settee. The rain hit *forte*, and Albert got curious.

Who are you?

He explored Kate. She stroked him, and Bernie felt spectacularly good. His new and old friend became buddies.

I could get used to this.

'Well you can't go home now,' said Bernie, as the rain set in. 'How do feel about some superb home-cooked Italian food?'

'I love Italian food,' smiled Kate, who suddenly found a cat on her lap.

'You've won a friend,' said Bernie.

He smiled at Kate and Albert, and Kate returned the expression.

'Now, something to drink; I've got a half-decent bottle of red.'

'Lovely,' she said, and resumed her romance with Albert. Bernie got busy in the kitchen. Kate called. 'Why is he called Albert?'

'He's the only cat who understands Einstein's theory of relativity.'

'Really?'

'He even understands Shakespeare.' Bernie popped into the room, and gave a hammy command. 'Albert — to pee or not to pee.'

Kate laughed, and more so when the cat walked out of the room.

'Dogs have masters, Albert has an attitude,' said Bernie exiting.

'You could have called him E = mc squared,' she called.

Bernie grinned. He liked this girl for many reasons. He liked her body. Her face, though not divine, had interesting beauty. Her brain was super interesting. He'd love to share his new drug invention news with her but for now he brought her a drink, and returned to the kitchen.

She hopped up and examined his book and CD/DVD collection.

This will tell me a bit about Mr Bernard Slim.

Two minutes later, Bernie called from the kitchen.

'You'll love this lasagna.' Silence from Kate. He popped his head in to the room. 'Everything okay in here?'

'Fine, but I'm wondering what this is.'

Curious, Bernie joined her. She pointed to the bookcase beneath one of the shelves. Bernie bent to see.

'Never seen that before,' he said. 'What is it?'

'It looks like a mini camera or some sort of microphone.'

'Bloody hell,' said Bernie making a closer examination. He tugged at the "thing" and it came free. They both examined it.

'You never said the secret service had an interest in Bernie Slim.'

He faked a laugh but his insides were churning.

'It must be something the previous owner put in.'

That didn't sound convincing.

They put the unusual discovery to one side, and enjoyed Signora Conti's superb lasagna. Bernie's salad was more trampled than tossed but the meal went down well.

The rain finally stopped, and Bernie walked Kate home. They were chatty and friendly, but both kept thinking about the hidden recording equipment. Bernie felt terrible that someone had invaded his privacy, and may already know about his new drug.

But did I talk about it aloud? What have I said on the phone?

At the entrance to her hotel, Bernie told Kate he'd really enjoyed their date. She agreed. He wished her luck with her *Marketing* meeting on Monday.

'When you're finished, ask *Reception* to give me a call. I'll pop down, and hopefully we can celebrate your new gig with *Labcope*.'

'Thanks, that'd be nice. Fingers crossed.'

He nodded and smiled. Their eyes locked, and Bernie made the move. Their lips touched, and Bernie worked hard at his technique of soft and gentle. The kiss moved up or possibly in a gear, and Bernie hoped his pasta sauce residue had long since evaporated.

Just as things got interesting, two residents burst out of the hotel, and almost collided with the romantics causing *kissus interruptus*. Bernie gave a grin, which simultaneously said *darn, oops* and *bugger*.

'See you on Monday,' he said and waited for an invitation.

'See you on Monday,' she said and turned into her hotel. He waved and headed back up Lennox Street.

Going home, his mind moved from kissing to microphones. Both were interesting although one made him sick to his stomach.

11

NODDY DIDN'T FANCY telling Murphy the bad news. 'Parisi's out, boss. The filth dropped all charges.'

Murphy spewed. His perfect plan exploded. Having murdered one of his own men, Brendan Murphy framed Luca Parisi in a classic sting. The police fell for it, and charged the Italian with murder. Now the prick was out, and not on bail; free, full feckin' stop.

Murphy's face showed a mix of incredulity and rage. More rage because *incredulity* had too many syllables for his bog-Irish brain.

'Word is, boss, some female lawyer, Jessica Reid, got him off.'

'That can't be true. And how the hell would you know?'

Noddy was shitting himself. He'd been interviewed — grilled more like — by some ex-cop working for Jessica Reid, and her head-kicking barrister. Noddy knew when to keep schtum, and this was one such time.

'In the pubs, boss, people are talking.'

'Well who the feck is Jessica Reid?'

'Member of parliament, boss.'

Murphy erupted. 'A member of parliament? Luca Parisi gets off thanks to the feckin' government? Are you taking the piss?'

Noddy felt pain. He dare not breathe a word of his run-in with that bitch, or he feared his big ears would part company with his big head.

'All I know, boss, is he's free, and the cops are lookin' for someone else for the murder of Hoops.'

'Someone else? Dey don't need someone else. I was dere. I saw da bastard shoot Hoops.'

Noddy thought about suggesting that Murphy should tell the cops he'd witnessed Hoops' murder. Noddy didn't have that thought for long.

'Right,' said Murphy, 'if da filth won't fix Parisi, I'll do it meself.'

'Are you sure, boss? Parisi still owes us, and the cops'll be watching him like a hawk.'

Murphy went quiet. Noddy made sense, not often, but now he did.

Dere has to be anudder way, thought Murphy, and then the idea genie flicked a switch in his Belfast-born brain.

The Irishman's fury contrasted with the Italian's joy. Luca was home free and loving it. He spread love and goodwill at home, and a shaky peace treaty was struck with his wife and mother.

But Luca had plans. Plans to import drugs from China or Europe; plans to smash the Irishman who stitched him up; and plans to reward the redheaded bimbo who saved his bacon. Luca got serious with Animal.

'Tell me everything about this Jessica bird.'

'You know as much as me, boss. Years ago she got me off some bullshit charge the pigs invented. I asked her to do the same for you.'

'And she's a politician in Melbourne?'

'Not just a politician; she's the boss.'

'You're kidding.'

'If her side wins in November, she'll be the Premier.'

'The Premier? My lawyer is the head honcho in Victoria?'

'If she wins.'

Luca's head drowned in ideas.

I need to be sweet with this woman. She could be seriously helpful.

'Invite her to lunch,' said Luca. 'Tell her any day is fine and, of course, everything's on the house.'

Animal's brain collapsed. 'Are you joking, boss?'

'Do I look like a fucken comedian? Tell her Luca Parisi is enormously grateful for all the help she gave him, and for exposing police corruption, and say Mr Parisi offers her the hospitality of his restaurant to her and ... is she married?'

'No idea, boss.'

'Well find out. And don't come back unless she agrees. Now piss off.'

Luca gave Animal many jobs, most involving crimes with violence, but asking a politician to lunch — that was a first.

Animal knew the way to Jessica's old office but she'd moved. Madam now occupied a bigger office, with more staff and more security.

Animal found Jessica's new location, and stumbled into Groundhog Day. Same reaction from receptionist. Same reaction from security guard. Same intervention from Genevieve.

In her office, Animal delivered Luca's invitation. Genevieve found it hard not to laugh, but dutifully promised to provide Animal with a response in the next few days.

'Ms Reid does have a fairly full calendar,' she said, standing, then ushering Animal to the lifts.

'The food's really good, Miss. Luca's got a top chef, and the squid in a sweet chilli sauce is fucken amazing.' He grimaced. 'Sorry Miss, it just slipped out.'

Genevieve farewelled Animal, and headed back to her room.

That's the last time I'll ever have to deal with Mr Animal.

She took her diary to Jessica's office.

'Who was that?'

Jessica's acute hearing matched her insatiable curiosity.

'Nobody,' replied Genevieve.

'Gen, my bullshit meter is twitching. Now who was it?'

'It was the lovely Mr Animal, that erudite bon vivant you once got off some drug charge.'

'Ah, Mr Parisi's bagman.'

'Yes, now can we get on?'

'What did he want?'

'Jesus Jessica, we've got a thousand important things to do, and you want to waste time on some poor man's gangster.'

Persistent and insistent best described the Opposition Leader.

'What did he want?'

Genevieve shook her head. Sometimes her friend and boss could be a right pain in the arse.

'On behalf of Luca Parisi, well-known drug-baron, the Animal wanted to ask you and your husband for lunch in his Lygon Street restaurant, where apparently the squid starter in a sweet chilli sauce is fucken amazing.'

'I don't think I should take Myles.'

Genevieve almost collapsed. Just talking about an irrelevant criminal was a shocking waste of time. Contemplating breaking bread with said outlaw was so far beyond the pale, the fence was in the next hemisphere.

'You shouldn't take anyone. You shouldn't even *think* about going.'

Jessica went walkabout. Genevieve hated these times. Her friend avoided eye contact when she wanted to win an argument. Jessica spoke.

'I'll take you. Find a free lunch time, and accept the invitation.'

Genevieve despaired. 'I don't know where to start. Defending criminals is bad enough. Rubbing shoulders with them in full view of the public is electoral suicide. I can see the headlines. *Opposition Leader Dines with Mafia Boss. Lobster with the Mobster.* Do you want to win this election?'

91

'Now you know my rule on rhetorical questions. We'll need a private room or screened area. And we'll arrive via the back door.'

'Jessica,' sounded a desperate Genevieve, 'in God's name, why?'

'I'll get to see the murder scene first hand and, as always, I'm doing this because everyone, including you, sweetie, tells me not to.'

Brendan Murphy's new "get Luca" plan was simple; plant drugs at Luca's home or restaurant, and tip off the cops. Murphy hated "giving" drugs to his rival but needs must. If the plan succeeded, Luca would do serious jail time. Murphy told Noddy.

'I need a female druggie, good looking and smart, someone who can act a bit.'

Noddy shrugged. 'Boss, if you want sex, I know plenty of babes.'

'Shut up and listen. I need someone to fool Parisi's family, someone who's smart and can con her way into that fecker's home.'

Noddy got the picture. 'Okay, I think I know just the bird.'

'Tell her, if this works, she'll make more money in a day than she does in a year. Now get her.'

Noddy did. Jasmine, not her real name, studied psychology at Swinburne, and gyrated on a porn webcam by night. Online, she wore a cat mask to hide her identity, but had no qualms about exposing the rest of her body. Noddy brought her to meet Murphy.

'Boss, this is Jasmine.'

Murphy remained seated. Jasmine hesitated then did a spin to show off her body.

'It's not y'body, darlin'. I want y'brain. Now put y'arse on the grass.'

Jessica and Genevieve wore sunglasses, and dressed down. They took a cab to Carlton, and alighted well away from the restaurant. As arranged with Animal, they wandered down the lane, and waited at the rear of Luca's restaurant.

'This is insane,' groaned Genevieve.

'I think I'll have the squid starter. Fresh chilli sauce you say?'

The back gate opened, and there stood Animal.

'G'day ladies. Bloody good to see youse. Come in.'

They entered the yard, and Animal led the way. He stopped because Jessica stopped.'

'Is this where the killers hid?'

'Yeah. Then they grabbed the chef, and forced him to call Luca.'

Jessica looked around, smiled then looked at Animal. 'Let's eat.'

Animal escorted the women through the kitchen, and into the restaurant. Luca welcomed them with respect. He indicated a corner table, separated from other diners by expensive screens.

'Please ladies, be seated. Order anything you like, and if there's something you require which is not on the menu, I'll have the chef prepare it especially.'

'You're too kind, Mr Parisi. We'll share your best pizza. Now, please join us and let's talk.'

Luca was thrown. Future Premiers didn't make a habit of popping in for a pizza, and certainly not via the kitchen. He spoke to a waiter then sat. Animal hovered in the wings. Jessica cut to the chase.

'You wanted to say something, Mr Parisi.'

'Please, call me Luca.' Jessica said nothing forcing mine host to speak. 'Ah, you may not have received my letter, Ms Reid, but I wanted to thank you in person. I am seriously grateful to you for getting me off that false murder charge.'

'Not so lucky with the unlicensed firearms.'

Luca put up his hands. 'Mea culpa and that will never happen again. But I'm very grateful, and want to make a donation to your favourite charity.'

Genevieve jumped in. 'Are you offering a bribe, Mr Parisi?'

Luca looked aghast. 'No, no, no. I'm offering a donation to any worthwhile cause you choose; sick kiddies, lost dogs, save the rainforests, anything. You helped me, and I help you. That's the way I do business.'

'And what is your business, Mr Parisi?' asked a smiling Jessica.

'Well, you're sitting in it. I've had this restaurant for years.'

'So the criminal activities for which you were arrested and imprisoned in your youth are long gone?'

'Long, long gone,' said Luca, worried the conversation was heading in the wrong direction.

It stalled completely with the arrival of some homemade bread, and a drink waiter with the wine list.

Both women ordered mineral water, and Luca joined them. More banter, disturbing for Luca, followed before the pizza arrived.

The guests ate with their fingers. Luca lost control of the luncheon. With her mouth half full, Jessica took aim at Luca.

'Mr Parisi, what do you know about organized crime in our fair city?'

Bitch! I offer the woman some wonderful Italian hospitality, and she spits on my pasta. Well, fuck you, lady.

He went to push back his chair in order to speak his mind, when Animal stepped forward and "encouraged" his boss to remain seated. There was an uneasy pause before Luca replied.

'As I explained, all those bad things I did, happened years ago. Now I'm a law-abiding businessman with a wife and family. If you want information about crime families, you're asking the wrong man.'

Luca had no idea Jessica could spot a lie from another planet. The tense atmosphere simmered before coffee arrived, and Jessica returned to the fray, wrong footing the Italian yet again.

'So Mr Parisi, a man with your criminal background, how have you found the Victorian police?'

Luca struggled to stay calm. 'It's a long time since my tearaway days.'

'Bullshit,' replied Jessica jolting Luca. 'Only last month you were charged with murder.'

Luca surrendered. 'Okay, you want the truth. That shooting, here in my restaurant, shows just how corrupt the cops can be. They never tried to get to the truth. They just wanted me.'

'For selling pizzas?'

'They hate me because I'm successful.'

Luca's luncheon plan flew out the window. He wanted a powerful ally. Instead, the politician grilled him, giving nothing in return.'

The ladies who lunch sipped their coffee then prepared to leave.

'Mr Luca, there's a good chance I'll be the Premier next month.'

'I hope you are.'

'And if I find any corruption in the Victorian police force, I may call on your experience to help me clean up the mess.'

'Me?' said Luca, seriously thinking this was a wind-up.

'How does it go? *You set a thief to catch a thief.*'

Jessica owned the crook. She didn't need his money, although if the Party took tobacco funds, why not a drug dealer's loot? She toyed with the criminal. If Luca's luncheon had been a card game, Jessica left with the pot, leaving Luca stranded in his budgie smugglers.

Luca baulked. 'Are you offering me a job?'

'Hardly,' smiled Jessica. 'But I've always found the most informed people are those working at the coalface.' She dabbed her mouth, tossed her serviette on the table and stood. 'Thank you for lunch, Mr Parisi. I'll have my staff contact you about suitable charities.'

She slipped on her sunglasses, and headed for the front door, with none of this exit-via-the-kitchen garbage. Genevieve scrambled to keep up, and two waiters fell over themselves to open the door. Luca couldn't avoid the impression he'd been ripped off.

Lygon Street was crowded, and Genevieve took time to catch her boss.

'Never again, Jess, never again.'

'Nice pizza, but,' said Jessica hailing a cab.

Jasmine wore a sombre suit, flat shoes, glasses, and a plain wig as an unremarkable public servant. Her cover story seemed plausible.

Noddy had a cousin, a former Education Department administrator who'd been a naughty boy. He did Murphy a letter-writing favour.

A week before Jasmine dressed down, a letter arrived at Luca's home from the Department of Pre-School Education. No such department but hey, who cares?

The letter mentioned a combined pre-school, primary and secondary school to be built in Luca's suburb. Education officials were calling on residents with school-age children to explain the new super-school.

Jasmine, now an education official, rang the Parisi doorbell from out in the street.

'Hello?' Sheila's voice came from a speaker by the gate.

Jasmine let rip. 'Oh good afternoon, madam. I'm from the Education Department. May I ask if you have any toddlers in your home?'

'One. What do you want?'

'I don't want anything, madam, except to give your toddler the best chance to enter the brand new super-school being built in your area.'

'He's already got a kinder.'

'Ah, but this new school is a crèche, kinder, primary and secondary school all rolled into one. If you start your youngster here, he'll have the one school for life. Enrolments open next month, and your toddler can be accepted in the first intake.

'It's not my decision. His father will decide.'

'But does his father know about this fantastic project?'

'I'm not sure.'

'Did you receive our letter describing the new school?'

Sheila remembered her daughter-in-law talking about a swish new all-age school.

'Yeah, we got something, but I didn't read it.'

'I can explain it in five minutes, and you can tell your son and grandson all about it.'

Sheila paused and said nothing.

'Okay,' she said, 'but only five minutes.'

There was a buzzing sound, and the rock-solid metal gate swung open. Jasmine stepped inside. Ker-lunk, the gate locked behind her.

Sheila opened the front door, and Jasmine held up her fake ID badge with photo. Sheila gave it a cursory glance.

'Come in, and please keep quiet. I've just got my grandson to sleep.'

They headed to the lounge room, and Sheila had her back to Jasmine as she pointed to a chair.

'Have a seat.'

Sheila turned and froze. Jasmine held a pistol pointing straight at the grandmother. The phoney official spoke.

'Call out and you die.'

'You bitch.'

'Sit down, keep your hands out front, and shut the fuck up.'

Sheila decided. If she survived this latest outrage brought on by her son's criminal activities, she would leave his house, kill him, or both.

Jasmine took out her phone, and pressed SEND. The text was ready to go. In the next street, Brendan Murphy got the message, hopped out of his car, and set sail.

Sheila was marched to the front door and, with a pistol in her back, made to open the front gate and front door. They waited. Murphy appeared with malice aforethought. He too carried a firearm.

'Inside,' said Murphy, waving his gun. 'Sit and shut the feck up.' Jasmine and Brendan had the same dialogue coach.

'The grandkid's asleep,' said Jasmine.

'Watch the woman,' said Murphy, and set off into the house.

His plan was simple. Find an obscure hiding place, stash the drugs, tip off the cops, and then get the hell out of the joint.

He went into the main bedroom but found no tricky hiding place. Then to the bathroom where he spied a ceiling grate. *Perfect,* he thought.

He stood on a stool. He needed to remove the grate without making a mess. It proved tricky. He struggled, then bingo. The grate came free. He took the packet of drugs from his pocket, and placed it in the ceiling. Suddenly he heard terrible screaming; weird, hysterical screaming. Loud.

Murphy raced through his full repertoire of oaths as he frantically replaced the grate and the stool, and bolted downstairs.

As he got closer the noise increased.

What the feck?

He burst into the lounge room and saw Sheila, kneeling with arms wrapped around her scared-to-death grandson, who continued to howl.

Then Murphy saw Jasmine. She was lying on the floor partly hidden behind a settee. Murphy sprang to examine her. Blood seeped from her nose and the side of her head. She would need her cat mask for tonight's webcam. Just as Murphy went to turn and deal with the old bitch, he felt a pistol barrel press against the back of his head.

'Go ahead, make my day,' said Sheila in a more dramatic fashion than Mr Eastwood. 'Drop it.'

Murphy hesitated.

I can take this bitch.

Then he heard the sound made when you cock a Glock. Murphy put down his weapon. He could never live down being shot by a woman in the house of his bitter rival. Sheila kicked the gun across the room.

The frantic grandson had settled a tad having watched Grandma whack the woman, and now corner the man.

'Good boy, Ange,' said Sheila. 'Now go and get Billy's lead. It's by the back door. You know, when we take him for a walk. Go and get Billy's lead for Grandma. Go on.'

Angelo looked at his smiling Grandmother. She was in charge. The bad people were quiet. He set off then returned with the dog's lead, and gave it to Grandma.

'Good boy. Now I want you to go back to bed, and Grandma will come and read you a story. Okay?'

Angelo trusted Grandma. She loved him, and cared for him. Despite their frightening episodes, they were best buddies. He did as he was told.

'Listen bitch,' said Murphy, 'let me go, and I won't kill your feckin' family.'

'Listen prick,' said Sheila. 'Speak again and I'll put the first slug up your arse. Now put your hands behind your back ... slowly.'

Murphy was ready to explode. The pistol, constantly pressed against his skull, reduced his options to zero. Sheila worked smart.

With her free hand, she slipped the loop of the dog lead over Murphy's left wrist, then grabbed his other wrist and pulled it closer. She wrapped the lead around both wrists and pulled. This locked Murphy's wrists together. He struggled, and she pressed the pistol harder. That hurt. Murphy didn't move. With his hands bound tight, she stood and ordered him to stand, and move to the kitchen.

'I can't move, you daft shite.'

Sheila moved back a little, and aimed the gun at her grandson's fluffy toy, on the floor beside Murphy. Poor Teddy. She fired. Murphy shat himself. He didn't cry for his mother but veered in that direction.

'You're feckin' insane,' he screamed.

'Please keep the noise down, sir. I don't want the police here just yet.'

Murphy went all quiet. *Worried* became his middle name.

'Now get up and walk to the kitchen,' said Sheila, and this time the Irishman did as ordered. He stopped, facing the sink.

Sheila opened a drawer, and grabbed some masking tape.

Kneel,' she snapped, but Murphy refused to move. She pressed the gun against his bum crack, and the Irishman knelt sharpish.

'Head up,' she said. Murphy lifted his head as Sheila opened the cupboard door under the sink. 'Head in,' she said. The gun went to his head. 'Head in.'

Murphy's head disappeared inside the cupboard with his face up against scrubbers, sponges and sprays. Sheila used her knee to close the door trapping the Irishman. With her knee pressing hard against the cupboard door, silently she put the gun on the benchtop, and grabbed the tape. She wrapped tape around his wrists on top of the dog lead. He would need serious time and effort to get free.

'Head out,' she snapped, moving her knee. Murphy's head appeared, and in a flash Sheila had masking tape around his face covering his mouth. He gurgled and garbled. With speaking no longer possible, Murphy's humiliation was complete.

Not only captured by a woman, but by a feckin' old age pensioner, the mother of me sworn enemy!

Sheila hadn't finished. She was sick to death of the crap she'd copped from her brute of a husband, her criminal son, and now his lunatic enemies. Now she was in control. Now she would make a statement, and a big one at that.

She ordered her prisoner back to the lounge room, picked up Murphy's gun, made him wait while she wrapped tape around the unconscious Jasmine's hands and feet, then shoved Murphy to the garage, opened the rear door of the family's 4WD wagon, and pushed her prisoner. He had no choice, and ended up face down on the floor with the door slammed and locked.

The roller door and front gates opened. Sheila took off. She headed towards Sunbury, left the main road, and drove along a dirt track. She pulled in amongst a copse of trees leaving her car hidden from view.

She opened the rear door. Poor old Murph was bound and gagged, and all thanks to the bitch with wrinkles. She dragged at his feet. He made noises of complaint.

'Then crawl out yourself,' she snarled.

It was bloody difficult. Murphy wiggled his way out of the vehicle, and made to lie face down.

She's going to shoot me here and leave me. Feck!

Sheila set to with scissors, cutting Murphy's clothes. They were more Kmart than Ralph Lauren, and the garments proved easy to remove. His sweat glands got busy.

She cut up the legs of his pants, the sleeves of his shirt, and the rest of his garments. His not-changed-for-a-week underwear came away easily. The weather was mild but the ignominy and fear were white hot.

Before long, the Irishman was naked. This was top-shelf humiliation. It was the equivalent of a rusted-on ex-IRA hitman, kissing the arse of an Englishman, while thanking the Limey for hopping over to the Emerald Isle and rogering the Irish.

Suddenly Murphy felt a sensation on his back. Sheila had grabbed a can of spray paint from the garage before they left. She painted him then threw away the remnants of his clothes.

'This is for shooting up my family, you Irish turd.' Then she jumped up and down on his lower back, and kicked him hard in the ribs — thrice. His agony endured.

With her phone, she took photos of Murphy in various positions. He would never pop these prints in his family album.

All done, Sheila spat on Murphy, hopped in her car, and drove off, missing his body by a whisker. En route, she rang two TV stations and asked for the news department. Before long, cars and a helicopter were heading in Murphy's direction.

To put it simply, Murphy was fecked. He could hear cars, and when he managed to get to his feet, he thought about heading towards the road for help. What he didn't know was that on his back were the letters PEDO, courtesy of Sheila's body painting. She used American English but her message was clear.

Being a typical male, he was not keen on exhibiting his genitals to the world, but his hands would not oblige. Talk about privates on parade.

When he broke cover, he tried to get a car to stop, while at the same time, turning sideways or even raising one leg. No go, as John Thomas insisted on waving to the crowd. When he turned his back for modesty, he revealed a certain painted sign. The car accelerated, and left him exasperated in a cloud of dust.

Then he heard a helicopter, and unbelievably felt grateful for the cops. Alas, it wasn't his day as the TV chopper swooped in for a closer look.

99

As Sheila drove home, Luca and his wife arrived first. Once the garage door went up, they knew something was wrong. Luca ran to his secret hiding place for his gun, while Kellie ran inside, calling to her son.

In the lounge room she heard noises. Jasmine had come to with one giant headache. Kellie examined the trussed stranger as Luca arrived. Kellie raced to Angelo's bedroom while Luca "interviewed" the visitor.

Jasmine mumbled the facts about Murphy's plan, and Luca switched from rage to fear. The fear dropped when Kellie returned.

'Ange is asleep in his room. He's okay.'

Luca resumed his chat with Jasmine. 'Where's my mother?'

Before Jasmine could answer, the front gates and then the garage door opened. 'Watch her,' barked Luca. 'If the bitch moves, hit her with this.' Luca picked up a marble ashtray, which had previously become acquainted with Jasmine's scone.

Luca raced to the garage with gun drawn. His mother stepped out of the car, saw the gun and scoffed. Luca remained hostile.

'Where is he? Where's Murphy?'

'I'm fine, thanks for asking,' said Sheila, handing Luca the intruders' weapons, before walking past her son heading inside. Luca followed.

'Mum, where's Murphy?'

They reached the lounge room. 'Oh,' said Sheila, 'she's still alive. Is Ange okay? I sent him to bed.'

'He's fine,' said Kellie, not having a clue about what had happened.

Sheila took out her phone, and showed her son and daughter-in-law photos of the well-known Irish nudist.

'This is how you treat naughty boys. No bullets, no beatings, just good old-fashioned humiliation.'

Luca looked at the photos and remained speechless. Sheila spoke.

'This arsehole now has his arsehole in Myer's front window. His face and family jewels have gone, what do they say, viral, and his reputation as a kiddy fiddler is instant world news. And that, my son, is how you fuck your enemy. Now, I need a brandy.'

They didn't need to worry about Jasmine. She would never talk.

12

AT HOME WITH ALBERT on his lap, Bernie watched the news showing a naked man wandering beside a highway. All footage was from a distance. Guarded in their comments, the police appealed to the public for help in identifying the man. Apparently, drugs were involved.

The story failed to grab Bernie's attention. His mind buzzed with Kate's discovery of that listening device in his house. Who put it there? When? How did they gain access? He decided to risk a phone call.

Now the device has been found, surely it's safe to call Annuska.

She answered in her usual jaunty manner but quickly became serious when Bernie started to tell her about the discovery.

'I think you have the wrong number, sir. Goodbye.'

She hung up. This left Bernie in shock. Then his phone rang and he grabbed it and blurted.

'Annuska, we were cut off.'

'Annuska?'

'Oh, Kate, hi. I thought you were someone else.'

'So may one ask who this strange-sounding name belongs to? Not your wife or girlfriend I hope.'

Bernie explained. 'Hardly. She's 86 and a dear friend who's been helping me with a project.'

'She sounds fascinating.'

'She is, but I don't want to bore you with my work stuff. So how are you? I really enjoyed the art-gallery.'

'Are you sure?'

'I'm positive.'

They laughed then paused.

Why has she rung?

She explained. 'I just wanted to thank you again for arranging my interview tomorrow at *Labcope*.'

'No problem. I really hope it goes well.'

'Of course I'd like to get some work, but even if I don't, I want to tell you how much I appreciate your kindness, and how much I really like being with you.'

Bernie paused. 'Well ... ditto.'

'Wish me luck for tomorrow. Good night.'

She hung up before Bernie could reply. He enjoyed an endorphin rush. Despite his worries about spies, human guinea pigs, and the fate of his folks, Bernie had found himself a girl.

And I think she likes me.

Next morning he bounced into work and stopped. No Lois. Ms Never-Late was never late. Bernie's head filled with terrible thoughts.

Lois is late because she gave her mother the MCP, and the old girl's dead. Lois killed her mother, and out of shame, took her own life.

Bernie wanted to howl, and to compound his misery, the Hyphen appeared.

'No partner?' he smirked. 'On strike are we?'

'Good morning.' Bernie waited for an identical response. Nothing. 'I'm sure Lois will be here soon. Can I help?'

'I'm here to inform you the board has made a decision regarding the proposed cuts.' Bernie held his breath. 'You were asked to suggest areas where cuts could be made, and chose not to participate.'

'You mean we didn't volunteer for redundancy.'

The chilly atmosphere turned colder. Bernie stood up to the Hyphen who ignored Bernie's sarcasm, and continued his rehearsed spiel.

'I could wait for your colleague but perhaps she's heard already.'

Bernie ramped up his aggression.

'Heard what? We know nothing.'

'Reluctantly the board has decided to reduce staffing levels, and your colleague is to be let go.'

'Let go! What kind of expression is that? She's a human. You sack people. It's a helium balloon you let go.'

'Perhaps you could ask her to come to my office when she arrives.' The CEO turned to leave. 'Wait,' snapped Bernie.

The Hyphen stopped, and spoke again.

'The decision's final. There's nothing I can do.'

'Yes there is. I wish to resign.'

Ralph narrowed his eyes. 'Don't be ridiculous.'

'You want to cut one staff member from this department. I'll resign, and there's your saving. Lois can stay.'

'I can't allow it.'

'You can't stop me resigning. I can bloody well do what I like.'

'It won't save her job.'

'You said you need to cut staff. I'll quit, problem solved.'

Ralph floundered. 'This is quite unnecessary. Your work is valued, hers is not. *Labcope* needs young scientists with talent and ambition. You fit the bill.'

'So will you put that in my reference?'

Bernie enjoyed seeing the Hyphen under pressure.

Why give me this baloney? What does the bastard want?

The CEO backpedalled.

'All right, if you feel so strongly. I'll make some calls to the board, and see if we can retain your colleague. Only I advise you to say nothing. The board may not accept my recommendation, and then you will have dashed her hopes. Say and do nothing.'

He gave Bernie a strange look then left. Before Bernie could begin to figure out the politics of what had just happened, Lois arrived.

'Good afternoon,' said Bernie, teasing Lois about being late.

'Sorry, I have had a very strange morning.'

'You and me both. Now I want you to sit please, Lois, because I have amazing news.'

Lois immediately thought about Bernie's new drug.

'What's happened?'

'I have just stood up to the Hyphen.' The look on Lois's face made Bernie grin. 'It's true. He bowled in here to announce that you were to be sacked.' Lois put her hand to her mouth. 'It's okay, relax, you're fine. But I told the Hyphen that if you were sacked, I would quit.'

'You what?'

'And Mr Bully Boots surrended. He gave in without a fight.'

'Bernie, I won't have you resign because of me. I won't let you.'

'You don't have to. The Hyphen said I'm an asset to *Labcope*.'

'You *are* an asset to *Labcope*, a wonderful asset.'

'Hang on, listen. Ralphie boy painted himself into a corner. He gave me this great rap, and when I asked if he would put that in my reference, he went to water.'

Bernie mimicked the Hyphen. 'I'll make some calls to the board, and see if your colleague can be retained.'

Lois couldn't speak. Tears filled her eyes. 'Thank you,' she mouthed.

'Don't cry, Lois. Your job's safe. We've got the Hyphen over a barrel. And if he won't budge, I'd like to go somewhere else anyway.'

Her emotions broke free, and her tears flowed. Bernie struggled.

She dabbed her eyes and spoke. 'I'm not crying because of my job, or your wonderful sacrifice; I'm crying because of my mother.'

Bernie started to die.

Oh no. What have I done?

'Is she okay?'

'No, she's not okay. In fact she's far from okay.' Lois looked straight at Bernie. 'This morning, my mother apologised.'

The shock hit Bernie hard. 'You mean she took the drug?'

'I gave it to her yesterday when she came home. All afternoon there was no change. She blamed me for putting her in the hospital in the first place. She whinged about her food, and about the tidy house being untidy — all the usual things. Then last night as I helped her to bed, she floored me when she said "Good night".'

'That floored you?'

'She usually grunts a reply if I'm lucky. But last night she spoke those two magic words. I nearly fell over. I couldn't get to sleep. This morning I went in and did the usual, asked how she slept, did she want her breakfast now or later, and she just looked at me. I stopped and asked her if she was all right. Then it happened.'

Bernie could not have been more attentive.

Please be good news.

'She said quite clearly, "I'm sorry". Just those two words.'

'And?'

Lois couldn't speak. More tears. Bernie waited. Lois recovered.

'She apologised for being rude and unfair. She admitted her cruelty had been going on ever since my father died. And then she asked me to forgive her.'

'Oh Lois, that is better than fantastic. That is stupendous news.'

'I didn't know what to do. I haven't hugged my mother for years. It was like she became a new person.'

'I am so happy for you.'

'And it's all because of your wonderful creation, Mr Bernard Slim. It's all because of your "ridiculous" Moral Compass Pill. Now I know it's only one example, but what an example.'

'Well … it's not the only example.'

'What? You've had another one?' Bernie nodded. 'And?'

'Two others.'

'Two!'

'And both like your Mum. Two men broke down, confessed their wrongdoing, and promised to change their ways.'

'Oh Bernie, that's fantastic, the best news ever.'

She moved to him and they embraced. Even Mr Shy felt it natural and normal to celebrate his drug, and Lois's mother's new birth. The timing of their embrace might not have been ideal, because in the midst of same, the dreaded Hyphen entered the lab.

It was hard to tell if he was shocked more by what he saw, or by the lack of reaction to his arrival. The *R & D* staff didn't give a damn.

'I trust I'm not interrupting anything.'

Slowly the scientists parted. No embarrassment; only big smiles.

'Just some good news we were both able to share,' beamed Bernie, trying to humiliate his hated superior.

The Hyphen had told Bernie to say nothing about Lois being sacked. Seeing the couple embrace, Ralph assumed Bernie had blabbed. He had but they were celebrating something else — the repentant mater.

Bernie enjoyed watching the Hyphen being uncertain.

'I'm going around to the various departments with news of cuts to the budget.' Bernie and Lois felt a pang of nerves. 'You'll be pleased to know this department is to continue as before. Carry on.'

He left, and the two scientists did a kind of dance.

It was hard to get on with their work but they did, stopping often to discuss the humiliation they heaped on the CEO, the three human guinea pigs, and one in particular — the mother who overnight became human.

At lunchtime, the lab phone rang. Lois answered and handed it to Bernie.

'A female,' she mouthed.

'Hello,' said Bernie and grinned when he heard Kate's voice. 'How did you go?'

Bernie saw Lois looking at him, and his grin expanded. 'That's awesome. Okay, I'll meet you in *Reception*.' He hung up, and looked at his colleague. She teased him.

'Since when have you started taking calls at work from females?'

'That's for me to know and ...'

'... for me to find out,' laughed Lois.

Bernie removed his coat and glasses. 'I won't be long.'

Lois called after him. 'Take as long as you like, Mr Genius!'

Kate waited in the foyer. She stood as Bernie approached. They kissed gently then headed to the canteen. They didn't see the Hyphen on the mezzanine floor. He stopped when he saw Bernie. Meet Ralph the spy.

In the canteen, Bernie fetched the coffees, and caused a minor panic.

'No cinnamon doughnut?' gasped barista Enrico. 'Are you not well?'

'Shhhh,' from Bernie with a finger to his lips. He brought the coffees to Kate, and delighted in her good news.

'It's only a small job but it's a start,' she said.

'That's fantastic,' added Bernie. 'If they like your work, they'll give you more.'

'I wish,' added Kate.

'They'll like it. I like it and I'm the managing director,' boasted Bernie.

They laughed, and Kate popped a question. 'Bernie Slim, will you allow me to take you out tonight to celebrate?'

'Okay, but only if we go Dutch.'

She reluctantly agreed, sipped her coffee, and stared into his eyes. Bernie enjoyed life until he suddenly remembered something.

'Oh bugger, I can't. Tonight I'm going to see my friend, Annuska.'

'Ah, the secret girlfriend. Now the truth comes out.'

'When you get to know me, Ms Naismith, you'll discover I'm strictly a one-girl kinda guy.'

They sipped some more then Kate had an idea.

'How about I come and meet your secret lover, and after we can go out and celebrate?'

Bernie smiled. 'Good idea. And I'd love you to meet Annuska.'

He phoned his scientific friend, and asked if he might bring his girl.

Bernie and Kate made their way to Balaclava by Uber, and survived the front garden with the scientist acting as jungle guide. Annuska opened the door having begun smiling three seconds before.

'Annuska, this is my friend Kate,' said Bernie.

'Hello Kate, and please, come away in.'

In the lounge room they met Dorothy. Small talk dominated with Kate explaining her work as a freelance graphic artist, and the women taking a genuine interest. Things took a Pythonesque change though when Annuska launched her first salvo.

'Now Kate, I want you to know that you have broken my heart when you steal my lover, Bernie, from me.'

Kate had been warned about Annuska Outrageous, but even said warning failed to save Kate from a shock of sorts.

'Behave Sussy,' admonished Dorothy.

'No, don't behave, Sussy,' demanded Bernie. 'I never want you to change.'

More laughter until Annuska subtly signalled to Dorothy.

'Kate,' said Dorothy, 'as you're a designer, would you be interested in seeing my water colours?'

Kate was thrilled. 'You're an artist?'

'Well, I try.'

'You've kept that hidden,' said Bernie.

'I'd love to see your art,' enthused Kate.

'Be careful, Kate,' warned Annuska. 'She once asked me to come and see her etchings before she seduced me.'

'Ignore the mad woman of Balaclava,' said Dorothy leading Kate from the room. The door closed, and Annuska instantly turned serious.

'Tell me everything,' she whispered, 'everything.'

For a moment, Bernie genuinely thought she was mad.

'Why are we whispering?'

'Quickly, while we are alone.'

'Did you plan to send Kate out of the room?'

Annuska shook her head. 'For a man who can create a marvellous new drug, you are sometimes particularly stupid.' Bernie frowned. 'We are living in a big, bad world, young man. Tell me about the microphone.'

Bernie related the tale, and Annuska interrupted asking questions.

'That is worrying. Now please, tell me about the human guinea pigs.'

Again Bernie gave details and, with each case, Annuska grew more excited, peppering him with questions.

'This is marvellous, Bernard Slim, marvellous. If what you say is true, I think you have created something remarketable.'

Bernie wanted to do a Dorothy, and say *remarkable* but continued.

'You must stop giving me all the credit, Annuska. Your notes from your years of research were the basis for my experiments. And then your comments helped me refine the final product.'

Annuska leant back. 'Thank you, but now we have the big problem.'

Bernie looked at her. 'You mean what to do with the drug?'

'I mean how do we keep the genie in the barrel?'

Bernie wanted to say *bottle* but needed to explain his thoughts. 'I've been thinking,' he said.

'Don't. Don't think, and don't act. Tell me, how many people know about the drug?'

'Ah, there's you and Dorothy, Lois my colleague, and me. My sister thinks *Labcope* have developed some magic-potion, but that's all.'

'What about Kate?'

'Nothing, I've said nothing.'

'Keep it that way.'

Bernie frowned. The drug results were sensational, but alongside his euphoria, he caught Annuska's fear.

The door opened and in came Dorothy, alone.

'What have you done with my love rival?' demanded Annuska. 'You have seduced her, and treated our friend Bernard with contempt.'

Dorothy ignored Annuska. 'She's powdering her nose. Now coffee, young man? I may even run to a cinnamon doughnut.'

'Just the one?' laughed Bernie.

Dorothy pointed at Annuska. 'You, behave.'

She left the room, and again Annuska dumped her flippant remarks, becoming super serious again.

'I tell you, Bernard, I am scared. If your drug can do what your first tests have shown, our lifes may become very difficult.'

'I hope not. I never want you or Dorothy to come to any harm; the exact opposite in fact.'

'That I know.' She smiled and patted his hand. Her fondness for the young scientist mingled with her feeling of foreboding.

Kate entered singing the praises of Dorothy's art. Dorothy entered singing the praises of her local bakery. Bernie's eyes lit up at the sight of the grub. Sadly, though, his heart refused to sing.

13

THE ELECTION DREW NIGH, and Jessica copped flak, the harshest from her disgruntled colleagues. Politics is war, and civil war the most bloody. But Jessica triumphed, and became the Premier of Victoria.

For the newly elected Liberal government, celebrations were long and loud, and Jess and Myles arrived home in time for an early breakfast. Hubby checked on little Simone, thanked the nanny, fed the animals, and went to check on the Premier. Fully dressed but shoeless, she lay face down on her bed fast asleep.

On election night, Luca Parisi watched the counting of votes on the telly. As the change of government became obvious, Melbourne's drug lord pondered how he might engage with the new premier.

She knows the criminal law. If I help her expose corrupt cops, will that help me? Will that help make me the Mafia Boss Down Under?

Ralph slept badly on election night. Being the CEO of *Labcope* Australia failed to satisfy Mr Ambitious. His plan for an international appointment hinged on him doing something spectacular in Oz.

Head office needs an executive like me. How can I make it happen?

He needed a whizzbang scientific breakthrough, something that generated vast profits for *Labcope*. He sensed Slim and the Hungarian woman were doing something special. But what? *Speak to me, spy.*

Ralph considered bugging the *Labcope R & D* laboratory, but the company's security team swept the building, and would discover any device the CEO installed. He needed his spy to come good.

After watching the election telecast, Annuska and Dorothy retired. In the darkness they chatted about the result before Annuska changed tack.

'I haven't told you everything about the trials for Bernie's new drug, my darling, because I'm worried.'

'Blind Freddy can see that,' replied Dorothy.

'Young Mr Slim is a brilliant scientist. His Moral Compass Pill works with amazing results. But I fear he's swimming in shark-invested waters.'

'Infested.'

'His human guinea pig trials have been wildly successful. If those trials are expanded and produce identical results, Bernie's drug will change society and kind humans forever.'

'Humankind,' said Dorothy, who leaned over, kissed Annuska, then turned her back and went to sleep.

'Humankind forever,' repeated Annuska. 'Goodnight my darling.'

Not far from Balaclava, every word of this conversation was heard and recorded. The Hyphen's spy, opened a laptop, clicked on a particular foodies' site, and, as Peregrine, left a comment about the *Recipe of the Day*. As before, this coded message meant news for the *Labcope* CEO; seriously interesting news.

In Bernie's house, the scientist watched the election result with Albert who, having refused to vote, found the voices of commentators soporific.

'What should I do, old boy?' asked Bernie, fondling his cat's ears. 'More trials or should I get the formula patented?'

Despite Kate having discovered a listening device in this very room, everything Bernie said was heard and recorded. The Hyphen's spy had bugged both Annuska's and Bernie's abodes. By saying nothing, at least Albert didn't let the human out of the bag.

Kate took little interest in the election telecast. She was busy preparing work for Labcope, worrying about her future career, and the health of her mother. She thought about Bernie Slim, and her feelings. She knew he liked her. But did she feel the same about him?

Lois and her mother watched the ABC election night telecast, and civilized conversation filled the room. Lois continued to be shocked.

'I'm glad that girl has become the Premier,' said the former irascible parent. Mother spoke calmly, sensibly and politely.

'Did you know we have a connection with the new Premier?' replied her daughter.

'We do? What do you mean?'

The reformed harridan added genuine curiosity to her repertoire.

'The Premier's Chief of Staff is Uncle Stephen's goddaughter.'

'I didn't know that. How interesting. Why didn't you tell me?'

Lois worried. "Why didn't you tell me?" sounded potentially aggressive. Was it the first step on the slippery slope to sarcasm?

Is Mother having a relapse? Has the effect of the drug faded? Is she about to say something caustic and cruel?

Had Lois been brave, she might have spoken the following.

"You don't know about the Premier's Chief of Staff, Mother, because you never take any interest in your brother or his family."

Lois cringed expecting a blast from her mother. A blast? Are you kidding? Mother delivered a stunning reply.

'I really should take more interest in my dear brother. It's his birthday next week. We must go and see him.'

Had a feather been to hand, Lois might well have been poleaxed.

My God, if Mother's response is typical, Bernie's formula is a hit.

Kate called Bernie on Saturday night soon after the Premier conceded.

'Family problems; I need to fly to Sydney in the morning,' she said.

'You haven't asked my permission,' replied Bernie.

She knew he was kidding.

'Ah, so you like to control your women. I'm glad I discovered that before I fell for your charms.'

'My charms?' laughed Bernie. 'I've never had anyone say that before.'

'Now that I find hard to believe.'

His pulse began an *accelerando*. He continued.

'I hope things are okay. When are you back? I can collect you.'

'Not sure,' said Kate. 'My mother's not well. I'll book once I'm ready. I'll text you.'

'Are you sure?'

'No, I'm positive,' laughed Kate, and they both felt good.

The call ended with Bernie feeling both sad and glad.

Bernie looked at Albert. 'Is this love, young man? Has your heroic master fallen for this girl?' Albert yawned. Ah, the wisdom of felines.

Next morning, Sunday, Bernie enjoyed a lie-in when his phone rang, and he spoke without looking at caller ID.

'Good morning. What's the weather like in Sin City?'

'I have no idea.'

'Lois. I'm sorry. I thought you were someone else.' Bernie suddenly turned serious.

Why is Lois calling me at home on the weekend?

Panic invaded his dialogue. 'Is everything okay? How is your mother?'

111

'Are you sitting down?' Bernie stood. 'You will not believe my mother. Not only is she not returning to her wicked ways, she just keeps getting kinder and sweeter and more considerate.'

Bernie relaxed. 'That's fantastic, Lois, I'm really, really pleased.'

'We need to talk, Bernie. I've got an idea to test your wonderful MCP at another level.' He blanched. 'We can't talk about it on the phone or at work. Can we meet today? It's important.'

'Okay.'

'What about your girlfriend?'

'Ah, she's in Sydney. I thought you were Kate when I answered.'

'There's a coffee shop in Middle Park. How does 3pm sound?'

'Fine. But will your mother mind?'

'I'll text you the address. This is big, Bernie, bigger than big. Bye.'

Ralph lived in an apartment in The Righi, South Yarra, with the postcode being super important. Bernie lived on the other side or north of the river, and in jest, sometimes called Cremorne, North South Yarra.

Living a short walk from the Royal Botanic Gardens meant the Hyphen could stroll to his dead-letter drop locale. His recipe code sent him there. He collected his latest missive, and read with shaking hands.

> Target A created new drug with help from Target B. Drug known as Moral Compass Pill. Trials successful. Target A's girlfriend discovered listening device but new one installed. Both Targets unaware of their listening device.

The Hyphen walked home pondering this latest news.

What is this Moral Compass Pill? What are these trials? How can I get the formula?

Albert Park housed several coffee shops. Bernie cycled, and arrived wearing helmet, tracksuit and sweat. Lois beamed from her table. Bernie ordered coffee, and settled for a blueberry muffin. He joined Lois.

'You are a genius,' she blurted, too loud for Bernie's comfort.

'Shhh,' he whispered as other coffee consumers looked at them.

'Sorry,' replied Lois in a far softer voice. 'I'm still in shock. My mother's had a personality bypass. She's a new person, and everything you said would happen has.'

'I said "might" not "would". Now has she had any headaches?'

'At first, yes. But once she apologised, they disappeared, exactly as you predicted. I only gave her a small dose, so God knows what might have happened if she took more.'

'I'm so happy for you, Lois. What a difference in your life.'

'Yes, it's wonderful, but so is your drug. How many trials is it now?'

'Just three.'

'And every one a resounding success.'

Bernie nodded. He wanted to pinch himself.

Is this really happening?

'You must take out a patent,' insisted Lois, now his biggest fan. 'Immediately, first thing tomorrow.'

Bernie hesitated. 'I'll need legal advice.'

'Find a lawyer who deals in patents. I'll help if you like.'

Bernie sat stunned. Lois's enthusiasm scared him.

What have I unleashed?

But if Bernie felt overwhelmed by Lois and her suggestions, he was gobsmacked with her next comment.

'You have to trial it on someone important.'

Bernie's mouth opened revealing some muffin. 'Someone important?'

'If someone in the public eye takes the drug, we, and the rest of the world, can observe how it works.'

'*If* it works.'

'We'll know it works if a public figure becomes the latest guinea pig.'

Bernie imagined a prime minister, a famous footballer, or a member of a well-known royal family popping the MCP, and then having the world's media broadcast confessions of previously unknown "sins".

Lois is nuts.

'Lois, I'm thrilled your Mum has become a kind and friendly person, but I'm not sure about conning someone famous.'

Lois turned sombre. She almost hissed.

'Well you've changed your tune.' She attacked. 'I remember a certain scientist saying, "If that happened, society would change for the better all over the world." What's happened to that person?'

Both stopped talking. Both felt overawed. This MCP was bigger than Donald Trump's hubris. Lois had a human being for a mother, and Bernie had amazing results for his sci-fi invention. He got curious.

'So tell me about your famous person.'

'My uncle is godfather to the new Premier's Chief of Staff, and it's my uncle's birthday next week, and my mother wants to go.'

'Great.' Bernie didn't mean that.

'She hasn't spoken to her brother for years; used to call him an idiot.'

'And his goddaughter?'

'Genevieve Kovács is the Premier's sidekick. People say without her Chief of Staff, the Premier would never be Premier.'

'So how would this Chief of Staff be involved in any trial?'

'I spike her drink at my uncle's party, and we see what happens.'

Bernie felt sick. 'You can't be serious?'

'Never more so.'

'You do know that's illegal? We could go to jail for years.'

'You did it.' She was right. 'Bernie, this drug is too important. If these first trials are genuine, your MCP could change the world.'

He clenched his fists. This crazy idea looked set to explode. Fear took over. *Let me out*, he screamed in silence. They whispered their argument.

'Look, Lois, why don't I just hand it over to *Labcope?*

She looked at him unable to believe his change of heart.

'You're not serious. That is absurd; mind-bogglingly fucking stupid.'

He froze. Lois swore! She never swore. Now she almost begged.

'Bernie, don't quit now. At least, let me try this one final test. You've run two; let me run two.' They stared into each other's eyes. 'Please.'

He had massive doubts, and argued against Lois and her plan.

'We can't study this Genevieve's reactions. She's not a public figure.'

'True, but if the drug works, her behaviour will impact her friend and boss, and she, Premier Jessica Reid, is most definitely a public figure.'

Bernie exhaled.

His can of worms was open, and the wriggly blighters were off and running.

14

GENEVIEVE GOT LUCKY with her godfather. Stephen Rose encouraged his goddaughter to study economics. A top banking executive, he gave her invaluable introductions. Sure, she had brains and drive, but sometimes it's not what you know but who. Besides, nepotism, like the poor, will always be with us.

Uncle Stephen watched Genevieve's brilliant banking career with pride. When she switched to politics, he shrugged, and wished her well. Years later, and especially right now, everything looked hunky-dory.

Stephen's birthday pulled a crowd. His son and his wife and kids were there, even his former wife and her hubby. His goddaughter, Genevieve, and her hubby and their kids never missed. Several of his old banking buddies and two long-time neighbours dropped in. But the showstopper, the red-carpet scene-stealer, the hold-the-front-page arrival featured his niece, Lois and her miserable mother. Miserable?

Stephen hadn't spoken to his sister in ages, so much so he didn't recognise her at first. And when she spoke and smiled, and actually kissed her sibling, Stephen thought the world was about to end.

Niece Lois often popped in but they rarely discussed "Mother". Who wants to talk about complaining, self-pitying people who revel in rudeness?

And speak of the devil; here stood the mystery guest. Mystery was right as few recognized her.

'Hello Lois,' they cried, and kissed the scientist before waiting to be introduced to the gray-haired octogenarian.

Lois knew Genevieve well. Through Uncle Stephen, the women met on many occasions. With the party underway, they landed in the kitchen.

'I'm so glad your mother was able to come,' said Genevieve removing cling film from her tray of sandwiches.

'You and me both,' replied Lois. 'And by the way, congratulations on the election result.'

'Thanks.'

'So what's our new Premier really like?'

'Interesting,' said Genevieve and left it at that.

'To me, she comes across as a woman on a mission; strong but sensitive.' Lois changed tack. 'Oh sorry, I didn't mean to pry. It's just that I admire any woman who can shatter that glass ceiling.'

'Let's chat later. Right now my sausage rolls need rescuing.'

'Sure,' smiled Lois, and took her finger food to the party guests.

En route, a firm hand grabbed her arm. The host dragged Lois aside.

'Thanks for the heads up on your mother but, bloody hell Lois, what's with the Mother Teresa routine? Is she for real? She's not dying is she?'

'Not that I know but please, Uncle, let's be thankful for small mercies.'

'Small? She's been transformed. Has she found religion?'

Lois lied with ease. 'No idea. She's been getting less irritable for a while, and the other day, made a big apology for her behaviour. I didn't understand it or care why, I'm just so happy to see her happy.'

'Something's not right. You scientists are always inventing drugs. I bet you've found a cure for selfish whingers.'

Lois laughed to dismiss her uncle's claim. She now had proof that many a true word is spoken in jest.

Before Stephen's interrogation could continue, singing broke out.

A flaming cake appeared, and the birthday boy left to celebrate. Once the speeches concluded, the party started to wind down. The kids still had energy to burn, although the adults took the weight off their legs.

Lois spotted Genevieve, and offered the goddaughter a coffee.

'Here's what you need, Genevieve. There's even a little something special inside.'

Genevieve laughed, took the mug, and toasted Lois. They both sipped.

Lois told only some of the truth. A nip of brandy was in Genevieve's brew, but so too was a portion of a certain Moral Compass Pill. The women relaxed although Lois had a much, much faster heart rate.

Perhaps the craziest part of the party involved "Mother", who simply didn't want to leave. She ignored her brother for years, and now wanted to make up for all those missed birthdays.

Stephen made a face and Lois took the hint.

'Come on, Mum, it's time we got going.'

'Oh really,' complained the former tyrant. 'And just when we're having such a good time.' Lois got her mother to the front door where the siblings kissed. 'Now brother dear, you know where we live. Don't be a stranger.'

Lois and Stephen looked at one another.

Is she for real?
The visitors left, Stephen shut the door, and shook his head.
Whatever she's on, the manufacturer will make a mint.

Bernie and Maddy decided. The estate agent reckoned they could get 1.85 with ease. With so many interested bidders, 1.9, 2 or more might happen. But the best settlement would be 60 days, possibly 90. The siblings wanted the cash immediately.

So what about your developer mates,' asked Bernie?

'Not as much money but settlement within 30 days, sooner if you cut a deal.'

'How much money,' asked Maddy?

'1.8, maybe 1.85.'

Gus and Daphne needed professional accommodation right now. Their babysitter, Chloe, was going overseas. The choice was simple; find temporary respite now, or, move the folks to permanent residential care, if they could, immediately. But whichever choice they made, they needed money as soon as possible.

The agent left the "kids" to make a decision.

'We might not be able to find a respite place which will take both of them,' said Maddy.

'150 grand is a lot less money,' replied her brother.

'Bernie, we need to agree on a plan, and stick to it.'

'Well why don't we try developers and get as much as we can, but with a very quick settlement?'

Maddy nodded. 'I'm glad you said that. Dad, and particularly Mum, need immediate help. Will you tell the agent?'

Bernie did, and within days, a developer bought their parents' home of 36 years. He paid almost immediately but wanted vacant possession.

The adult children chose an expensive nursing home cum retirement village with a special wing for high care and dementia patients. Now came the tricky part — waiting for a vacancy. In the meantime, they found temporary respite care. Bernie and his sister felt sad and glad.

The developer submitted plans for demolition of the Slim family home to be replaced by two double-storey townhouses. This was the new gold rush. Demolish old homes, and make a mint selling dual occupancy.

Being a penny-pincher, the developer placed short-term tenants in the Slim home while everyone waited for council to approve the plans.

Next Monday, Bernie arrived at work early. He wanted news.

What happened with the new human guinea pig? Please don't be late.

Lois too arrived early. The look on her face told all.

'Well?' asked Bernie.

'We have trial number four,' she sparkled.

'And?'

'Cup of coffee, MCP stirred in, along with a drop of brandy.'

Bernie gasped. 'Alcohol? You gave the drug with alcohol?'

Lois panicked. 'Just a drop.'

'Lois, we don't know how the MCP reacts with alcohol.'

She felt ill. Had she blown the trial? 'I'm sorry. I thought it the best way to be sure she'd drink all the coffee. It really wasn't much brandy.'

'And she's the one person we can't watch.'

'But we can watch her boss. If the drug works, the Premier may make some statement about her Chief of Staff.'

'What, that she's dead because a combination of my drug and alcohol caused her to have a stroke?'

They stopped talking, and tried to work. Both breathed tension, and then things got worse when the door opened, and His Holiness the Hyphen entered. He sensed a strange mood.

'Somebody die?'

Bernie felt empowered to tell the CEO to get lost. He stopped just short of *Fuck off Ralphy!*

Mind you, had Bernie known the Hyphen was spying on him, and knew about his MCP; Bernie's language might well have been brutal.

'I'm just here to advise that security found a listening device in the building last week.'

Bernie froze and Lois nearly fainted.

'In here?' asked a worried Bernie.

'Why? Have you something to hide?'

The Hyphen looked straight at Bernie, daring him to confess.

He hesitated then did just that. 'Yes, I have.'

Lois felt ill. The Hyphen believed he'd struck gold.

'I helped my girlfriend get some freelance work with *Marketing*. Would that be considered insider trading?'

The furious Hyphen snorted, told them to be careful, and departed.

Bernie and Lois looked at one another.

'I think he knows,' she said.

Bernie put a finger to his lips and made a soft *shhhh* sound. Lois realised and closed her eyes. Things went from bad to worse.

People talk about the first 100 days of a new government. What's been achieved? How the electorate has reacted, and so on.

With Jessica as Premier, the talk began after the first 30 days.

Internal polls produced good news for the government. Jessica won everywhere. Being a happily married woman with a young child appealed to voters. Even being a successful lawyer prepared to take on any client scored a tick. Her policies and presentation appealed.

She luxuriated in her success. Her happiness surged. Life could hardly be better. Until.

Jessica and Genevieve held a daily briefing over breakfast. This morning Genevieve was late. Jessica went to her friend's office. Empty. She went to the outer office.

'Anyone seen Genevieve?'

'No Premier,' sang the chorus.

Jessica rang Genevieve's mobile. Message bank.

'Morning darl. Where are you? Call me. Oh, hope you're okay.'

Half an hour later, the Premier's worry beads got a solid workout.

Where the hell is she?

They tried her home, her husband, her parents, and her kids' school. Nothing. They were about to call the cops when a worried staffer arrived.

'Premier, I just parked downstairs and saw Genevieve in her car.'

Jessica panicked. 'What's happened?'

'I think she's okay.'

'Think? What do you mean *think*?'

'I waved and she didn't respond. I tapped on the window, and asked if she was okay and she nodded.'

'And?'

'I've come to tell you.'

Jessica moved as she spoke. 'Get security to meet me in the carpark.'

The Premier found Genevieve then got her out and upstairs.

'Absolutely no calls or visitors,' she barked with menace.

Genevieve Kovács was the Premier's Chief of Staff, right-hand woman, PA, best friend, head kicker, and staunchest supporter. But what she said and did that morning in her boss's office started a mini tsunami.

'I'm sorry, Jessica, but I have to quit.'

At first the Premier thought it was a joke. *It has to be a sick joke.* But the ashen look on Genevieve's face screamed serious.

'Are you ill?' gasped Jessica. Sisterly concern filled the room. 'Have you got cancer? Is it Justin, the kids, your parents? Tell me, darl, please.'

Genevieve spoke softly and slowly. 'We're okay. We're all okay.'

'Is it money? Have you been scammed? Have you accidentally killed someone?' Genevieve shook her head. 'You've gotta help me here, babe. Something really strange is happening.'

'I can't explain it.'

'Explain what? You're not sick. Your family's fine. There has to be a reason. You look terrible. Please, what's happened?'

Genevieve became agitated. 'I don't know. If I knew I'd say.'

Silence. Jessica went walkabout. Genevieve didn't care.

Jessica loved problems. She loved the challenge of having to solve things. But this had her beat. Genevieve's behaviour made no sense.

How can I help when I don't know what's wrong?

'Okay, let's work backwards. You were fine on Friday, and now you're not fine on Monday. What happened on the weekend?'

'Nothing special.'

'Tell me.' That came out wrong. Softer. 'Please.'

'We watched the kids play sport. My folks came over on Saturday night. We went to my godfather's birthday on Sunday. That's it.'

'And how did you feel? Were you sick or upset?'

Genevieve shook her head. 'Nothing, I was fine. Maybe I had a small headache on Sunday night, but that was minor.'

'And this morning?'

'I still had that headache.'

'And now?'

'It's worse.'

'Oh for crying out loud, woman. Get yourself to hospital.'

'It's not a normal headache.'

'Are you in pain?'

'Not as such.'

Jessica fumed. 'Jesus Genevieve, what the fuck is going on?'

'I feel terrible about all the things I've done to help you win office.'

Wow.

The silence roared. Jessica became a politician lost for words. The women looked at one another. Who would speak? Jessica spoke slowly.

'You feel terrible about what you did to help me win office. Is that it?'

'The lies, the dirty tricks, and especially that fake news about Myles being a paedophile. I feel so ... guilty.'

'Okay. I think I understand. But why now?'

Genevieve shrugged. Jessica rubbed her forehead. She wanted to explode. She hated being impotent. It wasn't so much Genevieve's mind-blowing comments, although they shaped as being catastrophic, but rather their out-of-the-blue arrival. No warning. Not the slightest hint this was coming. Genevieve's behaviour came out of left field — on Mars.

'Right,' said the Premier, 'you feel terrible about telling lies.'

'And running dirty tricks, and using people and ...'

'Yes, yes, all right, one at a time.' They paused. 'When you told lies before, did you ever feel guilty?'

Genevieve shook her head. 'No. I didn't.'

'When you thought up a dirty trick, like leaking that Myles was involved with child porn, what were you thinking?'

Genevieve concentrated. 'I was thinking it was a clever idea, it would trick your opponents, and could be used to get you the leadership.'

'So no guilty feelings at the time?'

Genevieve shook her head. 'None.'

'And you were fine on Friday when you left here?'

'Yes, fine.'

'Then something happened on the weekend. Something happened to your brain, your psyche. Are you on drugs?'

Genevieve flared. 'Screw you, Jessica. What do you take me for?'

'I mean prescription drugs. Have you seen a shrink, a therapist? Have you been watching telly evangelists? Is your marriage sound?'

'I may be sick, Jessica, but not stupid, and yes, my marriage is fine.'

A soft tap on the door interrupted their meeting.

'What?' yelled an angry Premier.

A nervous staffer entered with news of a possible terrorist event.

'All right,' snapped Jessica. 'I'll be out in a minute.'

Jessica's pain increased. She faced a problem for which she had no answer. If her Chief of Staff quit days after they took office, what would that tell the electorate?

I can't keep my staff. I'm a tyrant. No smoke without fire. I'm a loser.

But far, far worse, would be Genevieve confessing her lies and dirty tricks. Here's your death warrant, Premier — sign here.

'Okay,' said Jessica. 'I want you to go home and stay there. I'll have your GP and a shrink give you the once over. My driver will take you.'

'I'll be all right.'

'It's not a request, Genevieve. Now wait in *Reception.*'

From his desk at work, Bernie rang Kate. Still no response.

I hope she's okay.

He left another message, and battled on at *Labcope.* He and Lois had sent one another to Coventry. Bernie went to *Marketing,* and found Josh.

'G'day Buddy,' smiled the reformed womanizer. 'Thanks again for all your help. I couldn't be happier.'

'Great,' said Bernie. 'Look, I just wondered how you got on with that graphic designer.'

'Kate, she's fantastic. We'll certainly use her again.'

'That's terrific.' He paused. 'So you haven't spoken to her of late?'

'Ah, not since last week. Is there a problem?'

'No, no problem. Just wanted to know how she got on.'

Josh kept buzzing. Bernie mumbled about being pleased Josh was doing so well and left. At least one of his guinea pig trials looked good.

But where the hell is Kate? Is she back from Sydney?

After work, he decided to try and track her down. She stayed in a hotel in Lennox Street. Bernie entered *Reception*.

'Hi,' he said. 'I'm trying to get in touch with one of your guests.'

'And your friend is a guest here?'

'Yes, I dropped her off last Friday.'

'Well we can't reveal guest details. Have you tried phoning?'

'I have. Could I leave a note for her?'

'You could. Do you know her apartment number?'

'No. And I think she was moving out to live with her cousin.'

'Well, perhaps you could try her cousin's place.'

What place?

Bernie blew a deep breath, thanked the receptionist and left. He walked home, opened his front door, and heard a familiar voice.

'Mr Bernie, Mr Bernie.' His elderly neighbour appeared.

'Oh ciao, Signora.'

'I have the message to tell to you. Signorina Kate she knock on your door, and you not home.'

'Signorina Kate?'

'Si. She tell to me her phone is broke, and her mother very sick, and she go back to Sydney to look after her, and she will try to call tomorrow.'

Bernie felt fantastic. 'Grazie Signora, molto grazie. Now let me feed Albert, and then I will take Gary for his walk. Un momento.'

He did as promised, then phoned Annuska. He told her his love life had taken a big step. Subtle? No but she understood and bade him visit. He set off failing to spot The Hyphen's spy. Bernie had a tail.

In the privacy of her lounge room, Annuska heard Bernie's news about guinea pig number four. The eavesdropper listened nearby.

15

IN THEIR DARKENED BOUDOIR, Annuska and Dorothy chatted in bed. It helped them fall asleep.

'Our favourite scientist is taking more risks,' said Annuska.

'I worry, Nussy. Are you sure this drug is safe?

The listening device in their bedroom worked a treat.

'Bernie has a new guinea pig, a friend of the Premier,' said Annuska.

'A friend of the Premier? My God, it's getting out of hand.'

'It's her Chief of Staff, Ms Genevieve Kovács.'

'Kovács?'

'A good Hungarian name. They've given her the drug, how do you say, surreptitiously.'

Dorothy grasped Annuska's hand. 'Oh Nussy, what will happen?'

'If Bernard's conscience drug works on someone important, and this person confesses their guilty secrets, the whole world will know it is created, and then ... kaboom.'

'But will *you* be in trouble?'

'Perhaps, but Bernard will be in big, big trouble. He is sweet and so intelligent, but I fear, Dotty, the shit will soon hit the pan.'

Dorothy didn't correct Annuska. Hitting the pan or fan was irrelevant. Bernie faced a crappy future. His secret formula was poised to explode.

In the dark, the women lay still, the listening device even capturing their breathing. The Hyphen's spy typed a message on a certain Recipe site. In code it translated as:

Dead letter drop tomorrow.

Dr Pauline France found her way to the Premier's home.

'Come in, Doctor' said the Premier, and led the psychiatrist to a study with décor suitable for your average millionaire.

Jessica forgot her manners, failing to offer her guest a drink.

'I can't thank you enough for doing this, and at such short notice.'

'Happy to help,' smiled the medical professional.

'As you know, I'm seriously worried about Genevieve. She's not just my Chief of Staff; she's been my best friend for years. Tell me, has she had some sort of breakdown?'

'She's certainly not well.'

'God almighty; tell me the worst.'

'Something dramatic happened, I'm guessing, in the last 24 to 48 hours. She feels tremendous guilt about things she's said and done; some of the things going back many years.'

'Why? Will she recover? God, I'm sorry, I'm in a mess. Forgive me, would you like some tea or coffee; something stronger?'

'I'm fine.'

'Please, go on.'

'We need to find out what's triggered her unusual behaviour.'

Jessica started pacing the study. She stopped, and sat again.

'I'm sorry. Have you ever had a patient with these symptoms?'

'Not as such. People feel guilt for all sorts of reasons but with Genevieve, there doesn't seem to be a specific reason.'

'What do you recommend?'

'Her GP has prescribed a sedative, and written a referral to a neurologist.'

'Do you think she's likely to do anything ... silly?'

'Like harm herself?'

Jessica nodded. She couldn't say the word *suicide*. But if truth were told, Jessica was far more worried about Genevieve telling the world about every lie, leak and dirty trick she'd committed on behalf of her pal, the Victorian Premier. Topping herself would actually be a solution.

Forget about hubby and the kids; it's my head on the block.

That night, Jessica sat on her husband's bed and talked; the atmosphere similar to one in a bedroom in nearby Balaclava. Worry.

Next morning Bernie woke and checked his phone. A text from Kate.

Sorry. Mum v ill. Still in Sydney. TTYL.

Albert put in his breakfast order, and Bernie kept thinking about Kate. He worried about her worrying about her mother.

Kate's shorthand appealed. Bernie's knowledge of the Periodic table far outweighed his ability to decipher the Twitter Dictionary. When he checked, her *Talk to You Later* shorthand made him smile.

At the same time, Ralph's laptop failed to work. He used his phone to check his emails, and a certain web site for recipes. Server down. Several swear words later Ralph went for his morning jog on the Tan, the 4K running track around the Royal Botanical Gardens. He took out his anger and frustration via exercise. He would be late for work but didn't care.

In their lab, Bernie and Lois worked abnormally. They were frightened to say anything about the MCP. According to The Hyphen, their workplace may be bugged.

'You need a break, young man,' said Lois. 'Go for a walk, and try and stop worrying.'

They looked at one another and grimaced. Not knowing was bad. Not being able to talk about it was worse.

Bernie checked his phone for a text from Kate. Nothing.

'I'll take your advice, oh wise one.' He removed his safety glasses and coat, and grabbed his jacket. 'I'll call it a very early lunch, if that's okay.'

'Take as long as you like. I'll call if anything happens.'

She winced realising her words sounded suspicious.

He bought a salad sandwich, and a bottle of water from the deli in St Kilda Road, and headed up the hill towards the Shrine of Remembrance. He passed the Observatory, and headed into the Gardens proper. As he passed the Ian Potter Foundation Children's Garden his phone rang.

'Maddy, what's up?'

'I'm fine but you sound strange.'

'Me? No, I'm fine. I'm out getting some fresh air. What's news?'

'Great news. Our preferred nursing home just rang, and they can take Mum and Dad this week.'

'This week? That can't be right. How come?'

'Huge slice of luck for us. A couple, just like Mum and Dad, vacated overnight. The wife's had a stroke, and the husband died yesterday.'

'That's terrible.'

'For their family, yes; for us, it's perfect.'

'What can I do?'

'We now have power of attorney. We need to sign the nursing home paperwork, and make a deposit. Any chance you can get time off?'

'Sure. I'll call you once I'm back in the office.'

'Okay. Bye.'

'Oh and well done you.'

He felt good for the first time in ages. He wandered around the lush environment, found an empty seat, and ate his sandwich.

The Gardens were crowded with groups of children on school excursions, with tourists, and workers like him. Lunch eaten, he headed back to work, dodged some unruly kids, and then got a massive shock.

The Hyphen had a bad morning. Workman carrying out renovations in the office next to his drove him mad, his PA went home feeling ill, and the company accountant announced he was taking early retirement.

By the time Ralph dealt with these issues, he was back online. He checked the Recipe web site, and saw the message from his spy. Minor panic. He told the temp filling in for his PA that he had urgent business, would be back in half an hour, and could be contacted on his mobile.

He crossed St Kilda Road, and headed for his dead-letter drop.

Bernie froze. He couldn't believe what he saw.

That's Kate.

The woman was fifty metres ahead, and walking out of the Gardens.

I'm sure that's her.

He thought about calling out.

No, it can't be.

She followed the winding path and disappeared. Bernie ran. He took a short cut across the lawn then dived into a garden to save time.

He burst into the open and stumbled on some picnicking Japanese tourists. Trying to avoid standing on people, he fell decorating his strides with sushi. The elderly members of the picnickers screamed, attracting other visitors wishing to help or just sticky beak.

Bernie apologised profusely, offered to pay for any damage, and finally made his humble exit. So much for the mystery woman.

He headed back to work when he saw her again.

It is Kate. Shit.

She walked away from him then stopped suddenly, to read a board with rules of behaviour within the Gardens.

This morning she texted me from Sydney promising to call. Now she's in Melbourne, a stone's throw from Labcope.

Bernie walked towards Kate.

There must be a simple explanation.

He stopped dead. The dreaded Hyphen was walking towards him.

Bernie moved to the side of the path, dropped to the ground, and fiddled with a shoelace. People walked around him. He couldn't see Kate. He hid trying not to look suspicious.

Be still my thumping heart.

He peered around bodies and through legs, and saw an amazing sight. The Hyphen and Kate stood side by side reading the same board.

Is that a coincidence? Should I confront them? And say what?

People were everywhere. Then the Hyphen headed towards Bernie. The CEO was scowling as he passed the kneeling scientist.

Bernie decided to confront Kate. Then his phone rang. He grabbed it but kept his eye on her.

'Hello,' said an anxious Bernie.

'Hi stranger, it's your favourite graphic artist.'

Bernie stared at Kate. She stood side on to him, fifteen metres away, with a phone to her ear. He stood.

'Oh, hi Kate. Where are you?'

'Where am I or how am I?' She laughed.

'I've missed you,' said Bernie thinking he sounded insincere.

'Likewise. Listen, my Mum's out of danger, and I'll be back in Melbourne tonight. I'd love to see you if you're free.'

'Sure, that'd be great.'

'Why don't I call you when I'm back in town?'

'Great. Look, I can pick you up from Tulla. What time's your flight?'

'Thanks but don't bother. I've moved in with my cousin, and she's already offered to be my chauffeur.'

'Okay, no worries.'

Bernie's brain had trouble coping. Kate continued.

'Listen, I've gotta fly. I'll call you tonight. Bye.'

Bernie's phone went dead as he mouthed *Bye*.

Kate headed out of the Gardens then suddenly turned, and headed back towards Bernie. Panic. He dropped again, fiddling with a shoelace.

He faced the fence, and prayed he wasn't spotted.

'I can tie my own laces,' said a little kid pointing to his sandals.

'Great,' muttered Bernie.

Just stay there kid and give me cover.

The boy's mother took her son's hand and led him away. Bernie, still kneeling, looked behind him to see Kate. She followed the Hyphen, and was swallowed up by the vegetation.

He stayed kneeling, then stood and set off for *Labcope*.

What the hell is going on?

Ralph fumed. His day from Hell couldn't get any worse. He needed news about Bernie Slim's invention. When Ralph finally got back online, he discovered there was a new dead-letter drop.

He didn't know his spy had one of those mornings too. Ralph walked into the Gardens, and suddenly saw his spy walking towards him. He fumed — strictly no face-to-face meetings. Okay, it wasn't a meeting as such, and happened due to unforeseen circumstances.

The spy was late making the drop, and the CEO was late collecting it.

Alone, he read the hidden letter, and the news gave him a boost. Ralph discovered that Slim's drug impacted the brain, and a leading figure in the government was an unwitting guinea pig. It involved the Premier's 2IC, which made the whole thing super serious.

I have to get that formula. If it works, Head Office in the States will offer me the keys to the executive washroom in downtown Philadelphia. Okay, so how do I get the formula? Think outside the box, Ralph.

Jessica took the phone call in her office. The Hyphen was on the blower.

'Good afternoon, Premier. We haven't met but I have some important news about your Chief of Staff and her health.'

Ralph said as little as possible over the phone but enough to have the Premier demand his presence within the hour.

He entered Jessica's office.

'Thank you for coming Mr Hetherington-Smythe. Please take a seat.'

'Actually it's Doctor Hetherington-Smythe.'

'My apologies, sir. Now please, what do you know?'

He told Jessica everything about a rogue chemist who secretly created a new drug, which attacks the conscience of those who consume it.

'We have strong information, Premier, that your Chief of Staff has unwittingly been given the drug.'

'I assume by "strong information" you mean your spies?'

Ralph reacted. 'I'm here to help you, madam.'

Jessica's uncanny knack of discerning lies kicked in.

'You're here, sir, because you want my help in sorting out your rogue scientist. He has the formula and you don't. Am I right?'

'Perhaps.'

'Oh, cut the crap, Doctor. What do you know about this drug?'

'Nothing,' replied a seriously frazzled CEO.

'Allow me to explain. It makes you feel guilty, want to apologise, and confess your sins.'

She knows more than I do. 'Yes, I know that,' said Ralph. *Liar.*

'So it's a cyanide capsule for politicians and greedy executives.' He nodded. 'And I take it you can't demand your geek hand over his recipe?'

'I could but he won't. He's not a company man.'

'I like him already. Do you know the formula?'

'No.'

'Can you get it?'

'No.'

'Do you know where it is?'

'No.'

Is there an antidote?'

'No.'

'So what *do* you know?'

'The rogue scientist is Bernard Slim, who either has the formula notated and hidden, or it's locked away inside his head.'

'If you had the drug, could you figure out its contents?'

'Possibly, but not how it's created, and not straightaway. And we're not absolutely sure it works.'

Jessica mocked him again. 'Oh it works, Doctor, and unbelievably well. I saw living proof yesterday, right where you're sitting.'

Ralph shifted. 'Perhaps you could have the police arrest my employee, and demand he reveal the formula.'

'I hope that's not your best idea. I mean apart from the minor matter of the separation of powers, what charge did you have in mind? Messing about with Bunsen burners?'

The CEO loathed being ridiculed. He tried another tack.

'We could take civil action against Slim, claiming that, as an employee of *Labcope*, the company owns the material he created.'

Jessica slipped on her lawyer's hat. 'Did he produce the work in your time, on your premises, and using your facilities?'

'We're not sure about that.'

'You're not sure about anything. Look, civil cases take forever and your scientist will have patented the formula, set up a shelf company in the Seychelles, and sold franchises universally before you even get to court. In short, Doctor, you're screwed.'

That was it. Ralph stood. He'd had enough.

'I didn't come here to be insulted.'

'No, you came here because you're over a barrel. We both are. Now sit down and help me find a solution.'

He sat. Jessica went walkabout quizzing her visitor.

'How good are your spies?'

'Very good.'

'Can they get the formula?'

'Perhaps.'

'My God, it's politicians who can't or won't answer questions.' She spoke with emphasis. 'Can they get the formula?'

'We're working on it?'

Jessica fumed and swore. More scorn and humiliation for Ralph.

Why the hell did I come here?

She kept at him.

'What about sex?' Ralph blinked. 'Can you set a honey trap, get fake footage of him with a kid, bribe him, kidnap his family, threaten him with castration, or torture his granny? Have you tried the basics?'

Ralph stuttered. 'We've only just discovered the situation.'

'Well if you're the CEO, your minions must be Neanderthals.'

That was it. She'd gone too far. He stood in a fit of pique.

'Premier, this ridicule diminishes you and your office. I thought you'd be interested in helping your colleague. I now know otherwise.'

He headed for the door but stopped when she spoke.

'Okay, keep your rug on.'

Ralph froze.

How does she know I've had a transplant?

'I'll have a word with the Police Commissioner.' Ralph looked at her. 'But we need to work together on this. Tell me everything the moment it happens.' He nodded. 'Now write as many details as you can about your scientist, his colleagues, family, and the formula.'

She handed him a notepad. He wrote while she paced. He finished and offered the pad. She read it then placed it on her desk.

'Thank you Dr Hetherington-Smythe. Let's hope this matter can be contained with a minimum of damage.'

She walked to the door, and offered her hand. He shook it, and she smiled like a politician wanting his vote.

He left, furious.

Bitch.

Jessica went to her satchel and opened a little black book. She dialed.

Bugger the Police Commissioner.

'Hello,' she said. 'I want to speak to Mr Luca Parisi.'

16

BERNIE COULDN'T WAIT to tell Lois his news about Kate. But where? The canteen seemed safe.

They sat alone, speaking softly. As Bernie told his tale, Lois's face showed surprise, shock, and then anger.

'The lying bitch; she's a spy working for the Hyphen.'

'It looks like it.'

'What are you going to do?'

'Not sure, but at least we've found the bad guys. Annuska told me that *Labcope* employs spies, and the company knows everything.'

'She's right.'

Back in the lab, the scientists struggled to work. Bernie kept thinking about Kate, and his thoughts surged when the Hyphen entered.

'There's been a directive from the States requiring a list of all new projects be they on-site or off-site. Have you declared all your projects?'

All three knew this was bullshit. The Hyphen stared at Bernie and Lois. They turned mute. The CEO fumed.

'I would remind you of the terms of your employment.'

'Well I'm up-to-date,' said Bernie. 'How about you, Lois?'

'Absolutely.'

The Hyphen looked at them, his frustration at bursting point. He turned to leave but stopped when Bernie spoke.

'Did I see you enjoying the Botanic Gardens at lunchtime today?'

A sliver of angst seeped from the CEO. 'You didn't.' He tried to exit.

'I was sure I saw you with an attractive young woman.'

The Hyphen produced steam. 'I wasn't there.' He stormed out.

Lois looked at Bernie who put a finger to his lips.

She moved to him and whispered. 'You're playing with fire, Mr Slim.'

He whispered. 'I know, and fighting fire with fire in the way to go.'

His phone rang. 'Maddy, hi. Oh god, sorry, I forgot.'

She reprimanded him for not calling, and reminded him of the priceless offer from the nursing home, and that their parents' babysitter, cousin Chloe, was heading overseas next week.

'Yes, I know, I know. Look, I can get to your place by 5.30.'

She agreed and ended the call. Bernie grimaced.

Lois worried. 'Problems?'

'Possibly, but nice problems. It's the *Labcope* spies who worry me.'

Luca Parisi had never been to Parliament House, let alone the office of the Premier. A trusted staffer brought him in via the back way.

Jessica smiled. 'Mr Parisi, thank you for coming. Please take a seat.'

The Premier oozed sweetness and light. That mood evaporated.

'Now Luca, I'll cut to the chase. I'm up Shit Creek without a paddle.'

Luca tried to speak but failed.

'I need the formula of a new drug before it hits the streets.'

Luca sat transfixed. *She knows about a new drug and I don't?*

'It's not a Class A drug, but something far worse.'

To my face, again she calls me a crim. What the hell is she on about?

She explained.

'Tell me, what happens to colleagues who double-cross you? No, don't answer. Imagine if one of your drug dealers found Jesus or veganism or Seventh Day Bike Riding, and gave up dealing drugs. Imagine if they confessed their crimes, begged for forgiveness, and publicly implicated you in all their wicked ways. Would you be a happy camper?'

Luca's thinking crashed. Just being here and talking to this person had him hooked. What she now said blew his mind.

'I'd be dead.'

'You and me both, comrade. So be very afraid. There is a new drug which impacts the conscience — something neither of us ever use — and it changes anyone making them a guilt-ridden, garrulous do-gooder. They suffer splitting headaches which only disappear if they blab about every dirty deed they've ever performed. How's that for starters?'

Luca still struggled to speak.

This shit can't be true.

Jessica hammered him. 'Criminals and politicians need this drug like a hole in the head. So we must find the formula, and bury it on Mars, yesterday. Comprende?'

Luca nodded and finally joined the conversation. 'Sì.'

'The woman who dined with me at your restaurant, my Chief of Staff, has taken this conscience drug and now wants to sing like a birdie.'

'Ouch.'

'Ouch indeed, so this is where we join forces — The Premier and the drug baron.' She smiled. 'Nice title for a novel.' She stopped smiling. 'So, wotcha reckon, Lukey? Not about the novel; about the new drug?'

Am I awake? Is this shit really happening? She just called me Lukey!

'Now if you agree to work with me — notice I said *with* and not *for* — there's a catch. If you get caught doing whatever you have to do, this conversation never took place. In fact even if you *don't* get caught, this conversation never took place. And if the Gendarmes come calling, you chummy, are on your Patrick Malone. Do I hear another Comprende?'

More nodding from the Italian. This setting, this conversation, this information and proposal, were so unusual he struggled — big time.

This woman can talk underwater.

She pointed to a copy of the current *Herald Sun*.

'There's an envelope inside that newspaper.' He moved to pick up the paper. She barked. 'Not yet.' The naughty boy sat again. 'In it are details about the drug, and the scientist who created it, plus his colleagues, family and hangers-on. You have one job; find that formula. How? That's down to you. I understand you're pretty good at persuasion.'

'I'm very good at persuasion.'

'Good. Now rules. Don't mention my name. *Never* mention my name. What's my name?'

'Sorry, you are?'

'Good answer. Now when, not if, you find the formula, bring it to me. Tell nobody. And *when* you bring me the formula, you'll have "a friend in high places" — literally. Cross me, and you'll learn how I could teach the Cosa Nostra a lot about retribution. You know that word?'

'Cosa Nostra.' He nodded and smiled.

'That's two words. No, *retribution*.' He stopped smiling as she whispered something about a barbeque and his male member.

Luca tried not to imagine. She drew breath, and again smiled.

'Now, Luciano, my lovely, how does all that sound?'

He drew breath and grinned. 'I like it.'

He liked it a lot and, unfortunately for Jessica, he liked it too much.

'Excellent. Now take your newspaper and POQ.'

She went to the door, and he followed.

'Thanks,' he said. 'I like a challenge.'

'If this drug goes rogue, mate, we're toast.' She looked at him. 'This conversation never took place.'

With his right index finger, he tapped his nose.

Maddy drove her brother to their parents' home. The siblings discussed the all-important offer from the nursing home where both their parents were to be accommodated. But Bernie's mind was elsewhere.

Why did Kate lie to me? Did she plan to meet the Hyphen? Is she working for him? How am I going to handle her tonight?

Cousin Chloe answered the door. Their parents were delighted to see their kids. Daphne seemed almost normal. Chloe took her aunt to watch TV while Bernie and Maddy went over the details with their old man. Gus didn't say a word. They looked at him. He started to cry.

Maddy spoke. 'Oh Dad, don't be upset.' She started crying.

'We know what the house means to you, Dad, but we really think this is the best way,' said Bernie.

Gus recovered. They watched him. 'Bugger the house. I'm just so grateful I've got two fantastic kids.'

There wasn't a dry eye in the house.

With papers signed, and hugs and kisses dispensed, Bernie asked to be excused. He desperately wanted to get home. He caught an Uber.

I need to sort out Ms Kate Naismith, assuming that's her name.

Turning into Chestnut Street, Bernie's phone rang. It was Kate.

'Hang on,' said Bernie, 'I need to pay the cab.'

'Is it convenient?'

'It's fine. I'm just home. Hang on.'

Bernie opened his front door, and Albert served him with a writ for *dinneris lateus*.

Still on the phone, Kate was concerned. 'Are you okay?'

'Yeah, I've been to my folks sorting out their future.'

'How are they?'

'Good. Look, I'd really like to see you. Are you back in town?'

'I got in an hour ago.' She paused. 'And I'd really like to see you.'

'Can you come over?'

'I'm on my way. And I have cinnamon doughnuts.'

Bernie laughed. 'Thanks. See you soon.'

He fed Albert, walked Gary in record time, and then started searching.

Has my house been bugged? Did Kate really find that microphone? If she's working for the Hyphen, why discover the incriminating evidence? Was that a double bluff? What is a double bluff?

He found nothing. Kate was due. Then he heard a scratching sound. In the lounge room, Albert dragged soil from the indoor plant.

'Oh, Albert, how many times? Use the bloody litter tray.'

Bernie grabbed a brush and pan. He tipped the soil back around the plant then saw a small black plastic box. It sat easily in the palm of his hand. With batteries it was one of the world's smallest voice transmitters.

Well done Albert Poirot. Is this what I think it is?

The doorbell rang.

He scrambled to return the "thing" to its pebbles and soil position, and then headed to the door.

Kate stood there holding a bag of cinnamon doughnuts.

'I bring goodies.'

'Come in, come in.'

He stood back to allow her to pass, and the narrow hallway meant their bodies almost touched. She paused. He looked at her smiling eyes. He bent his head and kissed her. Albert trotted towards the open door.

Needing to foil the would-be feline escapee, meant an end to the romantic encounter, and all three settled inside. Bernie took a quick look at the indoor plant.

'Kate, I have a special request.'

'Really?' replied Kate with an upward inflexion.

He took her hand and led her from the lounge towards the bedroom.

Right, thought Kate. *So much for foreplay.*

'Nothing weird but this is really important,' said Bernie. He stopped at the bathroom door and indicated.

'After you,' he said.

Ah, he has a cleanliness fetish.

'In here?' He nodded. 'I hope this is not a scene from *Psycho*?'

He laughed. She entered. He followed and closed the door.

Curiouser and curiouser.

He moved to the shower and turned on the cold tap.

'Do you come here often?' she quipped.

Bernie put a finger to his lips, stood close to her and whispered.

'Do you remember finding that listening device in my bookshelf?' She nodded. 'Well I think there's another one. I think I'm being bugged.'

Kate looked puzzled but whispered her reply. 'Are you sure? And why would anyone want to bug you?'

Bernie paused then took the plunge. 'Can I trust you?'

'Well that really depends on what you've done. Do you need help to move a body?'

He half-smiled then told her everything; about the drug, what it could do, the trials, and about his spying boss, the CEO of *Labcope*. Kate looked astonished. Not over-the-top astonished, just really interested and slightly surprised.

'That's some story,' she said.

'When we go back outside, let's not talk about the drug or my house being bugged. Okay?'

'Sure.'

He turned off the shower, and moved to open the bathroom door. She stopped him. They were closer than close. He knew her secret, and despised her deceit. She believed he'd told her everything.

Thanks Bernie, you've saved me hours of listening.

They kissed with passion — a perfect example of lust over lies. Bernie wanted to move to the bedroom but anger killed his desire, and this refusal to seduce her triggered concern in Kate.

Does he know? If so, what does he know?

Back in the lounge room, Kate sat and examined the indoor plant.

Has that material been moved? Do I need the device anymore?

Bernie went to the kitchen saying nothing about the second bug. He called. 'Are you really keen on cinnamon doughnuts?'

'I sure am.'

'You do know they're bursting with calories, sodium and fat.'

'I do but you've turned me in to an addict, Bernie Slim.'

He laughed. 'And your coffee is white with one sugar?'

'Spot on.'

Bernie added the milk, the sugar and a good serve of powder from his latest batch of the MCP. He stirred the brew then placed the coffees and doughnuts on a tray.

She was perusing his books when the supper arrived.

'Find anything interesting?'

'This and that.' She looked at him and put a finger to her lips. He twigged. They were not to mention listening devices or spies.

'Your coffee smells divine,' she said.

They sat, and Bernie served his guest. She placed her coffee on the table in front of the settee, and started nibbling her cinnamon doughnut.

He ate too, and sipped his coffee.

I'm drinking, Katie, please join me.

She kept eating, ignoring her coffee. He made conversation.

'So how's life with your cousin. You must give me her address.'

'No way; she's gorgeous — and a man eater.'

'Really?' said Bernie, forcing a laugh as Mr Cool.

He sipped. 'I called at your hotel the other day.'

Kate felt a twinge of panic.

'Oh?'

'I was worried. I hadn't heard from you. I remembered where you lived, and wanted to see if you were all right.'

'Yeah, sorry, but with my mother seriously ill in Sydney, and losing my phone, I was in a mess.'

'I thought your phone was broken.'

'No, lost. But I've found it, and we're all good.'

He's testing me. He knows something. But what?

'Anyway, it's great to have you back in Melbourne, although it feels as if you've never been away.'

He definitely knows something.

Bernie needed her to drink the damn coffee. He raised his mug.

'Well, here's to us.'

She picked up her mug, and tapped it against his. With her spare hand she unobtrusively handled her phone, and triggered a fake call.

'To us,' she said, and placed the mug against her lips.

Her phone rang, and she put down the mug.

Shit, thought Bernie.

'Hello Jo.' Kate's face contorted. 'Oh no! Have you called a plumber?' Kate looked at Bernie. 'Okay, don't panic. I'm on my way.'

She ended the fake call, stood and apologised.

'I have to go. Major emergency. My cousin's flat is flooded.'

She headed for the door. He followed.

'What's happened?'

'The flat above has some major leak, and there's water everywhere.'

'Can I help?'

'Thanks but no. And I'm really sorry.'

'No problem.'

He opened the door, and she hurried out.

'Call me,' he cried.

'I will. And thanks for the coffee. Bye.'

Bernie closed the door. 'Bugger,' he said.

That sounded like a real emergency. But I think she knows I know.

'Damn.'

Animal drove and Luca navigated. In leafy South Yarra, they headed east along Domain Road past real estate way beyond the driver's budget.

'Left at Punt, then second on the left,' said Luca.

'Who is this guy?' asked Animal.

'He's the boss of the scientist who invented the drug; the guy who went to see our favourite Premier. The guy who's gunna get me that formula.'

'Now boss, don't forget it was me what got you involved with the beautiful Jessica.'

Luca snapped. 'Left, left, turn left.'

Animal drove down Punt Road turning left again for The Righi. Not everyone gets a street name with the definite article.

'Park here,' ordered Luca. The car stopped beside two words in big letters — NO PARKING.

'What's the plan, boss?'

'For you, it's stay here and shut up.'

'No muscle?'

'Not for this guy. The scientist who invented the drug may need a slap. Wait here, pretend to be reading the paper, and look normal. Pretend you're an Uber driver.'

Animal grinned. He thought Uber was a country. Luca walked to the address given by Madam Premier — *my friend in high places* — and pushed the buzzer.

The main door opened, and behind the security door stood Dr Ralph Hetherington-Smythe. He loathed cold callers. In fact he loathed any callers, and had a sign by his letterbox and buzzer. *No Hawkers.*

'Can't you read?' said the homeowner.

'She said you were a prick.'

Ralph closed the door. Luca pushed the buzzer.

From inside came a voice. 'I'm calling the police.'

'Jessica sent me.'

There was a pause before the door opened again, just enough for the owner to survey the scene.

'Jessica?'

'You know, the sheila up in Spring Street; some call her the Premier.'

Ralph clung to ultra-cautious. Luca gave him heaps.

'Look, Shit-for-Brains, do you want the fucken formula or not?'

Formula — the magic word. Ralph unlocked the security door, and stood back. Luca wandered into the hall admiring the paintings.

'I know nothing about art. What's this stuff worth?'

Ralph indicated his sitting room. We'd call it a lounge. Luca entered and sat. The settee was genuine class from old money. Luca's décor came from drug money. Regardless of how much money he possessed, Luca could never buy class.

'So,' said the visitor, 'we've both got the same goal. You want the formula to make a mint. Me and the Premier want it to stay in business, and out of jail.'

Ralph felt his chest tighten.

Do I have a criminal in my home?

'What has the Premier told you,' asked Ralph?

'You mean apart from your useless spying technique?'

Ralph endured a mix of rage and fear.

Now I'm being insulted in my own home.

He stood.

'If you can't be civil, you can piss off now.'

He sounded like a wimp who failed Sand Castle Kicking 101.

Luca shook his head. 'Oh please, suck it up, Princess. The sooner you tell me what I need to know, the sooner I'm out of here and finding your magic formula. So talk to me.'

Luca had no gun, but his words and body language compelled Ralph to whack his crack on a Schinke velvet armchair from Italia.

Ralph told all. He had no choice. His spy delivered valuable facts, but not the formula. To seal the deal, to get his hands on the pot of formula gold, he needed muscle.

'Right,' said Luca. 'I can make your scientist sing.'

'If you can't get the formula or the drug by regular means, you may have to consider the extreme option.'

Luca looked at the serious CEO. Then the gangster laughed, again mocking the *Labcope* executive. 'Jesus, mate. Don't ever audition for *The Godfather*.' Ralph despised him. Luca switched moods. 'So, how can I contact you?'

'You can't.'

'Good answer. No calls, no digital footprint, no nothing.' Ralph nodded. Luca leaned forwards. 'Of course we could be bugged right now.'

Ralph's blood boiled. 'Don't patronise me. This place and my office are swept by professionals.'

Another mood swing by Luca. 'Nice one. I use *Bug Finder*. You?'

Ralph stood. 'I think you should leave.'

Luca went sarcastic. 'What, no coffee?' He headed for the door. 'Wish me luck, pal. If *I* win, *you* win.'

Luca opened the door then turned back. 'You ever see *Breaking Bad*?'

Ralph lied. 'I don't know what you're talking about.'

'Pity,' smiled Luca. 'Your chemistry, my network, megabucks. Ciao.'

Luca left and Ralph discreetly checked the street to see if anyone saw his visitor. The CEO's heavy breathing matched his rapid heartbeat.

Luca and Ralph made a very odd couple. Throw in the Premier, and there's a trio. None could lie straight in bed.

Jessica wanted the drug destroyed to save her skin. Ralph wanted it to win promotion to *Labcope International*. Luca wanted it to make money, and to impress his Mafioso mates in Calabria.

Did any of the terrible trio know what the others were planning? Did the Right Honourable Jessica Katherine Reid, MLA, know of this skulduggery? She's the clever one. But could she outwit the CEO and the crim?

'Where to?' asked Animal.

'Back across the river. Let's check out the main man.'

They drove down the Punt Road hill, crossed the Yarra, found their way to Chestnut Street and parked illegally. Luca put Animal in the picture.

'This scientist guy invented the new drug. We need his formula.'

'So, I go in, whack him, and grab it.'

'No. Just shut up and listen. There may be nothing to get. It might be all in his head. If we kill him we're stuffed.'

'I can make him talk.'

'No, you can make him scream.'

'Well how else we gunna get it?'

'We copy my Mum; we think outside the square.'

Animal laughed. 'I'm still laughin' at what she done to that Irish prick.'

Without warning, Bernie came out of his house, and Luca came alive.

'That's his house. That's gotta be him. That's the scientist.'

Animal panicked. 'Whadda we do?'

'Stay here, I'll follow. Just keep your phone on.'

Luca was no George Smiley, but walked quietly on the opposite side of the road some 20 metres behind Bernie. They headed north, and reached the railway line. Luca worried he might need to use public transport.

But Bernie turned left, and used the underpass, walked beneath the trains, and entered the supermarket where *Dimmeys* used to be.

Luca took a basket and followed. Bernie bought dry cat food, custard and milk, and headed home. Luca followed at a distance. Bernie took Albert's goodies inside, and Luca woke the dozy Animal.

'I know how to make Mr Scientist tell us his formula.'

Animal thought it was a guessing game. 'Ah, torture. I love the sound of breaking bones.'

'He's bought cat food. He'll give us the formula when we threaten to set fire to his pussy.'

Animal laughed. Luca had another idea.

'Or else his folks. He loves his cat, but can always get another. But he won't allow his dear old ma and pa to suffer. Let's whack the oldies.'

Animal grinned.

Back in his pad, Ralph worried. His plan had gone tits-up. Too many people knew about Slim's drug. Certainly it included Slim's buddy Lois, the Hungarian bitch, and now, thanks to Ralph's panic, the Premier, and some underworld gangster. They all knew the secret.

God knows how many more. If just one of them blabs, I've lost.

Ralph decided.

Dump the conscience-drug. No new career but I'll still have one.

He made a money transfer then went online to that cookery site and posted a new message in the Comments section of the *Recipe of the Day*. He typed.

I found all the ingredients and have finished the task.

For Kate, this meant *Job complete, payment sent.*

She too was worried. Almost certainly her main target had rumbled her. By triggering her phone in Bernie's flat, she managed to escape. To stay, meant drinking the coffee which was probably spiked.

Kate Naismith was a pseudonym. Her real name, Carolyn Briggs, remained unknown even to Ralph. She once had a promising career with the Australian Federal Police. That ended when she slept with a senior officer, and when the coitus ceased, the consequences were predictable.

As per the boys' rules, the female, the junior, lost.

Close the door on your way out, Bitch.

Carolyn used her AFP experience to work as a private detective, and soon discovered she could make nice money spying. She was good.

She looked okay, acted well, had several skills, and could create characters and scenarios to fool almost anyone. She fooled Bernie Slim until by accident she bumped into her employer in the Gardens. It was bad luck rather than a sloppy operation. Somehow the scientist had sussed her true identity. Bernie knew she was a plant.

Shit.

She checked her bank account and felt numb.

The bastard. That's not what we agreed.

She fired back a response on the Cookery web site posting the code.

My grandmother made exactly the same recipe.

This was the emergency code.

We must meet now.

The pre-arranged rendezvous was the Black Rock Yacht Club. Its car park beckoned late at night.

Ralph saw the code. He wanted no more to do with the spy but knew to ignore her could create trouble. He replied.

Homemade cooking is certainly the best.

This meant the rendezvous was on within 30 minutes.

Ralph pulled into the car park. Kate was already there. She walked to the Hyphen's 4WD Beamer, and stood alongside his window. He checked her then released the security lock. She walked around the vehicle, and climbed in next to him. He locked the doors. She was angry.

'Where's the rest of my money?'

'You blew it.'

'We agreed the fee with bonuses if I put in two listening devices.'

'You broke the rules by meeting me in the Gardens.'

'I didn't meet you; you were there.'

'You sent the code before you made the dead-letter drop.'

'I was late with the drop-off because my dog nearly died.'

Silence. Both fumed. He guessed but delivered the killer punch.

'Slim knows you're a spy.'

She couldn't argue. Ralph was probably correct. No, he was correct.

Both spies fumed. Ralph had a double dose of misery. Sacking his operative gave him no comfort. Without her, he had no chance of finding the formula. In Ralph's car, the silence had attitude.

'If you don't pay me,' started Kate.

'You'll what? Call the cops? Contact my CEO in the States? Do what you like. I don't care. You blew it. You're lucky to get what you did. I never want to hear from you again. Now get out of my fucking car.'

He released the door lock. She stared at him.

I could break his jaw.

She held her anger, got out, but left the door wide open, forcing him to undo his seatbelt, and clamber across. He was gone before she made it back to her car. She seethed.

The CEO had underpaid her big time. He'd never hire her again. She was hardly going to lodge an unfair dismissal claim with the Fair Work Commission.

I've got nothing to lose. Revenge is a dish best served cold. But how?

She scrolled through her phone. Being an ex-cop had advantages. She rang the head of the Dogs of War Bikie Club. Why a bearded bloke with more tatts than whiskers answered to Geoffrey had her beat.

'Geoffrey, hi, it's your friendly ex-Federal copper.'

He recognised her voice.

'G'day, babe. What's up?'

'I wanna do you a favour.'

Geoffrey roared. 'You're on. My place or yours?'

'We need a meet.'

They sat in a noisy Brunswick pub where she told him everything — the drug, the scientist, the bit players, the dangers and the benefits.

He didn't believe her. 'This is a windup.'

'You grab that formula, and you'll make a fortune, Geoffrey. All I want is the prick who ripped me off to receive a serious slap.'

'I've got the perfect slapper.' He beckoned to a brick outhouse stacked against the bar.

'Babe, meet our Irish enforcer, Brendan Murphy.'

They nodded. Had Brendan been bound and gagged, and dressed in his birthday suit, Carolyn might have recognized him. He once starred full frontal on various whacky web sites. But in mufti, he looked like any drug-pushing gorilla. She finished her instructions.

'The guy who needs a slap, Ralph the CEO, doesn't have the formula. For that you'll need Bernie Slim, the scientist. Here's a list of his cronies including a couple of old birds. They may have it or will know where Bernie keeps it. Copy?'

'We copy, hey Murph?'

The Irishman nodded.

He wanted back in the game. He wanted revenge on Parisi and his family, and anyone who'd even smiled at his naked humiliation. Meet the Ulster bareknuckle boxer on speed.

Geoffrey drooled over Kate and her offer, and for Brendan, if it meant a return to the drug trade, and gaining respect, he couldn't wait.

Kate kept pushing her message. 'Get the formula from Slim, then use it to flush out the bastard who runs *Labcope*. Give him a slap. You get the new drug, and I get my pound of flesh.'

Geoffrey ogled Kate. *I'll settle for a pound of your flesh, babe.*

They raised their glasses.

Bernie couldn't reach Kate. Her phone message told all.

This number is no longer available.

So, he knew her true identity, and she knew he knew, and that was it.

Goodbye Ms Spy. He thought about their first meeting.

She dropped those lemons to meet me. She approached Labcope because that's where I work. Is she a graphic designer? She conned me.

Kate, aka Carolyn, returned to her mother in Kew, collected her gear, and recovering dog, and headed home to the Dandenongs. She removed the wig and added the specs.

Roll on the next gig. Oh, and good hunting, Geoffrey.

The Premier called on Genevieve at home. The Chief of Staff looked drowsy. You would too with the medication she'd absorbed.

'Hello darl,' purred Jessica. 'How are you feeling, babe?'

Genevieve tried to smile. 'I still have these headaches, although the doctor says I'm fine. Can I tell you something?'

'Of course. If you can't trust your bestie, who can you trust?'

'I don't really want to quit.'

'And I won't let you.'

'But I can't come back to work until I've said sorry to all those people I've hurt over the years.'

Jessica fumed. *I need that formula and the bloody antidote.*

'Listen, darl. Some scientist invented a drug which plays funny buggers with your mind. You're a victim and been slipped a Mickey Finn.'

'What does the drug do?'

'I'm not sure. I think it affects your conscience. But hey, everything's cool. You're going to get through this. You're off to my beach house for a few days R 'n R. Walks on the sand, DVDs, and lots of snoozing.'

Genevieve looked confused. 'What about the kids?'

'Your Mum will look after the kids, and Janet, a wonderful nurse will look after you at Lorne. Just stay away, don't talk to anyone, and get better.' Genevieve nodded. 'Good girl,' said Jessica patting her friend's arm, and thinking. *I need to sort out this mess, pronto.*

Bernie arrived at work. Lois greeted him in hushed tones. He waved.

'As loud as you like, Lois; the spy's been outed.'

'What happened?'

'Last night, I tried to drug the lovely Kate.'

'No!' Lois opened her mouth. Bernie told all. War was declared.

17

LUCA DROVE ANIMAL to Gus and Daphne's former Hawthorn home. It was dark. The criminals parked beside St James Park. Luca no longer attended the scenes of crime. He stayed free. Animal took instructions.

'Get inside then call the scientist. Tell him if he wants to protect his folks, he's gotta rock up with the formula. Don't kill anyone. Just get that formula.' Animal got out. 'And get the right fucken house.'

'Gotcha.'

Animal crossed Barton Street, and walked up Lennox.

Get the right house, Animal.

He found it and knocked.

He heard footsteps and then an elderly female voice.

'Who is it?'

'Sorry to trouble you, love,' said the friendly Animal. 'I'm from the Gas Company. There's a gas leak, and we're tellin' everyone to turn off their appliances.'

Pause. Then the door opened and a face appeared.

'We were in bed.'

'I'm sorry, madam. Here's me ID.' He flashed the back of his credit card. 'Perhaps I could check your meter for you.'

He moved inside, brushing past the resident.

'Will we be all right?'

'Is it just you and your husband?'

'Pardon?'

'Who is it?' called a male voice.

Animal moved towards the voice. The old man was in bed. His wife appeared. Animal grabbed her frail arm, and shoved her. She screamed.

'Shut up,' snapped Animal. 'Stay there.'

'We haven't got any money,' said the man.'

Animal used his mobile. 'Shut up,' he snapped at the terrified pair. They were tenants on a short-term lease waiting for their new unit to be finished.

'Hello,' said the voice on the phone.

'Mr Slim, I'm at your parents' place, and you will come here, right now, with your formula or else.'

'Who is this?'

'Don't piss me about. Have a listen to your dear old Mum.'

Animal crushed the woman's fingers. She yelped in agony.

'Now that was your mother, arsehole. If you don't want her and your old man to cop a lot of pain, get here now — with that formula.'

The elderly residents added confusion to their fear.

'Wait, wait,' cried Bernie. 'Where are you?'

'I'm in your parents' fucken bedroom.'

'In Hawthorn?'

'Yes, now get here or they die.'

'You're in the wrong house.'

Animal stalled.

Shit. I double-checked the number.

Animal asked. 'What's the number of your parents' house in Lennox Street?'

Bernie told him and Animal relaxed.

'That's where I am, dickhead.'

'But they've moved. Last week. I don't know who those people are but they're definitely not my parents.'

Again, Animal stalled. Then he twigged.

'Nice try, prick. I'll give you 20 minutes before I start breaking bones.'

He held the phone close to the woman, and yanked her hair. Bernie heard a pathetic scream before the line went dead.

Bernie's mind buzzed.

What do I do? Call the cops? Does that mean my illegal drug will see me arrested? Who are those people? Could I save them, and turn this to my advantage? If I don't turn up, will they die?

He grabbed his bag, opened his Uber app, and ran to Swan Street.

In the cab, he scribbled in a notepad. In Lennox Street, he paid the driver, and knocked on the house he recently sold for his folks.

Animal opened the door, pointing a gun. Bernie raised his hands.

'Have you got it?' Bernie nodded. 'Give it to me — slowly.'

'Where are my parents?'

'Oh, so now they *are* your parents?'

'I want to see them.'

'Formula first.'

'No.' Bernie acted tough, although his hands shook, and his heart pounded. Animal relented.

If I shoot him and he hasn't got the formula, I'm stuffed. And the boss said no killing.

'Get in,' he said, and Bernie walked to the bedroom.

Two complete strangers huddled on a bed.

'I'm sorry,' he said. 'I'll get you out of here as soon as I can.'

Animal pushed the gun against Bernie's back. 'The formula — now.'

'I haven't got it.'

Animal exploded. He raised his gun undecided between shooting and smashing. The old folks recoiled in horror. Bernie blurted his response.

'It's here already.'

Animal paused. 'What?'

'I hid it in my parents' home.'

'Show me.'

'Not until I've helped my parents.'

'Tell me or I'll shoot your mother right now.'

He swung the gun pointing it straight at the woman. Everyone believed the gunman. Bernie persisted.

'You shoot anyone and you'll never get the formula.' Animal paused.

Luca will kill me if I don't get that formula.

'Let me help my parents, and then I'll give you what you want.'

Animal hated being beaten.

I'll give the bastard one last chance.

'Two minutes,' he spat, 'and no tricks.'

Bernie nodded. 'I'll make you a cuppa, Mum. And get you a beer, Pops. Stay there. I'll be right back.'

He squeezed past a threatening Animal, and headed to the kitchen.

What am I saying? I've never called my father, Pops.

In the kitchen, he made tea and, from his bag, produced two small bottles of beer.

Animal appeared, looking back up the hallway.

'Hurry up.'

Bernie kept busy. 'Please check on my parents. My mother's not well.'

Animal snorted, and headed towards the bedroom. Bernie opened the beers and tipped some MCP in to one. He put a small scratch on the label of that bottle. He took a mug of tea and the two bottles to the bedroom.

'Here we are.'

He gave the tea to the woman. 'Just as you like it, Mum,' he smiled at the woman and winked. She took it, mumbling her thanks.

'And a nightcap for you, Pops.'

Bernie looked at the bottles, and gave the one without the mark to the man. Animal didn't see Bernie wink at the old man.

I hope he likes beer.

The man took it. Bernie raised his bottle and toasted the couple.

'Here's to the best parents in the world.'

He raised the bottle to his lips then stopped. 'Oh I'm sorry. I'm forgetting my manners.' He offered the bottle to Animal. 'Here, as a sign of good faith.'

Animal looked at him, accepted the beer, and took a swig.

'Now get me that formula.'

They went to the kitchen. Bernie pulled out a cutlery drawer, and fiddled. Animal watched.

Have another swig, matey.

Animal obliged, then grew impatient.

'Come on, come on.'

Bernie made a show of finding the paper he put there five minutes ago, and gave it to Animal.

'This is it?'

'Yes.'

'All of it?'

'All of it. Now can I please go back to my parents?'

'A word of warning, pal. We know where you and your parents live. Tell the cops, tell anyone, and you and they are dead. Capiche?'

'I won't say a word. Just take the formula and go. I never want to see it or you again.'

Animal sneered, drained the bottle, and lobbed it at Bernie. Good catch. He flinched when Animal pointed his gun.

'Bang,' said the thug who laughed and left.

Bernie went to the bedroom.

'He's gone, it's all over. Are you all right?'

'Of course we're not,' almost shouted the man. 'Who are you?'

'My name's John and I've never seen that man before.'

'You had something he wanted,' said the woman. 'What was it?'

'I work for a mining company. He wanted our test result formula.'

'Will he come back?' asked the woman.

'And why did he think you were our son?' asked the man.

'I've no idea,' explained Bernie. 'But please, you must leave. Is there someone you can stay with tonight?'

The couple chatted then told Bernie they would leave.

'I think that's really wise.' He offered to help but they declined.

'We'll be fine,' said the woman. 'And thank you for your help.'

Bernie apologised again and left.

If I call the cops, I'll have to explain the drug. The testing is illegal and I'll be in big trouble. Who was that criminal? And how did he know about the formula? This is out of control.

'Piece of piss,' said Animal handing the formula to Luca.

'Tell me you didn't kill anyone.'

'I'm a pro, boss.'

Luca looked at the scientific writing. It meant nothing to him. He set off for South Yarra. They parked, and Animal stayed in the car.

Ralph was watching an episode of *Breaking Bad* on DVD. The buzzer caused him angst. He hit *Pause*, moved to the hallway, and spoke behind both front doors.

'Who is it?'

'Father Fucken Christmas.'

Ralph recognized the voice. 'Go away. I'm no longer involved.'

'I've got the formula, Dickhead. Here it is.'

Luca pressed the paper against the outside door. Ralph quietly rejoiced.

I'm back in the game.

Both doors opened, and Luca strolled in.

'This time I'll have coffee, Mister Barista.'

Ralph glared, but did as ordered.

The man is a moronic criminal, but bloody hell, he's got the formula. Don't ask why, just take it.

While the coffee brewed, Ralph returned to his sitting room.

'You liar,' scoffed Luca, pointing to the scene from *Breaking Bad*.

Ralph picked up the remote, and killed the screen.

'Let me see the formula,' demanded the CEO.

Luca held it back. 'Say please.'

Ralph snatched the paper, and read.

'So?' asked Luca. 'Can you understand it?'

'Almost. I have a PhD in science, majoring in chemistry, and you, knuckle dragger, have shit for brains.'

Whoa! Ralph does have a death wish. Luca's body language screamed anger. He stood over Ralph. 'Is that the right formula?'

'Yes and no.'

Luca dribbled. 'What the fuck does that mean?'

'You've been sold a pup, Wog Boy. Big Pharma use this formula every day. This ain't new.'

'Y'mean it's useless?'

'Not if you've got a headache. It's a formula for migraines.'

Luca fought to control himself. He snatched the piece of paper, and shaped to smash the CEO. Furious, he stormed out leaving doors open.

Ralph followed him calling. 'Were you born in a tent?'

The CEO no longer cared what anyone thought of him.

Luca seethed.

That scientist is gunna give me that formula.

Bernie battled through a Balaclava garden jungle. He reached the front door and knocked. Lights came on and, in dressing gowns, Annuska and Dorothy opened the door.

'Come in, darling boy, come in.'

Bernie carried two items — an overnight bag, and a cat basket.

In a cab, 20 minutes earlier, he rang with the message that his 'love life was crushed'. Annuska ordered him to attend forthwith.

He indicated the cat basket. 'I'm worried about Albert. I didn't bring a litter tray.'

Dorothy turned practical. Within minutes a cardboard box, some newspaper, and soil from the vege patch, appeared in the laundry. Done.

Back in the lounge room, the women craved news. He spoke softly.

'Ladies, it's bad. The enemy is within. My girlfriend is a spy.'

'Kate?' gasped Dorothy. Bernie nodded.

The women were stunned. 'What's happened?' whispered Annuska.

'Before I explain, may I ask if you have ever discussed my invention?'

'All the time,' said Annuska.

'And where do these discussions take place?'

'Usually in bed,' said Dorothy. 'It's our ritual to chat about things before going to sleep.'

Bernie put a finger to his lips, stood and beckoned. They went to the bedroom. The women watched Bernie explore under the bed, on top of the wardrobe, behind the dressing table, and finally, on the windowsill.

Kate had pulled the same trick twice. There, in an indoor plant, Bernie produced a listening device. The women stared, gobsmacked.

Bernie removed the batteries, put the device in a padded envelope, then inside a drawer, and closed it. The trio repaired to the lounge room where Bernie told all.

'I am so sorry, ladies. Kate bugged my home and yours too. Please, forgive me.'

'I am the fool, the big, big fool,' groaned Annuska.

'It must have been when she used the loo,' despaired Dorothy.

Bernie told them everything — seeing Kate in the Botanic Gardens with the Hyphen, her Sydney lies, her fake then real listening device in Bernie's home, and the *piece de resistance*, the criminal and the unknown old folks in his parents' former home. The women despaired.

'I told you this from the start, Bernard. *Labcope* is a den of wipers.'

'Vipers,' murmured Dorothy, stressed at their situation.

Annuska began to cry. 'And you gave the criminal the formula.'

'Not quite. There is some good news.'

When Bernie explained how he gave the criminal a headache formula, the black mood lightened a little. Annuska took control.

'They will try again, Bernard. You are right to come here.'

'Thank you, Annuska, and you too Dorothy.'

Annuska spoke in a manner serious. 'I would invite you to share our bed, only Dorothy snores, and besides, she is a very jealous woman.'

The sudden silence puzzled Bernie.

Me, sleep in the same bed as Annuska and Dorothy?

The women grinned then giggled, and, for the first time in ages, Bernie joined them in laughing with gusto.

But they knew the situation was serious. 'Ladies, if there's been a listening device here, then my boss, the *Labcope* CEO who hired Kate, must know this address. I'm so sorry. I may have put you both in danger.'

The gloomy mood returned. Bernie checked the windows and doors. Annuska fetched a kitchen broom, and waved it. She did Winston proud.

'We shall fight on the beaches. We shall fight in the fields and in the streets. We shall never surrender,' she declared.

'Normally she rides that,' chipped Dorothy.

Their laughter sounded hollow, and eventually everyone retired.

Bernie slept alone. His usual sleeping partner, Albert, made do with the laundry. Both struggled in their new setting, but had they been in downtown Cremorne, things might have been far worse.

After fuming at his restaurant, Luca drove Animal back to Hawthorn and then to Cremorne. Both houses were black and empty.

Animal offered a suggestion. 'You want me to firebomb 'em?'

Luca snapped. 'Will you forget the bloody violence? We want the formula, not the cops.'

'So whadda we do?'

Luca drove south. 'We'll give that CEO prick a slap. He's hiding something. I'll tell him I have the real formula. He'll let me in, and then you rush him.'

'Slappedy, slappedy, slap,' grinned Animal.

They parked in The Righi where Luca explained.

'Just remember, we need him to talk. Okay?'

Animal didn't answer.

'Animal?'

'Sorry boss. Yeah, ah, I feel a bit crook.'

Luca didn't care. The South Yarra wise guy would know where to find Slim, and Slim would hand over that formula — or else.

'Shut up and get out of the car.'

They headed to Ralph's abode. Suddenly Luca was alone. He turned and saw Animal leaning on an expensive car.

'Jesus, Animal, stop muckin' about.' Luca went and grabbed him.

'I'm sorry, boss, I feel shithouse.'

Luca shook Animal who collapsed on the car setting off its alarm.

'Oh, for fuck's sake,' hissed Luca, dragging Animal back to their car. House lights came on, and locals appeared as Luca drove away sans headlights.

Did they see my number plate?

One local sticky-beak was Ralph Hetherington-Smythe.

In an angry silence, Luca drove Animal home. His Preston weatherboard was sad and dark, with no family inside or out.

'Get some sleep. I'll call you, tomorrow,' said Luca. 'Be ready.' The words, "I hope you're okay" or "Get some rest," remained unspoken.

Luca drove away leaving Animal in the street. The thug sat in the gutter, his face in his hands.

Jesus, my head is killing me.

18

ALBERT MEOWED. Breakfast in Balaclava did not appeal.

I want my old smells.

Bernie felt safer at Annuska and Dorothy's place, especially now that Kate's listening device was kaput, but he knew things needed sorting. His conscience drug invention threatened to explode.

'I'll be a tad late tonight, ladies,' he told the women at breakfast. 'I have to check on my folks in their new nursing home.'

Annuska worried. 'I think we need a big talk, young man. This situation cannot continue.'

'I know, and if it's okay, I'd like to stay here to look after you ladies; just until everything is sorted.'

'You are a gentleman, Bernie Slim,' said Dot. 'And we're very grateful.'

'We are. But your wonderful drug has grown to a life of its own,' said Annuska. 'Now we have spies, criminals and worse, the government.'

Bernie nodded. He knew it was serious.

'I understand,' he said. 'Tonight we talk.'

He spent time with Albert, said his goodbyes, and set off for work.

Luca counted cash at home. With Murphy finished, Luca's drug empire boomed, and this money would be "washed" in his restaurant tonight.

His mother appeared. 'You've got a visitor.'

Luca looked through the new reinforced-glass window, and saw Animal standing by the front gate. Luca buzzed his lackey inside.

'I told you to be ready, not to come here.'

'It's important, boss.'

They went to Luca's study.

'You look like shit. What's up?'

'There is no easy way to tell you, boss.' He paused. Luca stopped counting, and looked at Animal. 'I gotta quit.'

Luca sat stunned. 'What?

'You remember how crook I got last night. Today I'm totally ratshit.'

'What's wrong with you?'

'I dunno.'

'You quit, and you're dead.'

'I gotta quit.'

'You've gotta death wish.'

'You don't need me. I'll be a gardener. Lots of work around, boss.

'A gardener!?'

'I'm sorry for all them people I hurt, boss. And I need to find 'em and apologise.'

'Apologise? You can't even spell it.' Luca twigged. 'Hang on, hang on.'

'Geez, my head hurts.'

'Have you got this conscience disease?'

Animal shrugged; ignorance being his strength. 'Dunno, boss.'

'You have. What happened in that house with the scientist?'

'Nothin'. He give me the formula, and I left.'

'Did you eat or drink anything?'

Big pause.

'You idiot. What did you eat?'

'Nothing.'

'If you're lyin', I'll kill you.'

'I might have had a beer.'

'In a bottle?'

'Yeah.'

'Did you open the bottle?'

'No. He did.'

'Did you see him open the bottle?'

Big pause.

Luca grabbed Animal's shirt, and roared. He wanted to grab Animal's throat. 'You've been drugged, you fucken moron.'

Animal looked like he wanted to cry.

'Please boss, I wanna go back to bein' a gardener. I can get work with me brother.'

'You wanna confess to murder.'

'No, boss, no way.'

'You can't help yourself.'

'I can, I know I can.'

'The only way to stop the headaches is to blab to the people you bashed.' Luca screamed in frustration. 'To Murphy's mob!'

'I'd never do that, boss, never, *never*, I swear.'

'Too bloody right you won't. I'll fucken kill you first.'

154

'Help me, boss, please. You've gotta help me.'

Luca had a problem. A blabbing Animal on the loose would be trouble. He thought aloud.

'I'll fix it. I'll find that scientist and get something to fix the pain.'

'Yes, please boss, please.'

'Get home and stay there. Speak to anyone, and I'll kill you.'

Luca pushed him towards the front door.

'Thanks, boss. But hurry up will ya?'

'There's gotta be a drug to reverse the drug. I'll get it. Now go!'

Jessica answered her phone. It was the nurse caring for Genevieve.

'Janet? How are things in Lorne?'

'Bad news Premier. She's gone.'

'What?'

'Your Chief of Staff has escaped.'

Jessica went walkabout.

'I told you to never let her out of your sight.'

'It was only a few seconds.'

'Where is she?'

'Don't know. We set off for the beach, and at the gate she said she'd forgotten her hat. She didn't return so I checked, and that was it.'

'And?'

'I think she caught a cab to Melbourne.'

Like Luca, Jessica screamed in frustration.

Luca rang the Premier, and was put through.

'Mr Parisi, what a coincidence. I was about to call you.'

'We have a problem.'

'Join the club.'

'We need a meet, madam. Still no missing item, and now the problem has spread.'

'Comprende. So, we meet in my carpark in 30 minutes. Be there.'

Jessica's bad mood grew darker. Her best friend had gone rogue. If Genevieve confessed her sins, most of which involved the Premier, Jessica was a dead woman walking.

To make a bad situation worse, the only person who could fix the problem *was* the problem.

Only Genevieve can fix Genevieve.

Jessica phoned the top cop in the state of Victoria.

'We have a serious problem, Chief Commissioner. Can you be in my office in 45 minutes?'

He could.

Was Jessica insane? She chose to deal with the law and the lawless, with the lawkeeper and the lawbreaker. Surely that way madness lies.

But that's how I've always worked. I walk the tightrope. Take risks. I tackle a massive problem with a massive solution. None of this tip-toe-around-the-edge crap. I always attack head on.

Mind you, any political journalist would give their texting thumb for the scoop on this tale. The headlines wrote themselves.

Top Cop arrests Drug Boss in Premier's carpark

Or

Drug Boss shoots Top Cop in Premier's office.

Jessica met Luca underground. The conspirators moved to a corner of the car park. Cue the Deep Throat setting. She spoke first.

'My Chief of Staff has escaped.'

'Snap,' said Luca, and Jessica thought he was taking the piss until he explained Animal's situation. Luca explained Animal's back-story.

'We trapped the bloke who invented the drug, but he tricked Animal who drank a spiked beer. Now the stupid bastard wants to confess to multiple assaults, and murder, plus the odd kidnap. If he blabs, I won't be finding your formula, ma'am, I won't be in the country.'

'Well my drugged Chief of Staff was under wraps until today. Now she's free and nobody knows where. If the press gets a sniff, I'm history.'

'You could be my friend in low places.'

The man has half a wit, thought Jessica, who made a special request.

'I don't suppose your man could remove my woman, with you sending your boy to join the fishes?'

It took Luca a few seconds to understand the request.

Did the Premier just ask me to have two people knocked?

'I can't believe I'm in this conversation,' he said.

'So tell me,' she said. 'How can we save our respective bacons?'

'Skip the country.'

Neither knew what to say. Their careers, their lives were in the hands of people who'd consumed a drug manufactured by a slightly overweight cat-lover keen on cinnamon doughnuts. Bizarre didn't even come close.

'We might be okay if there's an antidote,' said Jessica.

'I thought of that,' said Luca. 'We kill the effects of the original drug.'

'Saves a shootout,' said Jessica, who had never even touched a firearm. 'But does an antidote exist?'

'Everything points to Slim,' she said. 'You capture him; force him to hand over the drug and formula, and hopefully, its antidote.'

'I told you, we tried that using his old folks as hostages.'

'And?'

'He pulled down our pants.'

'What about bribes, or threats to other family members, lovers, pets, treasured possessions?'

Luca admired the thinking of the politician.

'When you give up politics, Premier, you can come and work for me.'

Jessica grew impatient. She hated Luca being relaxed.

'We're running out of time. Put Slim under pressure. Make him sing.'

'Right, and that's your only idea?'

'No. I've got a friend of yours upstairs. Apart from you setting up a hit squad, the Chief Commissioner looks like my only option.'

Luca's jaw collapsed. 'You are kidding?'

'Desperate times, Luciano, desperate measures.'

'You've got the crims *and* the cops working on the same job?'

'I thought I'd call the two-pronged special op, *Get Bernie.*'

Luca shook his head. He wanted the formula of Bernie's drug. He could make a squillion blackmailing anyone with power or money. He could impress the 'Ndrangheta in Calabria. But could he trust the Premier? He made a demand.

'I'll consider your snuff movie, but I control the whole operation.'

She looked at him, and shook her head. 'No way, Jose. You look after the boat rentals, and I'll run the army.' She pointed at him. 'You head-kicker, me mastermind.'

He watched as she walked away. No one from *The Washington Post* huddled in the shadows.

The Chief Commissioner was decidedly middle-of-the-road. He had no academic record, no study trips to Harvard, was never fast tracked, just old-fashioned policing in country Victoria with steady progress through the ranks. *Steady hand* summed up Raymond Constable Metcalfe.

Jokes about his middle name ran forever.

'He's a cop called Constable.'

It was his mother's maiden name.

Ray was already in the job when Jessica became Premier. They enjoyed a few cordial meetings but were hardly intimates. Jessica had no idea how to broach her delicate problem, and more importantly, how the man might respond.

His history of corruption did not exist. So could she trust him?

Once he was seated, she told her tale — the rogue chemist, his deadly drug, the terrifying trial results — in particular with her Chief of Staff — and the shocking health consequences for the victims.

Mind you, the families of most of the human guinea pigs were singing the praises of Bernie's brew, far and wide.

But hey, let's just answer those parts of the question which suit us.

'Very interesting, Premier,' replied Ray, 'but perhaps it's more a case for the Therapeutic Goods Administration or, more locally, your own Health Minister.'

Jessica saw she was dealing with either a professional buck-passer or someone who never rocked the boat.

'Let me ask you something, Chief Commissioner. Would you like your senior ranks to consume this so-called conscience drug? Would you be happy to have senior policemen and women, under your command, confess to corruption, dodging speeding fines and taking backhanders?'

Ray didn't like her tone, but the thought of some of his highest ranks standing in the County Court, not as expert witnesses, but as defendants, put the wind right up his traditional white boxers. His response changed.

'I take your point, Premier.'

She invaded his personal space making him more uncomfortable.

'I'm an experienced lawyer, Commissioner. I know the Law and wouldn't dream of trying to influence the police or judiciary.'

Jessica could lie with conviction. She continued to fool Ray.

'We're talking exceptional circumstances here. This drug could wreak havoc on our political parties, the government, the judiciary, and the police — your police. Would you want that on your watch?'

You cannot beat a good leading question.

Ray didn't hesitate.

'Of course not, Premier.'

'This scientist, Bernard Slim, has allegedly broken a number of laws involving the manufacture, distribution, and testing of unapproved drugs. They are clearly dangerous, and could be potentially lethal. How would the public react if they discovered you knew about Slim and his drug, and did nothing about it?'

Is she threatening me?

Raymond decided.

She is threatening me.

He stood. 'Thank you Premier. If you could give me the relevant details, I'll oversee the investigation myself.'

Preparation being her middle name, Jessica handed him a folder.

'Thank you, Ray.'

Ray?

'I have every confidence in your ability to act swiftly and decisively. Please keep me informed of any arrests.'

She didn't say *progress*. She said *arrests*. He departed thinking the woman was almost certainly a caring and concerned politician.

God, she was good.

Dr Hetherington-Smythe sat in his high-backed executive chair. The last few days would never be recorded in his diary. He'd been sunk by a spy, threatened by a thug, and shafted by a scientist.

Well if he thought that was tough, he needed to strap himself in as the fertilizer tippy-toed towards the fan.

His PA knocked and entered. 'There are some visitors for you, Dr Hetherington-Smythe; two police officers.'

Now had the PA told her boss his apartment was on fire, the Head of *Labcope International* had died, or Bernard Slim was on the roof threatening to jump, Ralphie could not have shown greater interest.

Police? Here? To see me?

It is worth noting that when Joe or Jo Blogs get burgled, it might take hours, even days for the local plod to turn up. But when the Premier intimidates the Chief Commissioner, two of his finest are on the case within an hour. Mind you, the police station and *Labcope* are almost next-door neighbours.

Two plain-clothed officers entered, introduced themselves, sat and began asking polite yet, for Ralph, terrifying questions. His mind raced.

Has that bitch of a spy dobbed me in? Will HQ ever hear about this?

'We've received information, sir, that illegal substances may have been manufactured on these premises,' said the male police officer.

Ralph tasted bile, and desperately wanted to spit.

'What can you tell us about Bernard Slim?' asked the female officer.

Jesus, am I under investigation?

'Ah, he's a scientist employed in our *Research and Development* section. Excellent worker, and been with us for several years.'

'And would you know if he'd produced any illegal substances?'

Oh no! When did I stop beating my wife?

'Of course I'd know. And I'm sure he hasn't. This is a prestigious international pharmaceutical company, a leader in world medicine.'

I am under investigation.

'May we have a word with Mr Slim, please?'

They said "please". Can I refuse? Do they need a search warrant? Oh dear, goodbye promotion; no, forget that, goodbye career.

'Of course,' said Ralph, and led the police to Bernie's domain.

They entered the lab, and Lois turned, surprised at the visitors.

'These are police officers,' said the Hyphen. 'Where is Mr Slim?'

Mister Slim? When did the Hyphen ever call Bernie, Mister Slim?

'He's not in today, sir. He's taken leave to be with his elderly parents who've recently moved into care. Can I help?'

The Hyphen looked at Bernie's desk. 'What is his current project?'

'I'm surprised you ask that, Dr Hetherington-Smythe. Bernie and I gave you our monthly updates only yesterday. But being such a busy CEO, perhaps you've not had a chance to peruse them as yet.'

The Hyphen's eyes fired daggers. Lois rejoiced in her put down.

Ralph wanted to escort the police from the building and his life.

'It appears you've had a wasted journey, officers. Will that be all?'

'Not quite, sir. We'd like to examine Mr Slim's workplace.'

'Do you need a warrant?'

Oh no. Immediately Ralph regretted having asked that question.

'Are you refusing to cooperate with us, sir?'

Under his breath, Ralph said *fuck* ad nauseum. The CEO looked helpless only because he was helpless.

'Of course not,' he said. 'I'll leave you with Miss ...' He floundered.

'I'm Lois,' said Bernie's colleague. 'How can I help?'

The Hyphen retired to chew glass, the police examined Bernie's desk, and Lois worried. She gave truthful answers denying any knowledge of so-called illegal drugs being created in this laboratory.

'I've known Bernie for years. He's a brilliant scientist.'

The police didn't know what they were looking for. Orders came down from on high with little information or briefing. And besides, the police were in a giant pharmaceutical company with drugs everywhere. How the hell could they tell if anything was illegal? They couldn't, so thanked Lois and left. Within seconds, she was on the phone.

'Bernie, the police were here.'

'What?'

'The Hyphen brought two officers to examine your work-space.'

'Bloody hell.'

'They asked if I knew anything about manufacturing illegal drugs.'

Bernie's heart started sprinting. 'And?'

'Oh Bernie, give me some credit. I said I've never seen you preparing anything here which wasn't part of *Labcope's* work. And I raved about you being a dedicated scientist.'

'Thanks Lois. You're a star.'

'But I think you should keep helping your folks.' She spoke slowly. 'They really need you, Bernie. *I don't.*'

There was a long pause.

'I think I love you, Lois.'

She smiled. 'I'll see you when your holiday is over next week. Bye.'

Bernie swallowed. He hung up and felt his mind work overtime.

First a spy.

Now the cops.

What next?

The police left *Labcope*, drove to Cremorne, and parked in Chestnut Street. They knocked on Bernie's door, even peering through a window.

They were leaving when Signora Conti came out to check her letterbox. The police pounced.

'Good morning, madam. We're looking for Mr Slim.'

'He not here in the day. He go to work.'

'What time does he come home?'

'Different time. But he will be coming tonight to see his friend, Gari.'

'Oh, Mr Slim has a friend called Gary?'

'He love Gari and Gari, he love Mr Bernie.'

'Have they been friends for a long time?'

'A very long time. They go together many time. I do not see them when they go but I know they love the other one very much.'

'Thank you, madam. You've been very helpful.'

The police started to leave but stopped when the Italian widow called.

'When they come home, Gari always give to Mr Bernie a beautiful kiss.'

The police returned to their car noting their suspect was possibly gay, and in a relationship with an unknown male called Gary. As they drove away, Bernie's "lover" barked for his midday snack.

19

GENEVIEVE did a runner. She escaped from Jessica's holiday house in Lorne, and made it back to Melbourne. Genevieve wanted answers, and from one person in particular.

It was dark when she knocked on a door in St Kilda. When it opened, the Premier's Chief of Staff could barely stand.

'Please, you've got to help me.' She collapsed.

Lois called. 'Mum, come here! Mum!'

The two women struggled to help Genevieve inside, and place her on the settee.

'Brandy,' said Lois helping the visitor get comfortable.

Mother fetched brandy, and Lois held the glass.

'Here, Genevieve, drink this — slowly.'

With brandy swallowed, Genevieve lay back, looking at the women.

'Who are you dear, and what's happened?' asked Mother.

'Ask your daughter,' said Genevieve, her head hurting like hell.

Tension simmered, and Lois knew the jig was up. She sat next to the visitor, holding her hand.

'I am so sorry, Genevieve.'

'You slipped me a Mickey Finn.'

'I did. It was a wicked thing to do, and inexcusable. But if you saw the impact of this new drug, and how it can change people from being cruel and breaking the law, to being kind and law-abiding citizens, you might understand why I did it.' She paused. 'Please forgive me.'

'Will I die?' Genevieve started to shake.

'No, no, no. And you'll recover immediately if you take simple steps.'

'Lois, who is this lady?'

'You know, Mother, it's Genevieve, Uncle Stephen's goddaughter.'

'Oh yes, so it is. How are you, dear? Is my brother all right?'

'Mum, why don't you pop the kettle on?'

'Oh, righty-o. Would you like a chocolate royal, dear?'

Mother left, and Genevieve ran through the events.

'It was the coffee you gave me at Stephen's birthday.'

Lois nodded.

'What have I ever done to you? Tell me.'

Lois hung her head in shame.

'Nothing,' she whispered. 'And I'll understand if you call the police. In fact, I wish you would. I've not taken that drug, yet my conscience is playing merry hell.'

Genevieve wanted details about the MCP. Lois told her everything; Bernie's idea, the ingredients, Annuska's research, and the other trials.

'But is there an antidote?'

'I don't know. All we know is that if you admit the things you now feel guilty about, and ask for forgiveness from the people you've wronged, the headaches disappear almost immediately.'

'Have you any idea what you're asking?'

Genevieve felt terrible; terrible because of her aching head, and terrible about the recommended cure. Lois tried to help.

'I know it's difficult,' said Lois.

'Difficult? Try impossible. If I go public, the government falls. How's that for difficult?'

Lois nodded. Shame, regret and sorrow mingled. Then she revived.

'I'd like to tell you about Mother. You may not remember, but for years, she behaved abominably; never spoke to her brother, your godfather, and treated me like a naughty child. Then I gave her the same drug I put in your coffee. The next day she broke down, cried, apologised, and begged for forgiveness. Now look at her. She's become the kindest, most considerate person I've ever met.'

Right on cue, Mother entered with a tray of tea and bikkies plus something, or rather someone else. Mother looked happy.

'Look who's come to see you, Lois; another of your friends.'

Luca Parisi grinned. Lois was gobsmacked. Genevieve shrugged.

Why not? No show without Punch.

'Mr Parisi,' said Genevieve. 'What a surprise. Lois, do you know Melbourne's leading drug dealer?'

Mother fussed with the tea, while Luca subtly opened his jacket revealing a gun in his belt. He spoke.

'I'm surprised to find you here, Genevieve. I've come to see Bernie's scientific colleague, Lois.'

Mother held up a cup and saucer.

'Do you take milk, love?'

'Milk, one sugar,' said Luca.

Two minutes ago, he slipped in the back door, charmed the old lady, and announced himself as a friend of her daughter. Mother delighted in meeting new callers.

I never knew Lois had so many friends.

Luca addressed the women on the settee.

'Now ladies, you must know why I'm here. I want Bernie's formula. He's shot through, which means you, Lois, will call your colleague and get him here pronto, or else I'll have to play the bad guy.' He patted his hidden gun.

Mother, blissfully unaware of the criminal in their midst, handed out the tea, and the plate of Chocolate Royals.

You could call it an unusual tea party.

Annuska and Dorothy took it in turns to pat Albert. Talk about fussing. His Lordship warmed to this treatment in his new abode.

The doorbell rang.

'Bernard's early,' said Annuska. 'I thought he was visiting his parents.'

'I'll go,' said Dorothy. Annuska heard the door open, and then silence.

'Now, now,' called Annuska. 'No hanky-panky in the hallway.'

No response. The door closed with a bang. Albert sat bolt upright.

'Dotty?'

Silence in the hall. Nobody entered. Annuska's mouth went dry. Her fear became terror when Dorothy stumbled into the room followed by a brute of a man brandishing a large knife.

Albert vanished and Annuska screamed.

'Shut the feck up,' snarled Brendan Murphy, former drug dealer, failed nude model, and unsuccessful rival of Luciano Parisi.

Murphy shoved Dorothy who fell on the settee. The elderly and frail females genuinely believed they might be murdered.

'Which one of you bitches is the scientist?' Neither spoke such was their shock and fear. 'Which one,' roared Murphy?

Annuska half raised a hand. 'I am a scientist.'

'Now listen, bitch. You'll save a lot of agro if you give me the formula right now.'

The women thought the intruder was there to rob them or, horror of horrors, rape or even murder them. Talk of a formula brought confusion.

Murphy had no patience. He thrust the blade towards Annuska.

'Give me the feckin' formula.'

Annuska stuttered. 'What formula?'

'I think he means Bernie's formula,' whispered Dorothy.

Annuska understood.

'I haven't got it. We haven't got it.'

'But you know about it. You helped that Slim guy make the feckin' thing. Now where is it?'

Closer came the knife. To the women it looked huge. It was huge. One slash, one thrust meant horrific wounds or death.

Dorothy showed pluck. 'You can search the whole house but you won't find it because we haven't got it. We've never seen it, and we don't know how to make the drug.'

'That's true,' added Annuska, reaching out and holding Dorothy's hand. 'Only Bernard knows the exact formula.'

Murphy fumed. Here was his chance to get back in the game. If he could give this conscience drug formula to Geoffrey from the Dogs of War Bikie Club, Murphy would save face. No more the goose of a gangster humiliated by some old battleaxe, Brendan could again stand tall, and show his face to the world.

But it all depended on getting that formula.

Okay, Plan B.

'Get y'phone.' The women froze. He waved the knife and screamed. 'Get y'feckin' phone.'

Annuska stood, and moved to the phone. Dorothy cried.

Murphy snatched the phone from Annuska, and flicked the knife at her. She screamed and fell back in her chair. The thug put down the knife, daring the women to make a move. Hardly.

Reading a phone number written on his arm, Murphy punched the digits on the keypad. He hit *speaker,* placed the phone on the coffee table, and picked up his knife as the ringing sound filled the room.

'Hello Annuska or Dorothy,' greeted Bernie.

The women's terror mixed with a smidgeon of hope. Murphy roared.

'Listen, you maggot, I've got y'lady friends, and unless you get here in ten minutes, I'm gunna start playin' *Stab the Bitches.*'

Silence. Bernie couldn't breathe. It was happening again.

'Please Bernard,' cried Annuska.

He recovered. 'Okay, I'm sorry I gave you the wrong formula before.'

Murphy was confused.

Wrong formula before?

'This time I'll give you the right one. Just don't hurt my friends.'

Murphy stuck to his plan, and held the phone towards the women.

'Speak,' he commanded.

'Hello Bernard. It's Nussy.'

'And Dorothy.'

They were in shock; Bernie piled on the bravado.

'Be brave, ladies. I'm on my way.'

Murphy yelled at the phone. 'Make it quick, prick, or both these slags go under the knife.'

He plunged the blade in the arm of a chair. Instinctively both women gasped.

'Get here!' roared Murphy.

Lois took control. 'Mum, I need to talk to my friends. We'll pop into the kitchen, and you can watch the television.'

'Are you sure?'

'We won't be long.' Lois turned on the TV, and helped Genevieve to stand. Luca followed the women.

'Nice move, Lois. Now to business.'

Lois checked on Genevieve. 'My friend is not well.'

'No thanks to you and your magic pill,' replied Luca.

Both women realised he knew as much as they did, perhaps more.

'Jessica sent you,' said Genevieve.

'She's worried, darling. You're her best friend.'

Genevieve scoffed. 'But she'd sell her Gran to save her own neck.'

Luca remained calm. 'You are a walking time bomb, darling.'

'I won't talk.'

Luca laughed. 'That's true. You won't talk if you're dead.'

That comment sent the temperature plunging. Luca hadn't raised his voice or uttered overt threats — until now. Suddenly things were out in the open. He was the assassin; Genevieve the target.

Lois threw in a possible solution.

'What if Genevieve takes the antidote?'

Luca and Genevieve came alive.

'What antidote?' snapped Luca.

'Oh please, is there an antidote?' almost begged Genevieve.

Lois winged it. 'I know he's working on one. If Bernie gives Genevieve the antidote, there's no need for this to go any further.'

'Listen bitch, I'm in charge. Any antidote's the support act. I want the formula.' Lois looked surprised. 'Oh come on, Lois. Your buddy's drug is worth squillions. Everyone wants it; your CEO, and Genevieve's boss in particular. And not forgetting little old me. So hand it over now or something sad and bad is going down in your *bella casa* tonight.'

Lois spoke. 'I haven't got it. Only Bernie knows the formula.'

'Bullshit.'

Luca removed his gun. He pointed it at Lois then shifted his aim to Genevieve. Both women had no doubt he would use it. Bluffing was not in Luca's DNA. He removed a silencer from his pocket, and screwed it to the end of his gun. He pondered his next move.

If Genevieve dies, my friend in high places will love me forever.

Nobody spoke. The only sound came from the TV in the next room.

Luca moved to get a better shot.

'Formula, now,' he said, waving the gun at a trembling Genevieve. He pointed the weapon, and prepared to squeeze the trigger. He took a step back to avoid any splatter and ... crash! He collided with Mother, who arrived carrying the tray with the cups and tea goodies.

The elderly woman fell backwards. The tray and its contents chose their own landing spots, and Lois screamed, and ran to her mother.

Genevieve stood to help but Luca pointed his gun at her chest.

'Freeze,' he said, and she did.

'Lie still, Mum,' said Lois, helping her fallen parent.

Mother groaned. What a way to die. Lois worried even more.

She thought the old "Mother" would come alive, that her true nature would re-appear. Lois actually longed for miserable "Mother" to return.

Come on, Mum. Blame the world for your woes. Get angry.

'Oh dearie me,' she said. 'Aren't I a silly duffer?'

In that moment, Genevieve got an up-close-and-personal look at how Bernie's Moral Compass Pill really could work wonders.

Ralph suffered serious stress. A major revolutionary drug, created by one of his staff, in his company, and under his watch, threatened his career. His spy uncovered everything except the damn formula. Now the spy had failed him, and the police were involved. Talk about a cock-up.

He racked his brains for a solution.

If I can't get the formula, I must cover my arse.

He settled for one final throw of the dice.

It was a short drive from South Yarra to Cremorne.

Miraculously, he found a park, and walked to Bernie's house.

I'll confront him. I'll bribe and belittle him. I'll get that formula.

Ralph pressed Bernie's bell. No response. He waited, and pressed again. Still zip. The dark house stayed dark. He tried knocking. Nothing.

Shit.

Ralph stepped into the well-lit street. Two men in suits approached.

'Excuse me, sir.'

Ralph knew he should have stayed south of the river. At least the muggers here wear suits.

'We're police officers.' They showed their ID.

'Yes,' asked Ralph? He regretted being born.

'Do you mind if we ask you some questions?'

'I certainly do mind. and I'll thank you to stop harassing me.'

Ralph started to walk to his car but stopped when a cop spoke.

'We can arrest you, sir.'

'What?' Ralph froze, adding fury to his annoyance.

'Do you mind telling us why you were visiting this particular house?'

'Of course I mind. It's none of your fucking business.'

Oh, why did I say that? If you are going to be abusive, Ralph, pick on students from Dublin going door-to-door selling electricity plans.

'The occupier of this house is of interest to the police, and we think you might be able to assist us.'

That put the brakes on Ralph's histrionics.

'Look, he's a work colleague, and I have business to discuss with him.'

'Work colleague, sir? Not a friend?'

Ralph spoke with exaggerated precision. 'Yes and no.'

'We would like you to accompany us to the police station, sir, to answer some further questions.'

'No,' said Ralph in a loud and angry voice.

He pushed past them. Oh dear. Wrong answer; wrong reaction.

At least he got a free ride in the back of the police car.

The Chief Commissioner answered his home phone. After-hours calls were *de rigeur* for the top cop.

'Good evening, Commissioner,' said Jessica Reid.

He knew her voice.

'Good evening Premier.'

Mrs Chief Commissioner looked over the top of her glasses as her husband raised his eyebrows.

'What progress have you made?'

'Some progress, madam, but still no document. We currently have a man in custody. We believe he's an associate, and possibly a lover, of the main subject of our investigation.'

'A lover?'

'A neighbour revealed the suspect has a male friend, and this man was apprehended trying to gain entry to the suspect's residence.'

'And still no sign of the drug's creator?'

'No, madam, but we hope the person in custody will provide the answer.'

'Keep me informed of any development; at any time, Commissioner.'

She hung up without a *please* or a *good night*.

Fortunately Ralph didn't hear that conversation.

Murphy grew more impatient. No sign of Bernie, and now the Ulsterman wanted a pee.

'I need y'leithreas.'

Anyone from Belfast would have pointed to the loo. In Australia, the locals were clueless. The Hungarian Aussie thought he spoke Chinese.

'Where's y'feckin' toilet?'

'Through the kitchen,' said Dorothy pointing.

Murphy heaved a chest of drawers against the double doors to the hallway and snatched the phone.

'Try anything an' I'll feckin' kill you — slowly.'

He left, and the women looked at one another. Both were teary. They wanted Bernie. They wanted peace. They wanted this man to go away.

'Meow.'

Albert appeared from behind the settee. The women fussed. They reached for him. He sidled closer.

What's going on? Where's my master?

They stroked Albert, and whispered kind words.

Suddenly a door slammed, and footsteps boomed from the kitchen. Albert panicked, and raced to escape. He crashed headlong in to the Belfast brute.

'Feck off!' yelled Murphy, and kicked at the cat. Luckily, the kick missed, but now trapped, Albert crouched and hissed. Murphy stooped to slash or stab the cat, which did what any cat could and would do in that situation.

Murphy screamed in pain as Albert the Slasher scored points from all three judges. Brendan dropped his knife and sucked his bloodied hand.

He swore, and stooped to pick up the weapon. Dorothy snatched a vase, and whacked the stooping Murphy's head. Annuska kicked his kneecap, and "the bigger they are the harder they fall" Murphy crashed.

En route to the floor, he struck his head on the table. Annuska, with her low centre of gravity, sat on him. Dorothy put the knife at his throat.

Shite, shite, shite. Not again.

Dorothy grabbed the phone, and dialed 000.

Annuska reached for Dorothy's knitting, dragged Murphy's hands behind his back, and proceeded to pull the wool over the Irishman.

'Not again,' moaned Murphy. 'Not feckin' again.'

Someone started frantically knocking and calling.

'Annuska, Dorothy, I'm here.'

The women rejoiced.

'Come round the back,' called Dorothy.

Moments later, Bernie burst into the room. What a sight to behold — two female octogenarians astride the Irish brick outhouse, now impersonating a beached whale with depression.

Not once, but twice, the former paramilitary hard man from the Falls Road had been reduced to this. Stitched up by female OAPs.

I'm on the first feckin' plane back to Belfast.

Bernie made Murphy more secure, and then helped his friends. What a night.

'Right, ladies,' said Bernie, 'we definitely need to talk.'

They heard a police siren, then a second. Bernie twitched.

'That sounds like the cops.'

'We called them,' boasted Dorothy.

'What?'

Bernie panicked.

Car doors slammed. Voices called. Torches flashed in the jungle.

The women looked perplexed.

'Bernard, what's wrong?' asked Annuska.

'I can't stay here. What will I tell the police? They may know about the Premier's Chief of Staff.'

A voice called from outside. 'This is the police. Open the door, now.'

Bernie headed for the kitchen.

'Can I escape through the backyard?'

The confused women nodded. More door banging.

'I'll call you,' cried Bernie, and vanished.

Dorothy opened the front door, and police officers entered with guns drawn. When they saw the muscled monster trussed and sobbing, head shaking and incredulity became all the rage.

'You two ladies overpowered this man?'

'We had some help from Albert,' said Dorothy.

The feline, who hated publicity, retired to his cardboard box in the laundry. Brendan considered prayer.

Ralph's fury smoldered. Failure was bad enough but humiliation?

I've been arrested for what? Visiting a work colleague? Outrageous doesn't begin to cover it.

'I wish to make a call, and need my mobile to locate the number.'

The desk sergeant passed the office phone, and Ralph's mobile. Everyone could hear. What's privacy?

Ralph found the number and dialed. The Victorian Premier answered.

'Hello.'

'This is Dr Ralph Hetherington-Smythe.'

'Good evening, Doctor. Have you located Bernard Slim?'

'No. In fact I've been arrested without charge, and would strongly suggest you do whatever is necessary to have me released immediately.'

Jessica paused. 'Please stay calm, Doctor.'

'I will not stay calm. I've had enough of this whole wretched business, and unless you take decisive action right now, I'll contact the media. Do you understand?'

'Stay on the line, Doctor. Where are you?'

He was within spitting distance of *Labcope*. Jessica called the Chief Commissioner. After a brief conversation, she spoke again to Ralph.

'I've attended to the matter, sir. You will be released shortly.'

'Thank you.'

'I am still seeking the document, and any assistance you can provide in the matter will not go unrewarded. I hope you understand that, sir. Good night.'

Almost immediately, a phone rang in the police station. The desk sergeant answered in a flat tone, which suddenly became deferential.

The phone call ended, and Ralph and his possessions were reunited.

'Can we offer you a lift, sir?' asked the arresting officer.

Ralph ignored him, and walked into St Kilda Road.

20

BERNIE FLED into Annuska and Dorothy's back yard, an ideal training ground for Bear Grylls. The scientist pushed through the overgrown garden. It was pitch black.

Where the hell am I?

Lights flashed from the side of the house, and a male voice carried.

'Check the back yard.'

'It's a jungle.'

Bernie blundered towards the back fence. The rails were on his side so he climbed and straddled the top. A torch flashed in his direction.

'I think I just saw David Attenborough,' joked a cop, getting close.

Bernie dropped next door. Hallelujah — lawn. Lights shone in this house, and the driveway gave access to the next street.

The scientist crouched, crept across the lawn then stalled. The back door opened, and a dog bounded towards him, its ferocious bark the entrée. Those teeth were made for chewing.

Bernie shooed the beast but such efforts were like a red rag to a bull — a pitbull. Pathetic kicks from Kung fu Slim. Fido fancied the intruder, and selected the finest leg in the shop. Ow! Bernie shoved his bag against his leg and lessened the war wound. His blood-dyed daks now featured air-conditioning. He whacked the hound, and broke free.

A clothesbasket on wheels slumbered beneath the clothesline. Bernie grabbed the basket as a battering ram cum shield. The dog hit the volume button. Lights came on in the backyard. The owner opened the back door, and summoned the canine. This meant a moment of distraction.

Bernie sprinted. He leapt a wire mesh fence, and landed in the driveway. The dog smashed against the fence, bellowing at Bernie, *Come back, coward.* The owner yelled to someone to call the police.

Bernie mimed a reply.

They're over your back fence!

Bernie chased freedom. He hit the street, looking both ways. *Six of one*, he thought and took off.

He crossed to the darker side of the street, and regretted having ever entered the darker side of drugs.

His chewy calf throbbed. Running was not his bag. Many cinnamon doughnuts cramped his style. What style? He paused for breath, and his phone rang. Leaning against a hedge, he puffed and spoke.

'Hello.'

'Bernie, it's Lois.'

'Oh hi, Lois. Sorry, I'm out jogging.'

Her voice screamed fear.

'Bernie, you've got to help me.'

He panicked. 'What's happened?'

'A madman's here with a gun. He's threatening to kill Mother unless I give him the formula.'

'Another madman?'

'What?'

'Can you call the cops?'

'No! He won't let us. Unless you come here right now, he'll shoot my mother. Please come here now, please.'

'Okay, I'm coming. I'm in Balaclava. I'll be there as soon as I can. Tell the madman he can have the formula.'

'Please hurry. Oh and Bernie?'

'Yes?'

'Can you bring the antidote too? The Premier's Chief of Staff is here.'

The line went dead. Bernie tried to think.

The formula <u>and</u> the antidote. What antidote? Lois lives in St Kilda. If I get to Carlisle Street I might make it. Have I got those placebo pills?

Ralph despaired. His life was spiraling out of control. No promotion to the States. No formula. No way of finding it. No support from his spy. And criminals and politicians were invading his privacy.

My life is finished.

It was a short walk to *Labcope*. He banged on the locked front door. Security approached and challenged him.

'Could I see your ID, sir?'

Ralph laughed when people said, "Don't you know who I am?"

'Sir? Your ID?'

'Don't you know who I am?'

Nobody laughed.

The security guard was relatively new, and didn't know Ralph from Adam. Besides, the boss rarely worked this late at *Labcope*.

Ralph exploded.

'Listen, you cretin, I'm Dr Ralph Hetherington-Smythe, CEO of this national company, and unless you let me in right now, you'll be unemployed in the morning.'

The security guard spoke quietly to his supervisor via two-way radio. 'Boss, there's a nutter outside threatening me. I think we should call the cops.'

Ralph, in his rage, didn't hear that conversation. He did hear the police siren as a patrol car pulled up behind him.

Bernie limped, and stopped for breath. His trouser leg was decorated with blood, and his daks started a trend in vertical ripped garments.

Why did I ever create that conscience drug?

He leant on a fence, and saw it — a kid's scooter; out in the weather, forlorn yet inviting. With not a soul in sight, he crept into the dark yard, and became a thief.

The scooter was way too small but in good working order. So with his bloodied leg astride the machine, the starter's flag dropped. The scientist took off with less strain on his lungs. Go Bernie.

At this rate I'll get to Lois in time to save her Mum.

Then he saw the police car.

Jessica rang the number again. The Commissioner knew who it was.

'Good evening Premier.'

'I haven't heard from you, Commissioner. I need to know what's happening.'

'We've made another arrest, madam.'

'Excellent. Please tell me it's Mr Bernard Slim.'

'No, it's Dr Hetherington-Smythe.'

'What! I told you to release him.'

'We did, and he's been arrested again.'

'Again? On what charge?'

'Threatening a security officer. The good doctor was attempting to force entry to the *Labcope* building.'

Jessica lost it — hugely.

'Oh for fuck's sake. That's his office. He's the CEO of *Labcope*.'

'We know that madam, and do have the matter in hand.'

'Are you running Victoria's Keystone Kops?'

Jessica risked blowing a gasket. Her career slid towards the gurgler.

And it was Groundhog Day in the police station as Ralphie got sprung yet again.

Jessica became desperate, and played the terror card.

'Chief Commissioner, I've received troubling information. This drug has attracted one of Melbourne's most violent criminals. Does the name Luca Parisi mean anything to you?'

'It does indeed.'

'Far be it from me to tell you your job, Commissioner, but I would suggest it is better to be safe than sorry.'

'With respect, Premier, you *are* telling me my job.'

Jessica rarely paused but she let the silence linger then struck.

'Remember, sir, if this conscience drug, and your fellow officers become better acquainted, your career, reputation and super, may well disappear.'

The Commissioner heard a dial tone. He considered the cavalry.

'Bernie's on his way,' said Lois, replacing her phone.

Luca growled. 'I don't like being lied to.'

'It's true. He's in Balaclava, and racing to St Kilda.'

She didn't know he was racing to St Kilda on a toddler's scooter.

'Either I get that formula real soon or somebody's gunna become a blood donor.' Luca produced his gun.

Mother had recovered, and was resting on the settee. In her new personality, she just couldn't help herself.

'Would anyone like another cuppa?' she asked. Mother turned, and saw Luca holding a gun. Her eyes popped, her jaw dropped. She pointed.

'He's got a gun.'

Lois went to her mother.

'It's okay, Mum. Everything's fine.'

'No it's not,' argued Mother.

This was more like the old girl. Was she backsliding? Had the MCP worn thin? She turned on her daughter.

'How dare you allow a gunman to enter my house?'

'I'm sorry, Mum.'

Luca snapped. 'Tell the old cow to shut it.'

Mother exploded. 'Old cow!'

Now we're getting somewhere. Here comes the "old" Mother.

Genevieve didn't care. She had something else on her mind.

'Is the scientist bringing the antidote? I need the antidote.'

The Chief of Staff suffered withdrawal symptoms — or something — and perhaps Mother required a second dose of the MCP.

Bernie hid in the shadows. The police car crept along, getting closer. It went past him. He exhaled a large serve of air. Safe. No!

The car stopped, reversed, and a torch lit the scientist and his scooter.

'Excuse me, sir,' called the police officer.

Bernie panicked. He had to get to Lois, and save her Mum, the Premier's offsider, and the rest of the world if necessary. He lost the plot.

Flipping the scooter, he took off. The police car swung around, and raced after the weirdo with the flapping trouser leg.

Being on the footpath meant Bernie could corner faster than the police, especially when they faced a stop sign. Did the police guidelines governing dangerous pursuits, include tearaways on a kid's scooter?

This was crazy. Bernie could not out-scoot a car.

It drew level in the next street, and the driver called to Bernie to stop. He knew he should but if they took him in for questioning, how could he save Lois and her Mum? If the cops took him to Lois and her Mum's house, the lunatic with the gun might go crazy.

I can't keep fooling gangsters. I have to give them the formula.

Bernie scooted flat out. It was dangerous. If something — a pet, a car, a person — came out of a driveway, a collision was inevitable.

The police car got ahead, slowed, and the passenger cop jumped out, and ran to Bernie.

'Oi, police, stop!'

Bernie didn't. The cop dived but the desperate scientist broke the tackle, crashed, and slid on the grass. Grass stains didn't improve his outfit. He recovered and took off. So did the cop who gained on the Formula 1 scooter driver.

There was a gap between properties, a narrow pathway with a metal barrier to stop cyclists racing into the street. Bernie managed to slow, negotiate the barrier, and then race along this walkway.

The running constable overshot, and by the time he stopped and got to the barrier, Bernie was scooting to safety.

The driving cop called to his colleague.

'Hop in. We'll get him around the block.'

The car screeched away. Bernie heard it, and looked back. Nothing.

He turned the scooter, and flew back to the barrier. No police car in sight. He crossed the road, and made a beeline for St Kilda, and his second appointment with a gangster.

With Ralph released yet again, he accepted a lift from the apologetic police. They dropped him in Cremorne by his car.

He stood in the street, and looked at Bernie's darkened house.

Will I try Slim again? No.

He drove home, collected his ID, and headed to *Labcope*.

Ralph didn't see the cop car in the corner of the underground car park. A police officer informed the Chief Commissioner a gent had arrived. He matched the description of the *Labcope* CEO.

In the foyer, the obsequious security guard welcomed the CEO, who flaunted his ID.

In his office, Ralph considered his options. He believed that Bernie might have hidden the formula in his laboratory. If so, Ralph knew he had to find the formula or destroy it.

Final throw of the dice, my son.

Ralph headed to the *R & D* lab.

Bernie dumped the scooter in Mother's garden and knocked on the door. Lois opened it, and dragged her colleague inside.

'Oh Bernie, thank heavens ... my God, what's happened?'

Luca arrived with gun drawn.

'It's what's *gunna* happen that counts. Now give me the formula.'

Bernie and Lois were pushed into the lounge room. The others were shocked at Bernie's appearance.

'Please, have you got the antidote?' begged Genevieve.

'What's happened to your clothes?' asked a concerned Mother. 'Come and sit down.'

Luca lost control. He had the gun but Mother the authority.

Genevieve lost it. 'Please, I have to have the antidote.'

Bernie fumbled in his pocket, and produced a vial with a few tablets. Lois glanced at them, then handed the vial to Genevieve.

'How many do I take?' She fumbled undoing the top and yelled. 'How many?'

'Just one,' yelled Bernie, 'and with water.'

Lois brought a glass of water from the kitchen. Everyone watched Genevieve nervously pop a pill then swallow.

Bernie and Lois made eye contact. Lois thought.

I know those pills. Are they what I think they are?

Bernie's nod was close to imperceptible. Placebo pills were common in many medical trials. The deception continued.

'Right,' bossed Luca, tossing his keys to Bernie. 'You drug makers get what's in my boot. It's the black Beamer out front. Now move.'

Bernie and Lois stumbled outside.

Mother protested. Her annoyance now mixed with fear; this was no party for Lois and her friends.

Luca called after the scientists. 'Try anything funny and the old bag gets it first.'

Mother gasped. 'Old bag!'

Genevieve flipped. 'I don't feel any different. The antidote doesn't work. I've still got a headache.'

'Shut up,' spat Luca, whose anger simmered. He walked to the front door and watched the others open his boot, and remove its contents.

Ralph pulled on some gloves, and entered the *R & D* lab. He worked with hardly any lights. He searched, his mind flirting with turmoil.

Is the formula on a disc or stick? In the Cloud? What about a laptop, tablet, or desktop? Is it in code? Can I encrypt it?

His thinking screamed. *Where is that formula?*

He left things exactly as they were, his addiction to tidiness ruling his life. He wanted that formula more than anything else in the world.

It has to be here. It is here. But where?

Ralph was right. Bernie did keep the formula in his lab, and a copy elsewhere. If only Ralph knew Bernie was a fan of Sherlock Holmes.

In *The Boscombe Valley Mystery*, Mr Holmes remarked that, "There is nothing more deceptive than an obvious fact".

The formula was staring Ralph in the face. The best place to hide something is often in plain view. Ralph walked past the formula every day.

Oh Ralphie, you may have a doctorate, but where are your simple skills of observation and knowledge? Despite his painstaking search, he found nothing. His thoughts turned to crime.

If I can't have it, nobody can.

Ralph prepared a bomb.

Jessica chewed her nails. Her days seemed numbered, her stellar career doomed. One lucky, plucky scientist had found a way to ruin her life.

Goodbye top job. Goodbye career. Goodbye politics and the Law. Her reputation faced disaster.

But quitting didn't appeal to Jessica. She pondered possibilities.

Get the formula and destroy it.

Get the antidote for Genevieve.

Get the formula and destroy it.
Get Genevieve to disappear.
Get the formula and destroy it.
Get Bernie Slim.
Get the formula and destroy it.
Become a nun.
Ah, but where there's life, there's hope.

Bernie and Lois struggled up the garden path guiding the contents of Luca's boot — Animal.

His mouth and hands were tightly bound. He was dazed, and his head hurt like buggery. The trio entered the room. Shock from Mother.

Genevieve grabbed Bernie's arm.

'How long before this antidote kicks in?'

'Take off his gag,' ordered Luca. Lois and Bernie obliged.

Animal spluttered. 'I'll never grass, boss, never, I swear.'

'And his hands. Then give him one of the antidote pills.'

Genevieve handed over one tablet. She clung to the vial. Lois offered water.

'Get that down you,' snapped Luca.

Animal swallowed. Everyone looked at him. He seemed confused.

'Well?' asked the man with the gun.

'I think I feel better.'

'I don't,' said Genevieve.

'You need more time,' said Bernie.

Luca ordered everyone to sit. He moved behind Bernie.

Mother fussed. 'Somebody will be in serious trouble over this.'

Luca ignored her and dealt with Bernie.

'Right, wise guy, let's have the formula.'

Bernie felt the gun on the back of his skull. He spoke.

'It's in my lab.'

Luca cuffed the back of Bernie's head. Ouch.

'No more lies,' spat Luca. 'You gave my man a useless formula before you drugged him. Look at him. He's not happy, and me, I'm annoyed. Now my doctor says I should never get annoyed. He reckons I lose control when I'm annoyed. And when I lose control, people get hurt.' He leant in close to Bernie. 'Would you like me to lose control?'

Bernie, along with everyone else, found it hard to breathe.

'No.'

'So hand over the formula — now.'

'I will give you the formula, the right formula, I promise, but I keep it in my laboratory.'

Luca seemed close to losing it. He hated these situations. His threats usually worked. Here they didn't. He searched for a solution.

'I'll give you a pen and paper. You write it down.'

'I can't remember it all.'

Luca's gun pressed against Bernie's head. 'Will this help?'

'I can't remember because it's complicated. I need all the ingredients, the right amount of each ingredient, and the correct procedure in mixing and cooking the drug. If I get one part of the formula wrong, the drug won't work.'

'That's true,' added Lois, trying to calm the furious criminal.

Luca wandered — a bit like Jessica on her walkabouts.

'So where is it in your lab? What's the special code to unlock the safe?'

'There is no code.'

'What, you just leave it lying around for anyone to see and steal?'

'Pretty much.'

Luca exploded. 'I warned you what'll happen if I get annoyed. If you're taking the piss like you did at your parents, so help me …'

'I'm not.' Bernie started sweating. 'I swear I'm telling the truth.'

'So why hasn't it been found?'

'Because Security look for bugs, and my boss is too clever by half.'

'You mean Ralph from South Yarra?'

Bernie nodded. 'If he's found it, we'd know.'

Lois joined in. 'He'd tell the world and claim it was his invention.'

'So if it's not in a safe, then where?'

'I hide it in plain sight.'

Silence. Lois shook her head.

Bernie Slim, you are amazing.

'In plain sight?' said Luca. Bernie nodded. 'Where?'

'It's on the back of the door in my lab.'

Lois stifled a laugh. Luca thought Bernie was stalling, lying or both. He again put the gun to Bernie's head, and growled.

'I'm getting really annoyed.'

'There's a calendar hanging on the door. We write in dates for jobs, meetings, conferences, etc. I've written the formula in amongst the other calendar stuff. It's all there, everything.'

More silence. Luca withdrew his gun. Bernie sounded sincere.

'Boss,' said Animal.

'Shut up.'

'I think I'm feelin' better.'

Genevieve agreed. 'Me too. I think I'm feeling better.'

Luca decided. 'Right, Animal, you drive.' He pointed at Bernie and Lois. 'You two come with me. We're gunna get that calendar.'

'I can't go like this,' said Bernie indicating his clothes. 'Security will be suspicious.'

'I've got something,' whispered Lois. 'Just don't let Mum see you.'

'Hurry, go,' snapped Luca.

Lois kissed her mother. 'Just going for a short trip to the office, Mum. Genevieve will stay with you. See you soon.'

Lois looked at Genevieve with hope. Genevieve nodded.

The 'new' Mother accepted her daughter's situation.

Bernie and Lois went upstairs. The two crims waited. Bernie descended wearing a pair of Lois's late father's Fletcher Jones trousers, and a cardigan with missing buttons and three moth holes. The trousers were beige and the cardy lime green. They were faded, too small and reeked of mothballs. It was not a good look.

'Bloody hell,' groaned Luca. 'It's fancy dress.' He pointed his gun at Genevieve. 'Contact anyone and your family disappears.'

The formula hunters piled into Luca's motor; a bimmer not a beamer.

Ralph finished making the bomb.

Okay, earning a PhD in Science didn't include Terrorism 101, but if anyone knew how to construct an explosive device, the Hyphen did.

He set the timer for one hour then took a final look around the room.

Is there somewhere I haven't looked? Is there some crazy place that prick might have hidden the formula?

Nothing jumped out at him.

He went to the door, grasped the handle and faced the calendar. Something caught his eye.

Of course. It's the wrong month.

Having OCD, Obsessive Compulsive Disorder, he flipped the page and, in so doing, missed the one thing he'd been chasing for weeks. He spurned the formula which had been staring at him every time he walked out of this very laboratory.

Oh dear.

Genevieve ignored Luca's threat. The moment the group left for *Labcope*, Genevieve called her boss. Jessica answered, breathless.

'Darling, where are you? I've been so worried.'

'Shut up and listen,' said Genevieve. 'I've taken a tablet which the guy who invented the drug reckons is the antidote.'

Jessica's heart skipped two beats.

'And?'

'I think I'm feeling better. And the formula's in the laboratory at *Labcope*. Luca Parisi has kidnapped the two scientists, and is taking them there right now.'

'Shit. Where are you?'

'I'm at my godfather's sister's place in St Kilda, 43 Mala Road.'

'Stay there. I'll have someone rescue you.'

'Luca threatened my family. Get the police to my home now.'

'Of course. Love you, babe.'

Jessica's priority was the formula. She rang the top cop.

Commissioner Metcalfe wanted to avoid an incident. The stakes were high. If this conscience drug worked as claimed, having even one senior police officer pop a pill could be disastrous.

Now that criminals were involved, it was time to bring in the Special Operations Group or SOG. They had serious firepower. Yes, if triggers are pulled and bodies shot, trouble will loom large — mountains of paperwork, enquiries, and trips to the coroner — but needs must.

The top cop dithered when the phone rang.

'Yes Premier?' he replied with dread in his heart.

Jessica told him about the kidnappers en route to *Labcope*.

That's it. Send for the Soggies.

Cry "Havoc!" and let slip the dogs of war.

21

ANIMAL DROVE TO *Labcope* with Lois beside him. Bernie and Luca sat in the back with Luca in charge of the arsenal.

'What's the quickest way to get inside your lab?' demanded Luca.

Bernie knew the drug dealer wasn't thick like Animal. This was serious; no tricks, no cons. Bernie told the truth.

'Park in St Kilda Road then walk in via the main entrance.'

'Just make your cover story good.'

They walked close together. Luca had a jacket over his arm hiding his gun. Animal, now out on Luca's parole, had his blade in a pocket. They stopped at the front door.

Harry from Security saw them and waved. Bernie and Lois were regulars. Both chemists held up their ID, and the front door opened.

'Good evening Bernie; good evening Miss.'

'G'day Harry,' said Bernie. 'Sorry to trouble you. We've brought a couple of colleagues from head office to see our latest trials.'

'No problem,' said Harry, 'if you could sign them in please.'

Luca looked at Bernie.

Skip this. Get upstairs.

Bernie tried some charm. 'Look Harry, these gents are from *Labcope* in the States. We're taking them to dinner in a flash restaurant. We'll be only five minutes, tops — please?'

Harry shrugged. 'Well, just for you, Bernie.

The quartet headed for the lift. 'Take the stairs,' ordered Luca.

As they climbed the stairs, Harry went to the reception desk and made a call. In his office, the CEO frowned.

Who's calling me at this hour?

'Hello.'

'Good evening, sir. It's Harry from Security.'

'Yes?'

'I thought you'd like to know Bernie and Lois from *R & D* are here.'

Ralph came alive but played it cool.

'So?'

'They have two visitors from America, sir.'

'From America?' Ralph tingled.

'But something's odd. Mr Slim said they were all going out to dinner.'

'That's not odd.'

'It's just, well, Mr Slim is dressed like a homeless person.'

'Call the police. No, wait. I'll do that. Alert the other security staff.'

'I *am* the other security staff, sir.'

'Well, alert yourself.'

Ralph hung up and panicked.

Slim and visitors from America. It can't be. That Italian gangster's here. They're going to the lab. They're after the formula. They know where it is. How can I get it? Will my bomb destroy the formula? What time will my bomb explode? Shit, shit, shit.

Jessica came alive. She made her driver break the speed limit racing to Genevieve's St Kilda location.

Jessica knocked and called. 'Genevieve, it's me. Open up.'

The Premier met Mother, who gushed at meeting the "Queen". Jessica wanted a private conversation with her Chief of Staff. The political chums moved to the kitchen.

'What are you doing here?' asked Jessica.

Genevieve explained about being drugged by Lois.

'We'll have her on a charge.'

'Have you sent the police to protect my family?'

'All in hand,' lied Jessica. 'Now what should I do about *Labcope*?'

'I'm fine by the way,' added Genevieve. 'But thanks for asking.'

She wasn't fine, although hoped the antidote would really kick in. Sometimes the placebo did work.

'Sorry. Look I need advice. How about we go to *Labcope* to congratulate the police when Luca and his mate are arrested? Good photo opp. *Premier gets hands dirty but triumphs in war on crime.*'

'Forget it.'

Jessica's underwear became tighter. A slither of anger appeared.

'Forget it? Listen sweetie, there's a formula out there which I need to destroy before it destroys me. And if I can't get it, then I need to ensure the Chief Commissioner does. So please don't tell me to forget it.'

'You want to be photographed when the drug baron is arrested — the same criminal you dined with in his restaurant.' Jessica started to boil.

'Not all publicity is good publicity, Jessica. My advice. Stay away. Deny everything.'

The Premier looked at her friend. That wasn't the advice she wanted.

She hissed. 'I have to destroy that formula.'

'Why? I've taken the antidote. Look at me. I'm fine.'

'You don't look fine.'

She didn't and knew it. Genevieve explained. 'Look, the old girl in the room next door took the drug, and she's made a stunning recovery.' Jessica remained skeptical. 'For years she behaved like a tyrant; even beat her daughter. Like me, her head hurt like buggery, and then bingo, she's as happy as Larry, and the kindest mother and sister in the world.'

Jessica relaxed. 'So the antidote really works?'

'Her antidote does. It involves confessing one's guilty secrets.'

Jessica stiffened. 'What?'

'She admitted her faults, apologised, and transformed her life.'

'I hope you're not thinking of doing the same.'

'I'm thinking of doing whatever removes this splitting headache.'

The Premier tensed. 'That could be a bad move, Ms Kovács. You wouldn't want your reckless behaviour to hurt anyone.'

'Oh, you mean like a certain Premier.'

'No, I mean like a certain Chief of Staff.'

Slap. Genevieve copped a metaphorical whack in the face.

The power of those words, and the look in the speaker's eyes, stunned Genevieve. Shock didn't even come close. She glared at her "friend".

'You bitch,' she whispered, then stood and returned to Mother.

Jessica stormed out, got in her car, and set off for *Labcope*.

The Commissioner's car swung into the *Labcope* car park. The Special Operations Group boys in black were there sorting their gear.

'Good evening, sir,' said Bentley, the SOG commander.

'What do we know?' asked the Commissioner.

'Security reckons two scientists, and two guests who we believe are criminals, are upstairs in the laboratory, with the CEO in his office.'

'What's your plan?'

'We believe the criminals are armed. We intend to secure the CEO, and then negotiate with the criminals.'

The Commissioner looked to see who might be listening. The others were busy elsewhere, but Bentley was led to one side for a lecture.

'We believe a formula for a new and extremely dangerous drug is in the lab. If I told you the power of this drug, you wouldn't believe me.'

The SOG commander looked at the Commissioner. The top cop would never work in standup; he was serious. He gave orders.

'We need to secure this formula.'

'Is that a target, sir, apart from the release of the hostages?'

'It is. At the very least the formula must be destroyed. Obviously the safety of your officers and the public is your top priority, but I cannot emphasize enough the importance of securing that formula.'

'How will I recognize it, sir?'

'If I knew, I'd tell you. It's what everyone is looking for. It may have a title, *Conscience Drug* or similar.'

'You want the formula, not the drug itself?'

'Preferably both. And all this is top secret. Tell nobody. Understood?'

'Sir.'

'Good luck.'

The "Sons of God" headed off to battle.

Ralph killed the lights in his office, and crept along the corridor. He stopped at the passage leading to the lab. Darkness. He heard voices and ducked back around the corner. He opened a cleaner's cupboard, and grabbed two mops. Did his tidiness compulsion rule his life?

He crept back towards the lab. A torch light shone. Footsteps. Code punched. Card swiped. Door opened. Door closed. Muffled voices.

Ralph resumed creeping. Squeaky shoes on lino. He crouched below the lab's main window and crawled, stopping just before the door. Lights spilled from the laboratory to the corridor. The voices inside grew louder. He knew them — Slim and that gangster who invaded Ralph's home. And they were discussing the formula.

It's in there!

Ralph crept closer. The narrow glass window in the door enabled him to see inside. He prepared to sneak a look then froze. The people in the lab were standing against the door, against the narrow window facing out. If he looked in, they would see him — couldn't miss him.

He drew the mops closer.

Genevieve shook. Well after Jessica left, the Chief of Staff struggled to comprehend the words uttered by her friend.

'You wouldn't want your reckless behaviour to hurt anyone ... like a certain Chief of Staff.'

This appalling threat from her colleague, her friend, her *best* friend, made a terrible situation, horrendous. No wonder Genevieve trembled.

Mother wanted to discuss Lois and her likely fate. Genevieve thought only of her family. *I cannot leave my kids without their mother.*

It was time to fight fire with fire.

She grabbed her phone, and dialed the one journalist she respected.

The SOG officers moved up the stairs. They studied a floorplan of the building, with the CEO's office their first destination. Rescue the boss. Then shut down the bad guys.

With dark uniforms, gas masks, night vision goggles, and automatic weapons, they looked terrifying. They *were* terrifying.

Using procedures rehearsed many times, they moved quickly and quietly. Hand signals gave the all clear, and sent officers through the next door. They approached the CEO's office.

Luca was desperate. Once he moved into organized crime, he never got his hands dirty. He left the dirty work to his underlings. But this was unique. The conscience drug formula screamed opportunity and wealth.

With it, he could extort high flyers. "Pay up or we'll spike your drink."

With it, he could manufacture and sell the drug, and have the market to himself. Anyone with an enemy to destroy would pay megabucks to ruin their rivals. But best of all, his 'Ndrangheta mates in Calabria would be impressed with his stunning and unique line of business.

We want in, Luca. Make us part of your brillante operazione.

'So this calendar has all the ingredients?' asked Luca.

'Everything,' replied Bernie.

'Nothing added, nothing missing?'

'Nothing.'

Luca examined the calendar. He saw the list of ingredients, which were hieroglyphics to him. The scribbled instructions too were gibberish.

'To be doubly sure, is there anything on or not on this calendar which would prevent the conscience drug being made?'

'No, it's all there.'

Luca turned to Lois. 'You agree, lady?'

Animal pushed Lois forward. Even with her scientific background, she couldn't be sure. Bernie showed her the smallest of smiles.

She looked at the calendar. 'Yes,' she said, quietly terrified. Animal pulled her back, flashing his knife.

Luca pressed his gun against Bernie's ribcage.

'You pull a swifty, Bernie boy, and I'll kill you, your girlfriend, her family and your family. Oh and not forgetting your good self — slowly.'

Bernie looked into the eyes of a killer. *This man does not make idle threats.* Bernie nodded.

'Right,' said Luca, 'let's go make the pasta sauce.'

Jessica's car drove into the *Labcope* car park. It was stopped by police. They looked in the back and saw the Premier.

'I'm sorry, Premier, you can't park here.'

'I think I can,' replied the politician.

The Chief Commissioner recognised the vehicle and intervened.

'I'll handle this.'

The police officer retreated. The Commissioner tried diplomacy.

'You might be better to turn around, Premier. It's not safe, and I can keep you informed of any developments.'

'Just show my driver where to park,' she replied.

She defied the top police officer in the state, who then became a traffic cop, pointing to where she could park.

The SOG officers closed in on Ralph's office. A few lights shone in the corridor but none in Ralph's suite. More sign language from the officers standing either side of Ralph's door. They were poised to attack.

Crash! Yelling and banging broke out. What's that? Where's that?

Ralph had slipped two mop handles behind the vertical bar used as the door handle at the lab. The door, which opened in, couldn't open.

Luca heard a sound, and pulled the door. It was stuck. He exploded, and pointed his gun.

'No!' screamed both Bernie and Lois.

'We're locked in,' roared Luca.

'That's reinforced glass. Shoot and you'll have ricochets flying at us.'

Luca pressed his face against the glass. 'Listen, whoever you are, open this door now or we kill your staff.' Pause. Silence. 'Do you hear me?'

Animal pushed Lois forward. Luca grabbed her, and shoved his gun against her head. Lois screamed.

'No!' cried Bernie.

Animal threatened Bernie with the knife.

'See,' roared Luca. 'I'll kill her unless you open this door right now.'

Another pause, but still no response. Then Luca nearly died. A face bobbed up. It appeared against the narrow window hard up against Luca's face. They were almost kissing. Luca stepped back in shock.

'Hello Arsehole,' mocked Ralph. 'Fancy a coffee?'

Luca aimed his gun straight at Ralph.

'Go on, I dare you,' yelled the CEO. 'Suck on your own bullets.'

'Fire and you'll kill anyone of us, including yourself,' shouted Bernie.

Luca raged. Ralph gloated.

'Now, Shit-for-Brains, here's the deal. You slide the formula under the door, and on my way home, I'll phone Security. If they're kind, you may be out in time for Christmas.'

'You're dead meat, mate,' spat Luca.

'I'm not your mate, *mate*. But I'll give you a tip. Either you hand over that formula, or you're toast.'

'Fuck off!'

Animal challenged his boss. 'Boss, we need to get outa here.'

'Shut up.'

'And here's the tip,' smirked Ralph. 'There's a device in your little lab which is due to go bang in about, ah, 13 minutes; unlucky for some.'

'Boss,' begged a worried Animal. His headache hit new pain levels.

'Ask the wonder inventor to check his beaker drawer,' called Ralph.

Luca looked at Bernie. 'Check your beaker drawer.'

Bernie moved to his cupboards.

'Slowly,' called Ralph.

'Slowly,' screamed Luca.

Bernie opened the drawer and discovered the device. A light blinked with a timer counting backwards. Luca looked.

'What is it?'

'No idea,' said Bernie. 'But knowing that bastard, it'll certainly work.'

Luca became desperate. 'Can we throw it out the window?'

'We can't open the window,' added Lois.

'And we can't tell if the device is stable,' said Bernie.

Ralph started singing. *'Why are we waiting, why are we waiting ...'*

Animal lost it. 'Please boss, if we stay here, we're dead.'

Luca refused to hand over the formula.

'The clock's ticking, gentlemen,' urged Bernie.

Luca wanted to argue.

'We give the prick the formula, and then he leaves us here to die.'

'Or we don't give him the formula, and we *will* die,' countered Bernie.

'Please boss,' pleaded Animal.

Bernie spoke quietly. 'Give it to him, and then we'll call Security and the cops.'

'Not the cops,' snapped Luca.

'I heard that,' called Ralph. 'Thanks for reminding me.'

Ralph pushed the handle on the two-way drop box. It was used to deliver and collect drugs without the need to enter or exit the laboratory.

'Please pop your mobiles in the chute. And remember, the longer you take, the quicker we get to Guy Fawkes night — ka-boom!'

Lois and Bernie quickly dropped their phones in the chute. Animal threw his.

Get me out of here.

Only Luca refused.

'Oh for Chrissake, man,' yelled Bernie. 'Give him your phone. Who are you? King Pyrrhus?'

Luca glared at Bernie. Furious, he slammed his phone in with the others, and Ralph pulled the chute through to his side. The phones were tossed on the floor in the corridor.

'Thank you,' crowed Mr Mock Sincerity.

Now the four lab rats were genuinely trapped.

Luca reached the lowest point in his life. He had to hand over, not sell, but give away the one thing he believed could make him a fortune, not to mention turn him in to a hero in the Italian Mafia.

Quadruple shit.

'The clock is ticking, Wog Boy,' gloated Ralph.

Enraged, Luca took the page of the calendar, knelt and starting pushing it under the door. His blood pressure sprinted higher.

'Good boy,' cried Ralph. 'Come to Daddy, come to Daddy.'

The top of the page appeared on Ralph's side.

'Please hurry, sir,' cried Lois. 'I have an elderly mother who really needs medical help.'

Ralph slipped into ecstasy mode. He grasped the formula, held it tightly, and started to pull. Then it happened.

Jessica got out of her car, ordered her driver to remain, and wandered over to the Commissioner. He now endured an intense dislike of the woman, and hated having her in his face, with a major op in progress.

'I really don't think you should be here, Madam.'

'I'm totally out of the way. No interference at all. Please carry on.'

'You do realise I could have you removed?'

'Ditto,' replied Jessica with a no-teeth smile.

He meant from the car park. She meant from office.

Bitch.

The Commissioner listened to his fellow officers, and to radio comments from the SOG upstairs.

After a few minutes, the police, concentrating on the job upstairs, saw Jessica wandering out of the carpark.

'Shit! Stop her,' snapped the Commissioner.

An officer ran. 'Excuse me, Premier.' He caught up with her.

'I need a pee.'

'I'm afraid you can't leave. There's a major operation in progress.'

'So you want the Premier to squat here? What, behind your 4WD? Got a bucket have you?'

The officer ran out of answers, and the Premier walked to the door marked *Stairs*, and left the carpark.

'Armed police. Don't move!'

The SOG officer shouted with a powerful voice. His words boomed down the corridor where the *Labcope* CEO knelt ready to receive a piece of paper. Not just any piece of paper — it was the formula for the highly-prized conscience drug.

The four people in the lab had mixed feelings. For two of them, the key thought was *rescue*. For the other two it was *arrest*.

The fifth person, the one kneeling in the corridor, felt an enormous urge to scream.

More stentorian tones came from the SOG. 'Lie down on the floor!' Ralph failed to follow the script. Louder. 'Lie down on the floor!'

He glanced at the men in black with their firearms. He acquiesced.

'Don't shoot,' he cried, fighting back tears.

My fingers touched the formula.

SOG officers moved in, their lethal weapons pointing at the CEO.

'Hands behind your back!' A shattered Ralph complied.

He firmly believed he had done no wrong, and this was his company. He fought back.

'Don't you know who I am?'

That line didn't work with the security guard, and it sure as hell didn't work with the SOG. One of their number replied.

'Unless you wanna get shot, sir, shut the fuck up.'

I'll take that as a 'no'.

The *Labcope* CEO tried on some bracelets. Not happy, Ralph.

Wonderful, he thought. *Just wonderful. So far this evening I've been arrested three times. Should that fact appear on my CV?*

Two officers helped the Hyphen to stand, and led him away.

During Ralph's capture, Luca retrieved the formula, and stuffed it inside his shirt.

Possession is nine tenths of the law.

The SOG officers looked through the narrow window in the door. They saw Luca with his gun to Bernie's head, and Animal with his knife to Lois's throat. Luca saw the police.

'Back off and nobody gets hurt,' called Luca.

The police stepped out of sight. One radioed to his commander in the car park. The other dealt with the quartet.

'Don't shoot. We are *not* coming in. Repeat, we are *not* coming in.'

'But we're coming out. Unlock the door and back away,' said Luca.

'That's a negative, sir. We are going to establish a landline to the phone in your room. Please be patient.'

'You're not listening to me,' screamed Luca. 'Either you do what I say immediately, or we start shooting the hostages.'

Animal *really* wanted to go be gardener. Lois cried, and Bernie felt sad. *I hope my folks don't hear that I've been shot.*

The SOG negotiator spoke.

'We can resolve this situation, sir. Please be patient. By the way, my name's Rick. What's yours?'

'Well if you won't open the door, Rick, I suggest you stand well back because there's a bomb in here about to explode.'

Rick found that comment interesting.

Bernie looked at the counter on the device and mouthed the word *six*.

Luca yelled. 'In six minutes!'

Jessica avoided the bodies inside the building, and crept upstairs. She didn't want the loo. She wanted that formula. She heard shouting on the floor above. One faint voice sounded like her luncheon pal, Luca Parisi.

She looked up the stairwell. All clear. She climbed.

On the next floor she waited on the landing. The shouting sounded close. The police and Luca traded insults and offers.

Waiting for something to happen wouldn't work. Hoping the formula would fall out of the sky would never work. Action is the key.

She opened the unlocked door.

22

THE COMMISSIONER SCREAMED. 'What?'

'The Premier is walking towards us, sir,' said the SOG member, his radio working perfectly.

It was all action at the *R & D* lab. Inside were two criminals and two hostages. Outside, SOG officers crouched in the corridor. A bomb was due to explode, and to add spice to the event, some loopy woman appeared, doing a superb impersonation of the Victorian Premier.

The last thing the police needed was a civilian wandering into the hostage scene. The fact that the civilian was the Premier, well, WTF!

'Madam, stop,' called a Soggie in his loudest/softest voice.

'I only want to help, officer,' replied Jessica, playing a cross between Joan of Arc and Mother Teresa.

The cop hurried to Jessica. 'This is a dangerous hostage situation, madam. The kidnappers are armed. Now please go back the way you came and stay there.'

Jessica paused. The officer was close to losing it.

'I will arrest you if I have to.'

Jessica slithered into her lawyer-like, bitch-like self. 'Not a good career move, soldier,' she said, then walked back to the landing.

The police scrapped the plan to communicate with the kidnappers via phone. With a bomb in the lab, speed ruled.

Luca tried to control the situation.

'Open the door and back away. We'll come out, and turn right. You stay left and do nothing. Do you hear?'

'We hear, sir, but we can't ...'

'The bomb is about to explode,' screamed Luca.

Bernie yelled supporting his kidnapper. 'I'm a scientist, and there really is a bomb in this room.'

Luca's anger mixed with his fear. 'Now open the fucken door!'

The commander nodded, and an officer removed the mops. All the police members moved back from the laboratory door.

Luca opened it, and signalled to Animal. He stood close behind Lois and, with a knife at her throat, eased her towards the corridor.

'Stand back,' screamed Luca.

Shuffling, Animal and Lois left the lab, and headed to the landing.

The men in black stood still, their trigger fingers twitching.

Luca and Bernie left the lab. Two couples now shuffled to the landing.

Luca spun around, making his partner, Bernie, face the cops. They moved awkwardly, shuffling backwards with Bernie as the shield.

'Warn them about the bomb,' urged the scientist.

'Shut up or I'll shoot you,' snapped Luca.

'Shoot me and you're dead.' Bernie could not believe he said that.

Animal reached the landing. Using his spare hand, he pushed the door. Lois went through followed by her captor.

Luca looked back to find the door. He pulled Bernie with him. They made their exit, and then it happened.

Ralph's firecracker went bang. SOG officers no longer stood. Glass exploded. Wood splintered. Smells wafted. Men groaned. Radios crackled. Coughing. Yelling. More yelling.

Luca and Bernie made it through unscathed — just.

Genevieve felt she had no choice. Fear for her and her family's safety brought enormous pressure. Only by telling the truth could she be free of her suffering. Confession is good for the soul. It worked wonderfully well for the old woman beside her. Genevieve wanted that happiness. Besides, if the issue goes public, Jessica would never dare do anything rash.

The Chief of Staff called the one journo she trusted.

'Hello, Gloria, it's Genevieve Kovács. Would you like an exclusive?'

The journalist hit *record* and Genevieve began.

'There's a scientist working for the pharmaceutical giant, *Labcope*.'

The journalist respected Genevieve. Anything she said would be worth repeating. Genevieve continued.

'This story involves a leading politician, a crime boss and a scientist.'

Suddenly a muffled scream was heard and then a thud-like sound.

Silence.

'Hello? Genevieve? Are you there?'

She was there but no longer able to speak.

Holding her walking stick with both hands, Mother stood behind the unconscious Chief of Staff.

'Nobody tells tales about my daughter,' whispered Mother.

Luca pulled Bernie through the door to the landing, turned to Animal and gasped. The woman hostage, Lois, had vanished. In her place, Animal's new hostage had a knife at her throat.

'Mr Parisi,' said Jessica, 'how lovely to see you again.'

'She grabbed me, boss, and pissed off the other bird.'

Bernie shook his head.

Criminals are mad; politicians insane.

Luca too shook his head. 'I said I'd get you a job. Right, down the stairs and no tricks.'

The quartet moved carefully. The explosion meant police were dead, dazed or distracted. From below, other police rushed to assist. Talk about the perfect cover for a getaway.

They reached the ground floor where the foyer was abuzz.

Luca thrust his gun against Bernie's spine.

'What's another way out of here? Come on.'

'There's the smokers' alley.'

'Show me.'

Bernie led them along a corridor. They entered a room marked *Store*, and then through another door to the outside. Cigarette butts abounded.

'Where now?' ordered Luca.

Bernie pointed. 'There's a small gap at the end of the alley.'

Luca urged them forward. Bernie told the truth; the gap was small. Anyone with even a moderate BMI would struggle.

The wiry Animal opened the battling. He squeezed through, and stood guard with his lethal blade. Luca ordered Bernie to follow. Trouble here.

Damn those cinnamon doughnuts.

Bernie made it. Then Jessica slipped through. She was slippery.

Luca's turn created a problem. What to do with his gun while his body underwent squashing? He ordered Animal to keep his knife against the Premier's throat then, keeping the gun in his upstage hand, squeezed through and joined the others.

'You can let us go now,' said Bernie.

'No way,' replied Luca.

'You've got the formula, your car's not far; and you don't need us.'

Jessica now knew Luca had the formula. Only by sticking with him could she hope to win the prize.

'Yes he does,' said the Premier. 'The police won't shoot Mr Parisi with the Premier by his side.'

Bernie shook his head in disbelief.

The world has many strange people but politicians are unique.

'She's right. Move,' snapped Luca.

St Kilda Road was buzzing with fascinated onlookers, gridlocked traffic and emergency vehicles. The quartet hurried away from *Labcope,* and reached Luca's car. Animal moved to the driver's door then stopped.

'Boss, it's no good. I can't do this no more.'

Luca's blood boiled. With the formula in his kit bag, and the cops in confusion, now was the perfect time to flee. Suddenly his faithful lieutenant turned wimp.

'Get in the car and drive,' snarled Luca.

Animal cried. 'I can't, boss. I can't do this stuff no more. I wanna be a gardener. Please.'

Luca cocked his gun. It was smart to shoot Animal. With the conscience drug in his system, the prick was a liability. Luca took aim.

Bernie moved, and Luca lost it.

'Freeze!'

The scientist kept moving to stop in front of Animal. Luca screamed.

'Get out of the way.'

Bernie refused.

'Move or I'll shoot you and then him.'

Bernie spoke. 'You can't shoot me, Luca. You need me to prove the formula works.'

Luca could not believe Bernie, and almost ran to the scientist.

'You told me everything was correct with nothing missing.'

'True, but unless you see how it's made, you'll never know.' Luca raised his gun. Bernie prattled away. 'Take me somewhere safe, and I'll mix the drug in front of you. You can see what I use and how. That way you'll have the formula, the drug, and the method.'

Luca hesitated. 'Last chance or you are seriously dead,' he growled.

'But one condition,' said Bernie.

'No fucken conditions!'

'Let this guy go.'

Animal stopped crying. He looked at Bernie and mouthed "Thank you". Luca fumed, paused, and then agreed. He tossed his keys at Bernie.

'You drive.'

Bernie shoved Animal. 'Go!'

The wannabe thug, thief and drug-dealer took a second to realise he was free. He ran.

Bernie drove with Luca and Jessica in the back.

'They're what?' screamed the Commissioner.

'Missing sir and we can't find the Premier.'

For the police, the incident at *Labcope* went downhill fast. No arrests, several casualties, and the conscience drug formula whisked away to parts unknown by a wanted criminal. Oh, and that interfering woman, the state's top politician, had gone AWOL.

Well, it wasn't all bad news for the boys in blue (or black). The CEO of *Labcope*, Ralph "the Hyphen" Hetherington-Smythe, was in custody — again — helping the police with their enquiries. Ralph was not happy.

The Commissioner felt one sliver of satisfaction.

At least I don't have to deal with that Premier. But where is she?

'Where to?' asked Bernie as he began to pull out on to St Kilda Road.

'I've got a lock-up past Campbellfield. Get driving.'

'That won't work,' said Bernie. 'The ingredients are at my house in Cremorne, and at my parents' empty house in Hawthorn.'

Luca hesitated. For him, things were desperate. His hands were dirty, and he had to disappear. It might mean buying a cheap wig and sailing to Italy, but with the formula and the conscience drug in his swag, Luca could find sanctuary and fame amongst his Calabrian chums.

'You're on thin ice, Mr Drug Maker. Don't push your luck.'

Bernie drove. He parked illegally near his home, and set off with Luca's words ringing in his ears.

'Any tricks and your beloved Premier dies. Try putting that on your conscience, Mr Conscience.'

Bernie let himself in and immediately missed Albert.

At least he's safe with Annuska and Dorothy.

He grabbed the essential items, and closed his front door. Gary barked next door. Bernie tiptoed to his gate, and returned to Luca, failing to spot the unmarked police car and its two occupants. From his home in Cremorne, Bernie headed east. Discreetly, the cops followed.

The scientist drove to Hawthorn, parked, and the trio entered the former, and now very dark and empty Slim property. Bernie played for time. He tried his key in the front door. No go; new lock.

'Maybe the back door,' said Bernie, and led the others down the drive. Luca's patience was in short supply.

The back door wouldn't open either. Luca pushed past Bernie, and turned the door handle. Bingo; one unlocked door.

'Get in, and no lights,' ruled Luca.

'Well how can he mix the formula in the dark?' asked Jessica.

'If the house is empty, lights will alert some nosy neighbour.'

197

'I do the mixing in the shed in the backyard,' said Bernie.

Luca fumed. 'Well stop wasting time and get in the shed.' He pushed Bernie outside but blocked Jessica. 'You stay here and make coffee.'

'Oh, charming. The caveman speaketh.'

'And understand, sweetheart, I know what you're up to.'

Jessica swore under her breath. She knew Luca was many things but no mug. She knew she had much more to lose if the conscience drug ever broke free. Jessica felt itchy. Her career was on the line, as was her life.

In the shed, Bernie turned on a soft red light his father used when working on his photography hobby.

Luca watched with interest as Bernie prepared to make a batch.

'So what happens after I make the drug?' asked Bernie.

'Shut up and work.'

'It's just that if this is my last hour on Earth, I'd like to know.'

'It'll be your last *minute* on Earth if you don't shut up and mix.'

Bernie shrugged and started. With all the ingredients on the bench, he held out a hand to Luca.

'What now?' asked the drug baron.

'This is the moment when the formula is handed to the scientist.'

Luca reached inside his shirt, and withdrew the page from the calendar. Bernie placed the document on the bench. He used a small torch to read his writing.

'I need to know every step,' said Luca. 'I have to be able to explain this stuff to any dumb drug-maker who isn't sure.'

'Good luck with that,' said Bernie. He held up each ingredient, named it, measured it and placed it in the bowl. He lit the Bunsen burner.

Luca was hooked. He asked questions, and moved in close. Bernie looked at Luca's gun. It was close. Bernie planned a heist.

He kept calm on the outside, but inside, his heart and mind went toe to toe. The shed seemed to shrink. Would it become his tomb?

If I make this batch, I'm no longer of any use. He'll use the Premier as hostage. So what happens to me? I've tricked him already. He can't leave me behind to call the cops. Can I get that gun?

Bernie worked through the steps of the formula with Luca fascinated. They approached the end of the task when a startled Luca darted behind the door and pointed his gun. Silence. A soft knocking was heard. Pause. Jessica spoke.

'I've made some coffee. Will Sir take it here or in the dining room?'

Luca opened the door. 'We're nearly done. Wait inside. And no lights.'

'I hope you like it black,' she said and left.

The Premier fumed but knew that when the music stops, the winner is the one holding the parcel. She had a plan.

Bernie had two opponents.

'How do I know this batch will work?' asked Luca.

'Try it.'

Luca aimed his gun. 'I've had enough of your crap. Tell me.'

'Think about it. You watched. I used the right ingredients, the right amounts, and the right process. If it worked before, it'll work again.'

Luca thought he had a brainwave.

'Of course,' he grinned. 'We can test it on you.'

'Well that's pretty stupid.' Bernie seemed to lose all fear.

If I'm going to die, I might as well go down stirring.

Luca added confusion to his anger. Bernie berated him.

'Work it out, Einstein. If I've made it correctly, and then take the drug, my conscience won't be troubled. If I've made it incorrectly, the drug won't work and my conscience won't be troubled. Stalemate, mate.'

'Just finish it.'

Bernie fiddled. His mind wandered. This shed was where his old man introduced him to Chemistry.

I never thought I'd finish up making drugs for the Mafia.

He thought of his mother now living in fairyland, not knowing her husband, children or grandchildren. He remembered stories about young men dying on the battlefield, calling for their mother.

Just before Parisi pulls the trigger, will I call for my Mum?

He thought of his Dad. When Bernie was a nipper, Gus taught him science stuff; his kind father, his wonderful, loving, patient father.

'Always handle with care, Bernie.'

'This is highly flammable, Bernie.'

'This combined with this produces a flash, Bernie.'

Tears formed in Bernie's eyes, because of his impending death, and because his mind filled with thoughts of the love his parents gave him — boundless, unconditional, selfless love.

'Have you finished?' snapped Luca.

Bernie crashed back to reality. 'Almost.'

Bernie's childhood lessons in this shed pinged in his mind. He reached for some potassium permanganate.

'What's that?' Luca wanted closure. 'That's not on your list.'

'It's a cleaning agent for the container.' Bernie lied with ease. 'The best drugs are useless with foreign bodies inside the container.'

Luca grunted, accepting the explanation.

Bernie explored his father's favourite cabinet.

'Hey, what now?'

'Sealant. I assume you'll be taking this to your Mafia mates in Italia. Do you want moisture inside the container, ruining the drug?'

Luca nodded assent. 'Get on with it.'

Bernie knew his Dad's supplies. Some of them had been used by Cain and Abel. Would these chemicals still work? He found an old bottle of propan-1,2,3-triol, and a couple of other items.

Have I remembered this correctly?

He made himself look busy. Luca grew impatient.

'Do you want the drug in small containers or one large one?'

'Whatever. Are we done?'

'Just about. The beauty of this conscience drug is that it's odourless. Sniffer dogs just walk on by. Here, have a sniff.'

Bernie stood back. Luca leant in and sniffed. Bernie flicked the liquid towards the potassium mixture and BANG! The flash struck Luca in the face.

He screamed, dropped his gun, and put his hands to his face. Bernie raced to get to the gun but was too slow.

'Back, back, back, hero,' said Jessica who was spying through the cracked window, and timed her entrance to perfection.

'I'm blind,' screamed Luca. 'I can't see.'

'Shut up,' hissed Jessica, and pistol-whipped the gangster for good measure. He screamed in slow motion.

'You'll be okay. It's only a temporary blindness,' said Bernie.

'Yes, shut up, Dago,' offered the Premier. Jessica could be all class.

She held the gun, Bernie came second — again, and Luciano slumped on the floor and suffered.

The Premier went all chummy. 'Now Bernie, me old mate, how's about you hand over the antidote to your wonderful invention?'

She moved to make sure Bernie saw the gun. He realised.

I'm now going to be shot by the Premier of Victoria. Surely, that guarantees a spot in The Guinness Book of Records.

'There is no antidote, madam; other than confession and apology.'

'Oh Bernard, please, you can't bullshit a bullshitter. I know my Chief of Staff and the lovely Animal both took the antidote.'

Continual wailing from Luca.

'No, you know they took what they *thought* was the antidote.'

Jessica froze. Panic stations. She sensed the scientist wasn't lying. Oh no! She only sensed. Had Jessica's great skill of picking lies deserted her?

Bernie continued. 'In scientific circles, it's the placebo effect. *Labcope* have a fine reputation for running trials using some of the best placebo drugs in the world. Have you discovered the anagram of the company?'

'You bastard.'

Oh great. I've outsmarted the crooked CEO, his spy Mata Hari, and the drug baron, only to be stymied by the psychopathic politician.

Jessica recovered. She may have lost the battle but she sure as hell had won the war. She grabbed the formula and stuffed it in her bra.

'Now the drug. Just the drug and none of your fireworks.'

In the dim red light, Bernie placed his latest batch of the MCP on the bench close to the Premier. She grabbed the potion.

'Well done, Bernie. Pity about the antidote. Still, two out of three ain't bad. Now, what does the script say about our denouement?'

'You're the boss.'

Luca's moaning was on a loop.

'How about Luciano shoots you and, to save myself, I wrestle the gun from the murderer and shoot Luciano. Sound okay to you?'

'Perfect. Just make sure you haven't breathed in the vapours from that little explosion.'

Jessica stopped. Two thoughts bombarded her brain. Is he lying? Has my ability to detect bullshit deserted me?

'Don't play games, smart arse.'

'There are traces of the conscience drug on the bench. The explosion sent particles floating in the air. Don't take deep breaths unless you want to cop the same headaches as your Chief of Staff.'

'You're lying.' Jessica's pulse switched to rapid. She breathed slowly.

'And you're the one with the gun.'

I wish I hadn't said that.

'Exactly. So think of this as coming from the Italian drug-dealer.'

She moved closer to Luca, still slumped on the floor, whimpering. Rubbing his eyes made his suffering worse.

'Been nice knowing you, Bernie.'

It seemed that time stood still. She aimed the gun then died.

The shed, the whole back yard, exploded with light — bright, dazzling, blinding light. A voice through a loud hailer split the night air.

'This is the police. You are surrounded. Do not move.'

Jessica decided. Firing now would not be in her best interests.

Bernie rejoiced — internally.

The police spokesperson gave explicit orders. Exit with hands raised.

Jessica hauled Luca to his feet, and shoved him out the door. He staggered and fell, whacking his head on a homemade garden swing. It danced above him. Police swooped on the hapless drug baron.

Bernie spoke calmly. 'You don't want to be caught with that illegal substance. Imagine the headline. *Premier charged in drug bust.*'

Jessica thought about it then placed the container on the workbench.

Announcing she would throw out the gun, Jessica did so then followed with her hands above her head.

Only one person remained.

Bernie picked up the drugs and ingredients, dumped them in the old sink, and turned on the tap. The police called for Bernie's appearance.

He wanted his former life, the one with Albert and Gary. He missed their cuddles and walks. Now this madness was over, Bernie longed for the old days; Signora Conti and her lasagna would do for starters. Black coffee and cinnamon doughnuts were right up there too. *Goodbye shed.*

He turned off the tap, opened the door and stepped into the backyard, his hands held high. He soon found himself in the back of a police vehicle being whisked away for a debriefing. That only took three hours.

Jessica missed the interview experience. Playing the victim helped. Being the Premier helped even more. She stood in the Slim backyard, beside the Police Commissioner.

'So, Madam, I assume you got what you wanted?'

'I did, Chief Commissioner.'

'May I see it?'

She produced the calendar page, and handed it to the police officer.

He shone a pencil torch on the document.'

'All Chinese to me.'

'And what would the Chinese pay for it, I wonder?'

He grimaced and tore the page in two, handing her one-half. He proceeded to tear his portion into pieces. She shrugged then copied him.

'I'll leave you to dispose of your material, Premier. Please don't litter. Now, can I give you a lift?'

'Thank you, Commissioner, I have my driver. Goodnight.'

'Goodnight,' said the top cop, who watched the Premier depart.

She took out her phone. Her Chief of Staff needed sorting.

At least the formula was dead.

Or was it?

23

AS SOON AS JESSICA left Hawthorn, she sped to St Kilda. Dealing with Genevieve dominated the Premier's thinking.

Having clobbered her guest, Mother set about caring for the victim. Lois, having escaped the *Labcope* siege, thanks to the Premier, arrived home, and could not believe Mother had attacked the Chief of Staff.

Lois immediately summoned an ambulance. The patient had "fallen down the stairs", and the wounded Genevieve departed for hospital.

Jessica arrived seeking her "pal". By now, Lois and Mother were in their nighties, which meant nothing to the Premier. She demanded details. When told the tale of the phone call to the journalist, and the wayward walking stick, she asked nothing about Genevieve's condition.

'Did she speak to the journalist? Did she?'

Mother still had her wits about her at this late hour.

'I stopped her,' said Mother. 'I won't let anyone say bad things about my darling, devoted daughter.'

Lois still had trouble coming to terms with her mother's personality makeover, which now apparently included a serve of thuggery.

Jessica felt a smidgeon of relief, but took off still in worry-mode.

The ambulance crew reckoned Genevieve had been assaulted. The doctor on duty at the Alfred Hospital agreed, and informed the police. Before they arrived, the patient had a visitor.

'She'll see me,' said Jessica to the nurse, who had been told to admit only immediate family.

Nobody stops the Premier. She entered Genevieve's room, and for the life of her, couldn't remember if the husband was Jason or Justin.

'Hello, darl,' she oozed, kissing Genevieve, and making the patient's headache even worse.

Genevieve felt crook, her mind hazy, but she could still remember the last time she and the Premier had a chat.

This woman threatened me and my family.

Jessica gushed. 'I'm going to look after you, babe. You're going to get the best care money can provide.'

The Chief of Staff kept having flashbacks.

You wouldn't want your reckless behaviour to hurt anyone ... like a certain Chief of Staff.

Before their chat could continue, two detectives arrived, and asked if Genevieve was up to answering some questions. She was.

Normally uniformed officers would investigate a possible domestic but with the ruckus at *Labcope*, word soon reached the Commissioner that the Premier's buddy was involved. He sent the detectives.

'Don't mind me,' smiled the Premier, settling in for the duration.

Wrong move. Word had come down from on high.

Under no circumstances is the Premier to be present at any interviews. She could well be a prime witness in any future trials.

The Commissioner wanted to include the following.

Besides, I wouldn't trust that bitch as far as I could throw her.

'Sorry, Premier; we must interview the witness alone,' said the cops.

Jessica wanted to argue but the look on the face of the police, the husband, plus her former bestie, ended all resistance. Jessica left.

She worried unnecessarily because Genevieve gave the police nothing. She "thought" her head wound came from falling down the stairs. She became a reluctant witness.

After her hospital stay, Genevieve's headaches slowly faded, as did her interest in making public confessions and apologies. Peace and quiet became her new mantra, meditation her antidote.

Did the MCP fade in time? Had her willingness to apologise been enough? Did *Labcope* have the best sugary pills in the world of placebo?

The Premier went public praising her heroic Chief of Staff.

'Genevieve Kovács is a brave and brilliant woman. I have no doubt she will soon return to serve the people of Victoria.'

Perhaps, but in the meantime, Genevieve hatched a plan.

The morning after the gunfight at the Slim Shed, early, Bernie knocked on Signora Conti's door. She was shocked, then worried, then delighted to be of assistance. Bernie used her phone. He could only guess as to where his mobile might be.

He rang Balaclava with more news than Yahoo on a busy day. He was fine, and his two favourite Balaclava babes were okay, well, glad to be alive. The only bad news involved Albert.

He completed an adoption claim. Life was sensationally grand in his new abode with human slaves on tap 24/7. Albert put in for a transfer.

Bernie rang his sister where her news topped his. Their folks were settled, and hubby, Brutus the Bastard, had been born again with nary a prayer or hallelujah in sight.

Then to Lois who found it hard to speak.

'I'm finished, Bernie.'

'We're both finished, Lois. Our lab doesn't exist.'

'I know most of your news thanks to the TV.'

'But wait till I give you the inside story.'

'And mine.'

Bernie began to panic. 'Pardon?'

'You know my meek and mild mother.'

'What's happened?'

Oh no! The first guinea pig failure.

'Would you believe Mother gave the Premier's Chief of Staff a whack with her walking stick to stop her telling tales to a journalist?'

'You're kidding. Tell me it's not true.'

'I think there's a new antidote for your MCP.'

'Lois, you're winding me up.'

She wasn't kidding, and when Bernie hung up, he had to go home and lie down to recover.

There was one last thing to do and that involved a trip to Hawthorn. He took the train, and climbed the ramp to Burwood Road.

He walked to the old family home. Last night he hadn't noticed the sign on the front fence. It was the usual notice about proposed changes to the property. Tell the local authority if you object.

In this case, the proposed changes involved demolition of the existing dwelling to be replaced by two townhouses. This activity is known as, "keep the name of your suburb but few of its landmarks, trees or houses".

Bernie was glad his folks wouldn't see the sign or its consequences.

The property was deserted. Who'd be a short-term tenant in a house invaded by drug dealers? The previous tenants had scarpered.

He wandered down the drive, and entered the kitchen. Not much reason to lock anything, although the world's homeless wouldn't say no to a roof like this over their head.

He wandered into his old bedroom, where memories whacked him left and right.

Life moves on, Bernie.

In the back yard, he tried sitting on the swing his father erected decades ago. His nephew and niece loved it today. Farewell swing.

The tree would become firewood, and the swing tossed in a skip.

He entered the shed, the scene of his childhood education, the setting for his drug creation, and for last night's soap opera.

The police had spent time giving the old building a forensic investigation. Bernie's mind wandered.

Will I be charged with some Class A drug crime?

Bernie didn't know the Commissioner gave orders to remove and destroy any drugs, dangerous materials or equipment in the shed. The police decided there was never any such thing as a conscience drug.

Move along; nothing to see here.

The only evidence needed to convict Luciano Parisi would come from police officers at the various scenes of crime, and from the lips of the Premier herself — an innocent victim in this whole sorry saga.

Now Jessica Reid was many things but innocent?

Looking around the shed, Bernie discovered even more memories from those old days, happy days.

Then he felt under the table, and from a hidden crack, he withdrew the only and much folded copy of the formula of his conscience drug.

It was a photocopy of the page from the calendar. The master copy had become confetti-like pieces scattered in landfill.

What will I do?

Bernie knew his formula was explosive. It certainly worked. If people from every walk of life came under pressure to admit their crimes, their wrongful actions, and even their simple lies, what would happen?

Would society be better?

If the MCP prevented crimes or hurtful behaviour, surely that's a good thing.

Ah, decisions, decisions. Talking it over with people like Lois and Annuska sounded sensible, even essential. He procrastinated.

I wish I didn't have to make a decision.

He heard voices and panicked.

Police? How do I explain being here?

He peered through the dirty window. Not police; hard hats and hi vis vests. He folded the formula, and slid it back inside the table.

'Morning,' he said stepping out of the shed.

'Morning,' replied the surprised workers.

Bernie saved them asking questions.

'I'm having a last look round. This was my family home. My folks lived here I think forever.'

'No worries,' said the boss.

'Do you blokes work on a Sunday?'

'It's our only chance to check out new jobs.'

Bernie became curious. 'So when do you start the demolition?'

'With the house, we have to wait for council approval, but it's just a matter of time. Now we're having a reccy, and a minor cleanout.'

'Well I'll let you get on,' said Bernie, starting to walk away.

'Is there anything you wanna take? The swing perhaps?'

Bernie shook his head. Then he stopped.

'Yeah, why not? The grandkids love this swing.'

One of the workers fired up a chainsaw. The men lopped the tree limb then cut the knots that Gus created last millennium. They wrapped the ropes around the plank, and handed the swing to Bernie.

'That's great, thanks.'

'We'll chop the tree and demolish the shed, so if there's anything you want to save, now's the time.' They prepared to start work.

Bernie's memories of his dad and the shed flooded back — his father's equipment, the things he made, the lessons, the fun, the science, that old red light, and the love between a father and son — all in the men's shed.

Then Bernie thought of his conscience drug, the trials, the crazy people chasing it, and the only copy of the formula hidden in that shed.

Grab the formula, Bernie. Hide it somewhere safe for when times are different. You never know when it might be needed. He decided.

'No, thanks' he said. 'Sometimes it's good to make a clean break. Bring on your skip and saw, and demolish away.'

As he walked down the driveway for the final time, the sounds of breaking glass and a chainsaw filled the air.

Right at that moment, his conscience was clear.

Epilogue

The Hyphen

Claiming ignorance of everything, Ralph avoided any police charges —his bomb destroyed the evidence — but not the censure of his employer. Head Office in the States ruled in favour of Ralph's early retirement.

He collected his super, sold his South Yarra apartment, and bought a B & B in the country. Today he gives science lectures at the U3A in Daylesford.

Luca Parisi

His dreams of great wealth, and respect from the Calabrian Mafia were dashed when the police went after him with a vengeance. Because Luca escaped that albeit false murder charge, the cops were pretty pissed.

The unlicensed weapons issue became child's play. The new list of charges was shorter than *War and Peace* but only just.

It included kidnapping, attempted murder, aggravated assault, false imprisonment, destruction of evidence, extortion with threats to kill, importing commercial quantities of drugs, tax evasion, trafficking in a drug of dependence, and use of firearms in the commission of offences.

Luca needed a good lawyer. He tried you-know-who but Jessica refused to take his calls. He thought about grassing on the Premier then remembered her reputation. He pleaded guilty, and gave up homemade gnocchi for porridge — the institutional variety.

Sheila Parisi

She teamed up with her daughter-in-law. Kellie went back to running a beauty parlour offering style cuts, colour/tinting and manicures. Little Angelo had the best babysitter in town.

Lois

She retired with her super and a generous payout from *Labcope*. Being kidnapped pays. With born-again Mother in tow, Lois packed her Mum and their bags, and she and the old girl sailed away on a world cruise.

Bernie

The head honcho from the States came Down Under. He sensed Bernie had skills and imagination to burn. Alas Bernie had no desire to climb the greasy corporate pole. A new CEO arrived from the US, and Bernie accepted a promotion as *Scientist in Charge of New Developments*.

Albert came to his senses, and moved back to Cremorne.

Annuska and Dorothy

The women went to the local animal shelter, and adopted two cats they named Bernie and Slim. Their namesake became a regular dinner guest in Balaclava.

Animal

He divided his time between mowing lawns, and trying to track down fellow thugs in order to apologise. He was better at gardening.

Once Genevieve left hospital, she discovered her headaches from the MCP had faded. This confused her. Was there an unknown antidote? Perhaps the placebo worked. Or did the whack to her head destroy or dissipate the impact of the MCP? Did the drug simply fade in time?

She pondered a return to work. *Why not return to banking?*

Jessica wanted Genevieve back in harness in Spring Street.

One Saturday morning, Bernie opened his front door.

'Hello,' said Genevieve, who was invited inside.

Bernie and his former human guinea pig chatted for ages. Bernie apologised profusely. He worried.

Is she wearing a wire? Has she come to accuse me, assault me, or report me to the cops or to Labcope?

It was none of the above. 'I have a request,' said Genevieve. 'May I have a small amount of your conscience drug?'

Whoa. Heavy.

'I'm happy to pay,' added the visitor.

Bernie shook his head. 'Sorry, it's all gone. That drug caused terrible grief.' He indicated his visitor. 'Present company a perfect example.'

'Let me tell you what I want it for.' She explained, and her explanation worked. He weakened.

'And you promise to only use it in the manner we discussed?'

'I promise, cross m'heart and hope to die.'

In his bathroom, Bernie found a small container of prescription drugs. The contents didn't match the label. It was the old "hiding in plain view" trick. He popped two capsules in a plain container.

In time, Genevieve returned to work for Jessica, and together, the old team pushed the Premier's ratings ever higher. Politically, life was good.

But Genevieve had a secret. She owned two *Moral Compass Pills*, a fact known only to her and a Mr Bernard Delahunty Slim.

The Premier suspected something. What, she didn't know. Was it her conscience nagging her? Did she have a conscience?

Her relationship with Genevieve never returned to that of the pre-MCP days, and whenever Jessica took tea or coffee with her Chief of Staff, a thought pinged in the Premier's brain. *Am I being drugged?*

Jessica feared what she and Genevieve never discussed — the dreaded conscience drug. Just the threat of the effects of the MCP kept the Premier on the straight and narrow. Well, in that general direction.

Bernie took Gary for his daily walk. The simple life suited them. Bernie's dream of a *Moral Compass Pill* was dead and buried; or so he thought.

In fact, his conscience drug was working flat out without ever being consumed. It was the power of its potential, the power of Bernie's idea.

A person with a new idea is a crank until the idea succeeds.

Labor to keep alive in your breast that little spark called conscience.
George Washington

The Detective Joanna Best Mysteries

www.cenfoxbooks.com

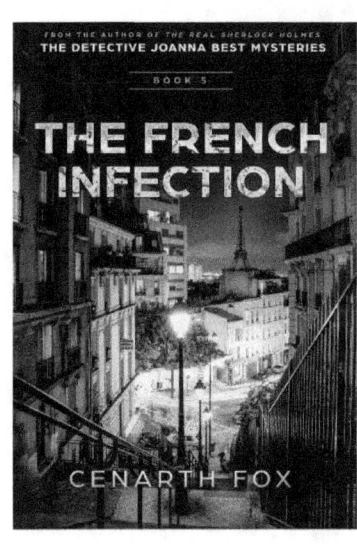